Harpey Mendelson

Harold L. Schmidt

ISBN 978-1-63903-570-0 (paperback)
ISBN 978-1-63903-571-7 (digital)

Christian Faith Publishing, Inc.
832 Park Avenue
Meadville, PA 16335
www.christianfaithpublishing.com

All Scripture quotations, unless otherwise indicated, are taken from the Holy Bible, New International Version (NIV)®. Copyright © 1973, 1978, 1984, 2011 by Biblica, Inc.™ Used by permission of Zandervan. All rights reserved worldwide. www.zondervan.com. The "NIV" and "New International Version" are trademarks registered in the United States Patent and Trademark office by Biblia, Inc.™

Disclaimer: This book addresses racial issues and uses strong and potentially offensive language. This is done in an effort to create awareness and make the contents more realistic. While the author has gone to great lengths to ensure the subject matter is dealt with in a compassionate and respectful manner, this may trigger or upset some readers. Please use discretion.

This book is a work of fiction. Names, characters, places, and incidents either are products of the author's imagination or are used fictitiously. Any resemblance to actual events or locales or persons, living or dead, is entirely coincidental.

Printed in the United States of America

For Sheila,
who loved this story from the very first sentence.

and

Zak and Sierra
All My Love

Then the Lord put forth His hand and touched my mouth and said to me, "Behold, I have put My words in your mouth"

—Jeremiah 1:9 (NKJV)

Coincidence is but God's way of choosing to remain anonymous.

—Rabbi Benjamin Blech

Acknowledgments

This book has itched at a scratch in my mind for close to twenty years. Now that it is finished, I realize how many people encouraged the central idea and cheered me on when I shifted from writing plays and musicals to working on this novel. Thanks to all who took time out of their busy lives to read drafts and provide feedback. It was invaluable.

Preface

⸎

1963

"Nixon Bliss thought I couldn't speak without borrowed words, that my useless legs dangled because I was made of wood. It makes sense to me now, the way his eyes fixed on me when my father lifted me out of the car, eyes that couldn't believe what they were seeing, an illusion, as if a magician had pulled a Jew out of a hat instead of a rabbit. I had no idea Nixon wanted to be a ventriloquist, or that I was the spitting image of Jerry Mahoney, or that Jerry Mahoney was Nixon's hero. My name is Isaac Harpey Mendelson, and I am a real boy."

Chapter 1

Sunday, June 7, 2020
Summer Sermon Series: Week One
Pastor Nixon Bliss

As a pastor and a ventriloquist, I have stood before my small congregation in Winslow, New Jersey, every Sunday for the past forty years, preaching the Word with my wooden partner, Moses, by my side. It was a rocky start at first. A smattering of curmudgeons and naysayers led by Ms. Nellie, who had been baptized at Miller Memorial Church in the summer of 1929, thought Moses and I were better suited for the circus than her beloved little church. After all, this was Sunday worship, not *The Ed Sullivan Show*, and after Jesus, Ms. Nellie thought Ed Sullivan was the best thing since indoor plumbing. But she grew to love the interplay between Moses and me, especially when Moses corrected me on a point or added a bit of spontaneous sarcasm, which he did often.

Constructed in 1861, Miller Memorial Church is small but meticulously maintained, its charm and sense of the sacred palpable. It has a white picket fence, flower boxes filled with lilies beneath its stained-glass windows, and the original old wooden cross atop its steeple. I have an affinity for old churches. They've heard more prayers and saved more souls than their modern counterparts. They have real wooden benches, the type that encourages shifting buttocks, straight backs, and attentive minds. We provide padding for comfort, but not so much as to encourage nodding off. We blend the old with the new.

It's 9:26, and as I prepare to take to the pulpit on a gorgeous summer morning, I take a moment to ask God to give me the words to make my sermon resonate with the audience. In the chapel, Gladys sets her calloused fingertips on the ivory keys of Buster, our antique pipe organ, an instrument of such monstrous girth it looks like a giant octopus has suctioned itself to the back wall of the church. Buster has the lungs of a heavy smoker. He wheezes and heaves, expectorates puffs of dust made visible by beams of colored sunlight filtered through the stained-glass windows. His massive pipes are so intimidating to children that Gladys decorated them with smiley faces to soften his persona. And Gladys, now in her seventies, with her back to the congregation hunched over the pipe organ, her bony shoulder blades protruding through the wispy fabric of her print dress, could easily give the impression that a vulture was at the keys playing "How Great Thou Art." But as the first notes of that old hymn fill the air, the majesty of Buster's commanding sound draws people to their feet, and the motley harmony of our zealous congregation lightens my heart.

The opening hymn complete, I lift one end of the wooden trunk that is home to my trusted sidekick, Moses, and wheel him into the chapel. The wheels clatter across the floor's aged planks. I move to the lectern, set the trunk down, and smile. The church pews are filled.

"Good morning," I say, and the collective response from the congregation, "Good morning, Pastor," energizes me. I open the trunk and lift Moses up onto the lectern. He sits as he has for the last forty years. Moses has a wild crop of gray hair, big eyes, and puffy jowls. For a guy over a hundred years old, he looks good.

"I didn't always want to be a pastor," I say. "Actually, since I was a boy, I wanted to be a ventriloquist. But God had other plans, didn't he, Moses?"

"Yeah, he made you the dummy."

It was the same opening we had used forty years earlier, and all those summers since, but it never ceased to get a laugh. Harpey would call this our "shtick," and so it was.

I turn to the congregation. "I longed to put words into my father's mouth. Now I am humbled to have my Father put His words into mine. I want to tell you a story."

"Uh-oh," Moses says.

"I'll be brief."

I swivel Moses's head toward the congregation. "We've heard that before."

The congregation laughs. I turn to catch Gladys's glance in her rearview mirror. She had two installed on Buster so she could watch the service without twisting around, which hurt her back. Wally Pritchett, who owned a salvage yard in the adjoining town, donated the mirrors. They had been part of an old Chevy Chevelle. Gladys refers to them as "transplants donated to her organ," and she ritually wipes them down before each service.

"Gladys, set your egg timer for forty-five minutes. I'll come in under that. Promise."

Gladys sets her timer and nods. This is the sermon I gave the first year I became pastor. Now, every five years, it is the sermon I give for twelve weeks as a recurring summer series. Some of our parishioners have heard variations of this sermon six times, but it remains one of their favorites. It is my story. I glance back at Gladys and smile at her reflection in Buster's mirror, turn to the congregation, and begin.

"I became a pastor because of a boy named Harpey Mendelson who moved onto our street in the summer of 1963, a summer my friends and I will never forget."

Chapter 2

———— ❧ ————

On June 22, 1963, I sat at our kitchen table, facing my two favorite boxes of cereal: Fruit Loops and Captain Crunch. I lifted both and noticed Captain Crunch was at that dreaded juncture where I'd end up with half a bowl of crumbs. "Sorry, Captain," I said and poured milk over my bowl of Fruit Loops.

My father stood at the kitchen counter and put four tablespoons of Chock Full o' Nuts into my mother's Farberware percolator. A gangly man with a slight slump in his shoulders, he had blue-green veins that stood out like tree roots on his sinewy forearms. His rough-hewn face was sturdy but not intimidating. He worked in a tape factory where his job was to ensure the correct amount of each ingredient went into the adhesive mixture. If it wasn't done with precision, the tape would stick too much or not enough. He measured the coffee grinds as if a pinch less or more would percolate an atom bomb. The percolator was my mother's most prized possession next to her Kirby vacuum cleaner, which was so expensive my father told her to park it in the garage because it cost as much as the Plymouth.

I didn't understand the distance between us, a fixed emotional orbit that kept us at arm's length despite my best effort to breach it. Neither affectionate nor talkative, he measured his words the way he measured ingredients, using only the precise amount needed to make his point. If you asked him a question, his answer was often one word, and I convinced myself his years at the tape factory caused adhesive to leak into his pores, making what he wanted to say too sticky to release. Such was the mind of a twelve-year-old boy who

My mother plucked at a rebellious lash. "I need to get this goo off. What we women won't do to be beautiful."

My father followed my mother out of the kitchen.

"Why wasn't I born into royalty?" Izzy said. She grabbed a bowl from the kitchen cabinet.

I hurried to my bedroom, got Mr. Mercury, and threw my best robot voice. "Got a big day at work today, son," Mr. Mercury said.

"Really?" I replied.

"Critical batch of adhesives. You want to hear how it's done?"

"Sure, Dad!"

My room was my refuge with my Hardy Boys mystery books, a jar of marbles, Mr. Machine, and Frogman. My walls displayed monster movie posters like *The Brain That Wouldn't Die*, *The Blob*, and *Attack of The Crab Monsters*. I had tons of shelves. When you're twelve, your shelves are a museum of all your worldly possessions. I proudly displayed my Matchbox cars, Duncan yo-yos, and monster models including Frankenstein, The Mummy, and The Creature from the Black Lagoon.

A voice startled me.

"Hey, you wanna kiss me?" Ellen Yancey pressed her face against the screen of my bedroom window. Before I could react, she yanked it away. "No way! I'm never letting a boy put his stamp lickers on me."

"Who said I'd want to?"

My mother said Ellen would break a lot of hearts one day. "That girl's as cute as a button. And those periwinkle eyes! She'll be the Noxzema Girl, mark my words." My mother thought Noxzema was the secret to eternal life. Ellen was eleven and a tomboy. She loved to play baseball, climb trees, and when playing baseball, she would spit like a major leaguer.

"You coming out? Billy set up the bases."

"Be right out."

We lived in Kendall Park, a middle-class neighborhood in Central New Jersey. "KP," as we called it, sat between New Brunswick and Princeton. It was mostly ranch houses back then and a magical place to grow up. Front lawns were littered with the accoutre-

ments of childhood: bikes, basketballs, dolls—and in the hot summer months—vinyl pools, lawn chairs, and sprinklers. It was a street
without boundaries. In the summer, lunch was served by the mother
with the most kids in her yard around noon. We ate hot dogs, Oscar
Meyer cold-cut sandwiches, PB&Js, and moon pies. We played
cowboys and Indians; kickball; baseball; red light, green light; and
hide-and-go-seek. We imitated villains and superheroes. At night, we
watched *Walt Disney's Wonderful World of Color*, *Rawhide*, and *Wagon
Train*. Izzy loved *Dr. Kildare*, my mother loved *Hazel*, and my father
liked westerns.

With a bike, you could get to the library, the shopping center,
ball fields, roller rink, and the 7-Eleven in less than twenty minutes.
You could walk or bike to school, and most of your friends lived
nearby. Our house was on a dead-end street that ended with a cul-
de-sac so people who got lost could drive around the circle and head
back out. When you're a kid, a dead end is prime real estate. It meant
few cars drove by to interrupt a game of kickball, stickball, or hopscotch. We had plenty of cracks to break our mother's backs and tar
bubbles to pop. The middle of the cul-de-sac was our safe zone, the
place we could go to share what we didn't want adults to hear. It was
our private island, and we spent a good deal of our childhood within
that small circle. On the downside, Kool-Aid stands were a bust. Not
enough through traffic, but for the most part, growing up on a dead
end rocked. I grabbed my baseball glove and ran outside.

"Took you long enough," Billy said.

Billy Finley was my best friend. He was built like a hydrant,
thick and stubby with short arms that made it difficult for him to dig
deep into his trouser pockets without pitching like a teapot. This odd
ratio of Billy's arms to his pockets gave us hope when we biked to the
7-Eleven and realized we were three cents short of being able to pay
for our SweeTarts or Fruit Stripe gum. Like me, Billy had a flattop
crew cut. Most boys my age got them in the summer back then.

"Dig deeper, Billy!" Ellen would plead, and more often than
not, Billy would tip, reach down, and find three or four pennies to
complete our purchase.

Billy stood in the center of the lawn on our makeshift pitcher's mound, practicing his windup. Ellen played outfield, pounding her glove before getting into position to await a fly ball. "Batter up!" she yelled.

Home plate was a piece of cardboard with a brick on it. I tossed my glove on the ground and traded it for Billy's Louisville Slugger. I thumped home plate and got into my batter's stance.

"Get ready for strike one," Billy said.

A gusty wind kicked up as a swath of high clouds drifted above us. The freshly cut grass smelled like summer. It was a perfect day for baseball.

Billy threw a knuckleball. I hit a pop fly high into the air. Ellen got under it, made the catch, and tossed the ball back to Billy. "One down!" she said. Ellen wore a Yankees cap a size too big for her head, and she constantly tipped back the brim to keep it out of her eyes. We were about to resume the game when a station wagon, a Rambler with New York license plates, pulled into the Kelly's driveway. We stopped playing. The For Sale sign in the front yard of the Kelly's old house had been covered diagonally with a sticker that said Sold, and we were awaiting the arrival of the new neighbors.

"The new people," Ellen whispered.

A man stepped out of the car. He was dressed in black and wore a skullcap on his head. He removed a small wheelchair from the trunk of the Rambler, opened it, and set it on the ground. A woman stepped out of the passenger side, and she covered her hat with both hands at a gust of wind. The man wheeled the wheelchair around to the rear passenger door, opened it, and reached into the back seat. When he emerged, he had a tiny boy, legs dangling, cradled in his arms. I stood there, transfixed by the sight of the new boy because of his uncanny resemblance to Jerry Mahoney. It was as if the wooden ventriloquist dummy I idolized had come to life!

Billy was transfixed for another reason.

"Jews," he said. The word "Jews" left Billy's lips with the same fear he displayed when we watched *Creature Features* on Saturday afternoons. When a creature appeared on the screen, Billy's eyes would widen, and he'd say, "Holy smokes, giant crabs," or "Aliens," or "Vampires." And now—"Jews."

"What's a Jew?" Ellen asked.

"They're weird. They go to church on Saturdays."

Ellen knitted her brows. "I didn't even know they were open on Saturday."

"And they don't celebrate Christmas."

That did it. Billy might as well have said they were cannibals.

"That can't be right," Ellen said.

"Who told you that?" I asked.

"My dad. His boss is a Jew, and my dad hates him."

"No Santa Claus? No Christmas tree?" I asked.

"Nope. They have some other holiday instead. Like I said, they're weird."

"Great, another Addy on the block," Ellen said.

Every neighborhood has a crazy neighbor to avoid. Ours was Addy Wolf, an elderly woman with wild curls of chalk-white hair that bounced on her head like bedsprings. She spoke in screams and whispers, directing her conversations at people that weren't there. She didn't have a husband, so we assumed she'd murdered him. He was a mannequin salesman, and once in the middle of the night, Addy was outside in her bathrobe, dancing with a mannequin on her lawn. Now Addy wasn't the only oddity on our block. Now we had... *Jews*.

"I wonder why the boy's in a wheelchair," I said.

Billy tossed the baseball in the air and caught it. "Beats me, but my dad's gonna have a cow."

Ellen tipped her baseball cap back out of her eyes. "He looks like that doll you like on TV, Nix."

"He's not a doll. He's a ventriloquist's dummy."

"Maybe it's him, and he just pretends he's a dummy."

"That would be cheating," I said.

Billy spun the ball in his hand. "Jews cheat all the time."

"Maybe he really can talk, and it's all a big fake," Ellen said.

"It's not fake, okay," I said, irritated by the conversation.

Ellen scrunched her face and glared at me. "You don't have to get all huffy about it."

A moment later, a moving van turned onto our street just as Mr. Finley came out of his house. Mr. Finley stood in the driveway with a can of Schlitz in one hand and a bag of Fritos in the other. His biceps were the size of bocce balls, and he walked as if he intended to squash something beneath his feet with each step. The man glanced over at Billy's father and acknowledged him with a nod. Mr. Finley's face turned red. He squeezed the can of Schlitz, and it burst in his hand. "Dammit!" he screamed.

Mrs. Finley whipped open the kitchen window above the sink and screeched. "Tucker! Language! And pick up that beer can!" She slammed the window shut. Mr. Finley kicked the can before begrudgingly picking it up.

The new boy's head rotated toward us. He smiled. His movements were jerky and mechanical, like a puppet.

"Holy smokes, I got goose lumps," Ellen whispered.

"He's weird, even for a Jew. This is bad," Billy said.

We had no idea how right Billy would be.

Chapter 3

———— ⁂ ————

1963

That afternoon, Billy, Ellen, and I hopped on our bikes and headed for the library. We all had Schwinns. Billy had a red 1957 Tiger, and I had a black Corvette. Ellen had the prize, a new Schwinn Stingray. The Stingray came out in June, and Ellen got one for her birthday in July. She could've asked for the Fair Lady model, but Ellen insisted on getting the boy's bike with butterfly handlebars and a banana seat. Billy and I had baseball cards clipped to our spokes to give our bikes an engine sound, but Ellen refused to clip anything to the spokes of her Stingray. We rarely went to the library in the summer, but after watching the movie *Alien Invaders* on TV, Billy decided we should get the book.

"The author wrote it as a warning because it could really happen. Look at Addy and the Jews that moved in. And Mr. Pepsin. What about his greenhouse? And my dad?"

Billy had a wild imagination. We all did. Billy and I loved horror movies and had running arguments about them. I thought the mutant ants in the movie *Them!* were the most terrifying, but Billy had nightmares after watching *Attack of the Crab Monsters* and thought they were the scariest.

"They cut your head off with their claws and eat your brain. Then they absorb your mind and start talking, and your entire neighborhood hears all your thoughts being spoken by a giant crab, even thoughts you would never speak out loud in a million years!"

"Like what?" Ellen asked.

"I'm not saying, but the crabs would. I'd rather have The Blob absorb me than get eaten by the crabs any day."

We loved watching scary movies but hated the nightmares they conjured up. At one point, Billy's parents fought because Billy's father started drinking too much. When you're young, you don't want to believe the people you love would hurt one another without a good reason, and for Billy, that reason became his belief his father's body had been invaded by an alien.

"My dad's not the same. My mother said she doesn't even know who he is anymore. Sound familiar?"

The notion his father's body was invaded by an alien would explain Mr. Finley's sudden bursts of anger. In *Alien Invasion*, alien life forms grow in giant pods and take over people's bodies. It was Billy's favorite *Creature Features*. We needed to get the book so he could help his father.

"We need to know everything about them, Nix. That's the only chance we have of stopping them. Know your enemy, right?"

We tried to take the book out a week earlier, but Ms. Crane, the librarian, informed us of an age restriction. You had to be in high school to check it out. This hurdle required a Plan B. So we rode back to the library and reviewed our alternate plan after locking our bikes to the bike rack. Ellen was our secret weapon. Billy gave her last-minute instructions.

"What are you checking out?"

"A book about Abe Lincoln for a book report."

"Not a book report. We're not in school. Mantis can smell a lie a mile away."

Ellen wagged a finger at Billy. "You shouldn't be stealing books."

"We're not stealing it. We're borrowing it," I said.

Billy finished spinning his bike lock. "We'll put it back before she ever knows we had it."

We walked into the library and Ms. Crane, known as "Mantis," because of her uncanny resemblance to a praying mantis, examined us like insects on a slide. She was freakishly tall with oblong eyes and a long neck. Billy believed she was the child of the Deadly Mantis and the Fifty-Foot Woman. Her glasses hung from a silver chain and rested on her chest, and she walked with her hands bent at the wrists and retracted inward. Billy said she had adapted to her environment because she practically never left the library. "Her wrists stay like that because she takes her glasses on and off a thousand times a day. And she's tall so she can reach the top shelves without a ladder. It's evolution."

The plan was for Ellen to distract Mantis while Billy and I grabbed the book. Ellen was the perfect decoy. She had an aura of innocence that made her immune to suspicion. Ellen walked up to the circulation desk and smiled. "Good morning, Ms. Crane. I was wondering if you could help me find a cookbook where the recipes aren't too hard?"

Mantis shifted her eyes to us then back to Ellen. "That would be in nonfiction. Follow me."

As soon as they were out of sight, Billy and I rushed to the bookshelf where *Alien Invaders* was located. Our library was small. We needed to act fast.

"Keep a lookout," Billy whispered.

"Okay, but hurry!"

Billy rummaged through the books behind me when I spotted Mantis and Ellen emerge from an aisle, but instead of going to the circulation desk, Mantis headed right toward us.

"She's coming!"

Billy fumbled with two books.

"Hurry!"

Mantis's heels clicked against the tile floor. She quickened her pace, turned the corner, and glared at Billy. "Are you boys trying to sneak that book out?"

"No, ma'am," Billy said.

"I wasn't born yesterday," Mantis said.

Billy was so nervous I thought he'd wet himself. "Yes, ma'am. Your birthday had to be at least sixty years ago, right, Nix?"

Mantis scowled. "I'm forty."

"It was an estimate," I said. "Billy's not that good at math."

Mantis pushed past Billy and slid her bony finger across the binders to scan the titles. She found what she was looking for and tipped *Alien Invaders* toward her. Satisfied, she slid it back in place.

"If you need a book in this aisle, you're to request that I accompany you to retrieve it."

"You got it," Billy said.

We hurried out of the library and walked our bikes to the street. We looked back to be sure Mantis didn't follow us outside. "Wow, that was close," I said.

"I switched book covers." Billy pulled the book out of his pants. "The book she saw was a western, and this"—Billy opened the book so Ellen could see the first page—"is *Alien Invaders!*"

"You did real good, Ellen," I said.

Billy put the book in Ellen's bike basket. "Yeah. You can read it after us."

"It was in your pants. I wouldn't touch it if Mr. Clean cleaned it."

"Your loss."

We hopped back on our bikes and headed home.

Chapter 4

1963

We stopped at the 7-Eleven on our way back to get Slurpees. Billy got brain freeze and walked in circles in front of the store with his head in his hands.

"My skull is cracking."

"You're supposed to sip it, knucklehead," Ellen said.

While Billy walked in circles, Rory Pitts showed up on his bike. Rory was the most predatory human being I ever met. My first encounter with him happened in the schoolyard when he cornered Adam Knowle, the runt in a litter of fifth graders at our elementary school. Adam spent his days seeking cover, moving cautiously through the halls to remain anonymous in fear of being bullied. The scariest part about Rory was you didn't have to do anything to end up on his bad side. Adam pleaded with Rory to leave him alone. As Rory's menacing shadow eclipsed him, Adam wet himself. It was worse than being punched because you can't control it if someone punches you. Wetting yourself is inexcusable and incited a level of cruelty known only to kids. I knew something terrible happened to Adam that day. Shame followed him as he ran from the schoolyard. I knew he would never be the same.

"What's with him?" Rory asked, pointing at Billy.

"Brain freeze."

"Not possible. You need a brain for that."

A phone booth was in front of the store. Rory grabbed my arm and yanked me toward it. His grip was legendary, and he had my arm squeezed to the bone.

26

"What gives?"

"Join me in my office." He pulled me into the phone booth and closed the door. "Here's the plan, dweeb. You're going to distract Winston while I pocket baseball cards. Do a good job. If I get caught, you get punched in the face. It's simple. Like your friend out there."

Winston worked the counter in the 7-Eleven. He got in a car accident and ended up needing a glass eye, so he had trouble keeping track of customers in the store. The bad kids took advantage of him and shoplifted stuff.

"I can't. If my parents find out, they'll kill me."

"If you don't, I'll kill you. I'm a definite, and they're a maybe."

I relented. I had seen Rory punch kids before, which always resulted in a black eye, fat lip, or cauliflower ear.

"Okay, but don't take too many, or Winston might get fired."

"Are you telling me what to do?"

"He's only got one eye."

Rory made a fist and pressed the hard bone of his knuckles against my cheek. "How would you like two black ones?"

"Not very much."

"Then shut up and keep Cyclops busy." Rory pulled the phone booth door open and shoved me out.

Once inside the store, I shuffled to the counter. Winston smiled. "Saw your friend walking in circles out there. Brain freeze. Gets them every time."

"Yeah. Some kids never learn." Beads of sweat gathered on my forehead. My heart raced. When you're twelve, stealing from a store is like participating in a bank robbery. It's not shoplifting; it's a heist. Winston lifted his eye from me and peered toward the isle where Rory was stuffing packs of baseball cards in his pockets.

"Do you have aspirin?" I asked.

Winston's eye stayed on the back of the store. "You're too young to buy aspirin. Eighteen or older. Can I help you back there?" he asked Rory.

"No, I'm good."

Winston's eye shifted back to me. He knew I was there to help Rory Pitts steal.

I mouthed, "I'm sorry."

Winston marched from behind the counter straight toward Rory, who appeared from the aisle with packs of baseball cards falling from his pockets. "Wait right there!" Winston said. Rory ran out of the store to where he had left his bike, but someone had moved it. In the minute it took for Rory to look around, Winston had him by the collar.

"Let go of me, or I'll poke out your other eye, you freak!" Rory yelled.

Winston dragged Rory back into the store.

Billy, Ellen, and I jumped on our bikes and took off. Now we not only had *Alien Invaders* to worry about, we had Rory Pitts.

When we got to our street, the new boy was in his wheelchair on his porch. His father was nailing something to the door below the doorbell. The boy waved as we passed. Ellen waved back. When we got to the cul-de-sac, we laid skid marks on the pavement and jumped off our bikes.

"Longest!" Ellen proclaimed.

Billy checked. "By an inch, so big whoop. And why did you wave at the Jew?"

"Because he waved to us."

"You're gonna be sorry."

I sat on the grass and summed up my situation. "I'm dead."

"Why? I'm the one who moved his bike," Ellen said.

"He said if he gets caught, it's on me."

"At least we're not in school. I don't think he'll come on our block," Billy said.

Ellen plopped on the grass and looked up at the sky. "Wanna mind bust clouds?"

Mind busting clouds was Ellen's favorite pastime.

"You can't bust clouds with your brain," Billy said.

"Sure, you can. All you have to do is believe. That's what my dad says."

Before I sat down by Ellen, I took *Alien Invaders* out of the basket on her bike. "Who gets to read it first?"

"Let's shoot for it," Billy said. "Odds or evens?"

"Evens."

We shot for everything back then. Each person shot out one finger or two, and you'd end up with an even or odd number. Two out of three won.

"Ready?" I asked.

Billy nodded.

"I'll call it," Ellen said. "One, two, three...shoot!"

Billy shot out one finger, and I shot out two.

"Odds!" Ellen said. "One, two, three...shoot!"

Billy shot out two fingers, and I shot out one.

Ellen looked to Billy. "Odds! Nix wins!"

"Darn it," Billy said.

"Don't worry. I read fast."

Sometimes, we didn't want to shoot for it. So for other matters of consequence, we played rock, paper, scissors, or asked Magic 8-Ball. Girls had an additional method known as the "cootie catcher" made of paper with flaps that had colors and numbers, and you'd pick a color, then a number, and it told you something like who you would marry.

"Time for lunch," Billy said.

"*Creature Features* at my house this afternoon?"

"My mom doesn't like me watching that stuff. It gives me nightmares," Ellen said.

"You say that every week," Billy said.

Ellen always came over. I loved it when she watched scary movies because, for once, she'd scoot close to me. The truth was, I was seeing Ellen Yancey more as a cute girl with adorable freckles on her nose than as an outfielder who could catch pop flies. It confused me because a part of me hated Ellen for being so cute while the other part daydreamed about what it would feel like to kiss her.

Chapter 5

2020

Of no surprise to those who had previously attended this summer sermon, Gladys plays, and the choir, which consists of Otis Oliver and twins Francis and Winnie Dern stands as abruptly as a choir whose average age is eighty can and sings "Puppy Love." Gladys presses the keys, and Buster puffs out the melody in grand style. As they sing, I thank God for my life, these friends, and the blessing of memory. Our ability to revisit the past is a precious gift. Old songs are a gentle tap on the shoulder, a voice that whispers, "Remember me?" I feel sorry for the younger generation. Their memories will be fragments of instant messages, texts, and video chats. They will never hear as many shared dreams, close whispers, or laughter as the older among us did. Tears fill my eyes. The pews are full, and beams of sunlight stream through the stained glass windows. Ms. Nellie's rose water perfume wafts past me. The congregation joins the choir in song. The emphasis on the words is playfully accusatory. Crying tears. Hoping she'd be back in my arms again.

It's a peculiar truth that parishioners believe their pastors never thought about things like kissing girls or, God forbid, s-e-x. But as Harpey said, "The Bible's full of sex. God tells the raw truth!" Harpey was wise beyond his years. We thought he might be an old man inhabiting a boy's body. Not so strange when you consider we thought alien invaders had invaded the neighborhood that summer.

The song ends, and Gladys smiles. "Back to you, Pastor."

I turn to Moses. "We're on."

"Try not to be boring," he says.

Chapter 6

1963

Billy, Ellen, and I sat on my living room floor in front of the Philco TV and watched *The Blob*. Ellen covered her eyes. "Is it gone yet?"

"No," I said.

"Tell me when it's gone."

Billy sat wide-eyed, sipping a glass of chocolate milk made with Bosco. "It's like a batch of Silly Putty went crazy and started eating people."

A group of teenagers ran from a movie theatre while *The Blob* oozed out of the building. If the gelatinous life form caught you, it devoured you.

Ellen leaned toward me. Her shoulder touched mine, and I tried not to move. I wanted it to last. My mother got a new living room set. The cushions were encased in plastic. If you sat on them, they stuck to you when you got up. So we sat on the floor on the braided rug with our backs against the couch.

When the movie ended, Ellen and Billy left. I went to my room to read. As I opened my book, muffled voices came from Izzy's room. I hurried to my closet and hunkered down in the corner. I kept a water glass in the closet so I could listen in on Izzy. I put it up to the wall and pressed my ear to the glass.

"There's a million fish in the sea, and you and Harry keep swimming back to each other like poodle magnets," Izzy said.

"I can't help it," Margaret Ann said.

I knew it was Margaret Ann because, when she talked, it sounded as if she had cotton balls up her nose. She was always whining to Izzy about her boyfriend, Harry Moore.

"My mother said I'm a tease and boys hate teases," Margaret Ann said.

"And how in the name of Pete are you a tease?"

"By wearing my skirts above the knee."

"First off, don't ask your mother about boys. The last time she dated, *American Bandstand* wasn't even on TV. Write this down. The secret to keeping a guy is to treat him like a prisoner of war. Keep him hungry but never let him starve. You give him enough food to keep him healthy but not so much that he gets fat and happy and thinks about possible escape."

I loved listening in on Izzy and Margaret Ann. It gave me the inside scoop on the secret life of girls. And when you're a twelve-year-old boy, that's nothing to sneeze at. Then I sneezed, and Izzy pounded on the wall.

"Ouch!" I yelled.

"Mind your business, nosebleed!"

I went back to my bed to read *Alien Invaders*. It was about a town where the people acted strange because aliens were taking over their minds and bodies. Billy believed it was happening on our block. I got through the first chapter when my father's car pulled in the driveway. I jumped up to my window as he got out of the car and walked toward the house. He moved as if he were on the last leg of a long journey. He held his tin lunch pail in one hand and grabbed the newspaper from the mailbox with the other. I ran to the door to meet him.

"Hey, Dad!"

"Hey."

He put his hand on my head for a moment as he often did and walked past me into the kitchen. He sat at the kitchen table and opened *The Town Post*. He turned the pages until he got to the Buy, Sell, or Trade section. I never understood why he was so interested in it because he never bought, sold, or traded anything.

"It's the gossip section for men," Izzy explained. "So they can be nosy about what the neighbors are up to while pretending to engage in commerce."

"Anything good?" I asked my dad.

"Same ol', same ol'."

My mother came into the kitchen and kissed him. "You look tired. Rough day?"

"Plant was an oven."

"Mr. Cappy said the humidity's almost 100 percent." Mr. Cappy was the local weatherman.

"How can you be wrong every day and still have a job? If he was in my business, nothing would stick."

"Now, now," my mother said, "let me get your dinner. Izzy! Time for dinner!"

This was an exercise in futility. Izzy couldn't hear a thing with her music blaring.

"Margaret Ann broke up with Harry again," I said.

"Mercy me," my mother said.

My mother was about to get Izzy when my father raised his arm in protest. It was his signal to my mother to let it be. Izzy's door opened, and Leslie Gore singing "Judy's Turn to Cry" blared through the house. Instead of turning down the record player, Izzy screamed over Leslie. "Tell me it's not fish sticks. If I eat one more of those, I'll grow gills!"

My father and mother shared the look parents share after their children become teenagers—the "what have we done?" look. I intervened. No sense in ruining dinner over the prospect of fish sticks.

"I got it," I said.

I told Izzy what we were having. She instructed me to tell the cook and court jester she'd be having her chicken a la king in her quarters with her faithful subject, Margaret Ann.

"Queen Izzy will take two plates in her quarters, one for her and one for her faithful subject, Margaret Ann."

My mother made two plates for the girls. I delivered them to Izzy's room and went back to the kitchen.

"How's your routine going, honey?" my mother asked. "Your father's so excited about your entry in the talent show." My mother often spoke for my father. Izzy said married people do that.

"After five years, they mold into one person. It's like demonic possession. There's a battle until one of them gives up their soul." Despite Izzy's explanation, the practice annoyed me. I wanted to hear from my dad.

"Good. But it would be better if I had an actual ventriloquist dummy for the act."

My parents shared another look. My mother smiled. "We'll see. You just keep practicing."

I didn't know it then, but they feared the tape factory might close, so they were saving money to tide us over in the event it happened. Paying six dollars for a ventriloquist dummy would be a burden.

After dinner, Ellen played hopscotch in the street. She wore pink shorts and a pink tank top with daisies on it. Her honey blond hair fell across her face as she hopped from one box to the other.

"The new boy's out."

I turned and looked at the boy seated in his wheelchair at the bottom of his driveway.

Ellen hopped as she spoke. "Do you think he's as weird as Billy says he is?"

"Beats me."

I tried to act as if I'd gotten past my apprehension of him. Was it a coincidence the new kid looked like Jerry Mahoney? Was it possible that Paul Winchell's sidekick wasn't a dummy but an actual boy that had been faking it all along?

Ellen made it across the chalk-lined hopscotch box and hopped back. She pushed her hair back behind her ears as her sneakers scuffed the pavement.

"He can't run or play on the jungle gym. It's not fair." Ellen balanced on one foot, bent over to lift a penny from a square, and continued across the board.

Billy came out of his house. He walked up the street, sipping a bottle of Orange Crush. Billy was a soda junkie. If he was out of regular soda, he'd drink his mother's Tab.

The new kid tracked Billy as he walked by. We met on the cul-de-sac and sat on the grass.

"We need to make a pact," Billy said. "We ignore the Jew. Spit shake."

Ellen looked at the boy sitting in his wheelchair. "I'm not hating someone because you say so."

"Fine. Be that way."

Billy looked to me.

I shook my head. "Not yet."

Billy threw back another swig of Orange Crush, swished it around like mouthwash, and swallowed it. "You guys will regret it. Just wait and see."

For the next week, we did our best to ignore the new kid as we went about the rituals of summer. We played baseball, rode our bikes, climbed trees, and paid special attention to the behavior of our parents and neighbors for any sign they were acting weird. In the evening, we met on the cul-de-sac to discuss it. Billy picked up a stick and popped a tar bubble. "My dad's getting worse. He screamed at my mom last night and told her she was a lazy, good-for-nothing, and then woke up this morning and acted like it never happened. What do you think of that?"

I didn't know what to think. I was too busy fixating on the new kid. His look and mannerisms matched Jerry Mahoney's to such a degree even Izzy commented on it.

"That kid looks like your dummy friend."

"Well, he's not."

"Yup, it's him. And that Winchell guy is full of crap, making us believe he's throwing his voice while he's a got a real kid sitting on his lap."

"Don't be stupid, Izzy. Just because somebody looks like somebody else doesn't mean it's them. You think they'd let him on TV if he was faking it?"

"Are you saying you think Mr. Ed can really talk?"

She had me there. They dubbed that. But I was sure Paul Winchell was no fraud.

Billy noticed me staring at the new kid. "Hey, how about casting an eye this way?"

"Sorry."

"I'm telling you, there're pods here, and we need to find them. If we don't, your parents could be next."

Ellen stood. "Stop saying that. You're scaring me!"

It was getting dark, and Ellen needed to be home when the streetlights came on. There were only two on our street, and Ellen knew they were about to light up that small area of the street between the cul-de-sac and her house.

Billy pointed to the new kid. "That's what should scare you. He's doing it again. What'd I tell you, huh?"

Before the sun went down each night, the new kid went inside.

"They might be vampires," Billy said.

Ellen jetted a hip out and snarled. "Stop it, Billy Finley!"

"If they were vampires, they'd come out when the sun goes down and go in when the sun comes up," I said.

The new kid wheeled himself into the house. "My dad says Jews bury their dead within twenty-four hours, or something happens."

"Like what?" I asked.

"I dunno. Maybe if they don't bury each other fast enough, they turn into zombies."

It sounds crazy now, but when you're a kid, your mind thinks crazy thoughts, especially after it gets dark and you just finished watching *Creature Features*.

"Now I'm scared. And it's all your fault, Billy!" Ellen said.

"I'll walk you home," I said.

"No. Just watch me and don't take your eyes off me."

That would be easy. Ellen walked toward her house, and when she got close, ran the rest of the way to her door. She turned to us and waved then went inside.

It was almost dark. Time for Billy and me to go on a secret mission.

Billy and I were avid fans of *The Hardy Boys* mystery series. I received *The House on the Cliff* for Christmas in 1960, the second book in the series. Since then, we had devoured every book in the set. We imagined ourselves to be the amateur sleuths, Frank and Joe Hardy.

"We need to be careful. No mistakes," Billy said.

"Got it."

A berm ran behind the houses on my side of the street and separated them from a farm out back. Old farmer James lived there, and he went to bed around six, so we never had to worry about anyone seeing us from the back side of the berm. It was a wonderful place to hide. You got a panoramic view of everyone's backyard. We settled in behind the new neighbor's house and watched. Billy peered through his dad's binoculars.

"See anything?" I asked.

A screen door opened and slammed shut. Billy shifted the binoculars to Mr. Pepsin's backyard. "It's Pepsin."

Mr. Pepsin was a retired schoolteacher who spent his time mowing, watering, and fertilizing his lawn. He hated weeds. He yanked them from his lawn like fat ticks on a beloved dog. He had a greenhouse in his backyard with cactus and other weird plants in it. Billy wondered if Mr. Pepsin might use his greenhouse to grow alien pods.

"It makes perfect sense. Pepsin's bonkers about plants. That makes him the ideal patsy."

Almost everything made perfect sense to Billy, even if it made little sense to anyone else. When he saw Mantis in church, he said it made perfect sense. "Where else would a praying mantis be on Sunday morning?" as if it were obvious. "Maybe Pepsin's invaded?" he said.

"I don't think so."

"Why?"

"He shoots up nose spray every five minutes. I don't think aliens need to clear their sinuses all the time." Pepsin was a nose spray addict. He always had a bottle of nasal mist in his pocket.

"Yeah, you're probably right."

Pepsin stepped into the greenhouse and flipped on the light. A single bulb dangled on a wire. The bulb swayed and illuminated the greenhouse, casting a shadow of Pepsin that hovered over him like a second presence. He was as thin as a matchstick and had a case of horseshoe baldness that left a thick ring of hair around the crown of his head. His shadow highlighted his bony, elongated fingers. He spoke to his plants, "Good evening, Margery. Victoria, you look wonderful tonight," and "Oh my, my Rosie, how you've grown!"

"Hear that? He talks to them like they're alive!" Billy said.

Pepsin's shadow wavered above him as warm gusts of wind kicked up; the vinyl walls of the greenhouse snapped like a bull-whip. Bits of hay flew up from the berm and the rusted chains on the metal swing set in the Mendelson's yard creaked as the empty swings swayed.

"That's creepy," Billy said.

"Yeah." I laughed nervously. "Creepy."

"We crawl on hands and knees to the window. No talking."

"Got it."

We crept past the rattling swing set toward the house. Pepsin was still whispering to his plants. The screen door on the porch swung open and slammed shut. We froze. We waited then lifted our chins and peered through a tiny opening below the window cur-tain. Our eyes grew as wide as manhole covers. Our new neighbors were performing a ritual. The man, the woman, and the little boy in his wheelchair were around the dining room table. Candles, three glasses, a bottle of wine, and a loaf of bread covered with a cloth nap-kin sat on the table. The woman lit the candles, waved her hands over them, covered her eyes, and chanted, "*Baruch atah Adonai, Eloheinu, Melech ha-olam, asher kid'shanu b'mitzvotav, v'tzivanu, l'had'lik neir shel shabbat. Amein.*" They each took a glass of wine, lifted it, and chanted again. Then the woman dipped her fingers in spilled wine and touched her eyelids. The hair lifted on the back of my neck. We dropped from the window and scampered on our stomachs back to the berm.

Billy's face was ashen. "Holy crap," he said, his voice cracking. "I told you! Man, oh man, this is bad, Nix. This is really bad!"

The swings in the Mendelson's backyard twisted and clanked in the wind as Pepsin's voice bellowed in the dark, "Grow, my little children! Grow!"

That did it. We both ran home as fast as our PF Flyers would take us.

Chapter 7

2020

The congregation sits silently for a moment. I turn Moses toward me and drop his jaw open.

"Something wrong?" I ask.

"Yeah. I need to change my drawers."

Laughter breaks the tension in the room. With Gladys, who played ominous notes on the organ, and Virgil Finn, who reprised his role as Mr. Pepsin and bellowed a bone-chilling "Grow my little children! Grow!" from the back of the church, we had drawn the congregation into the eerie feeling of that long-ago night when Billy and I peered in the Mendelson's window. Virgil, who took an early retirement last year at age sixty-two, cherished the opportunity to display his acting prowess. In his heyday, he had done voice-over work on commercials. His most notable was the time he was the voice of the raisin in a Raisin Bran commercial that aired during *The Wonder Years* in the late eighties.

"Those were the days," he'll tell you, with a sparkle in his eye that belies his age. Virgil is the church handyman and janitor, but his first love—aside from his wife, Ruby—is acting. Each year, he directs the church Christmas show, and you'd think he was directing a Hollywood movie. It was only July, and he already put out the call for this year's players. He's short, not quite five feet, eight inches, with a red beard, a crop of tightly wound red hair, and an infectious love for Jesus. A cross between an old biker and Santa Claus, one would never suspect he was once a prolific actor, or as he states, "My voice was."

As I stand on the church steps, shaking hands with my parish-ioners, I soak in their warmth and appreciation. Ms. Nellie pushes her walker, slow and steady, from her designated pew. Her frail arms tremble as she shuffles toward the exit. She is a vibrant spirit trapped in an aging vessel. Blotches of liver spots litter her forearms, and her fingers, gnarled and arthritic, grip the walker. Each step is a cautious adventure. She slides the four yellow tennis balls attached to the legs of her walker along the plank wood floor. On the front two tennis balls, she has PRAISE written on one, and GOD on the other. On the back two tennis balls, PASS and NO, are written in black let-tering. Ms. Nellie has lost some eyesight and mobility but not her sense of humor. She looks up at me and smiles, pausing a moment to calculate the distance between us, and then continues her journey. When she reaches me, she extends her hand to mine, and I clasp it.

"Wonderful, Pastor. Unlike me, that story never gets old."

"You're a blessing to us all, Ms. Nellie," I say and believe it with all my heart.

With services over and pleasantries complete, I return to the lectern, place Moses back in his trunk, and wheel him into my office. I plop into my leather chair and breathe. Sermons exhaust me. I turned sixty-nine this past April, but age has little to do with my post-sermon fatigue. I suffer from stage fright, and there is no more consequential stage than the pulpit. Actors have millions of dollars riding on their performances, but pastors have mortal souls riding on theirs. Actors answer to an audience; pastors answer to God. It is the reason many pastors I know ask God to provide the words that allow us to be instruments of his voice. It is, after all, His show.

As I close my eyes, there's a tapping on my office door. It's Opal McGill, the church secretary. I can tell from the tapping, which strikes the door as *tap...tap, tap, tap...tap...taptaptaptaptap*. Opal is hearing impaired, but when she taps on my door, it's like Morse code. I understand it like a second language. Something is up. I go to the door and open it. Opal has something on her mind. She signs so fast I can't keep up. It's like watching a chef at Benihana flash Ginsu knives. I signal her to slow down, and her face scrunches up in frustration. When Opal has something urgent to communicate, she expects you to keep up. She's excellent at reading lips if you enunciate, so I deliver my words with clarity.

"The collection plate, what?" I ask, having garnered that much from her signing. "Stop talking so fast!"

God has given Opal many gifts. Patience is not one of them. She rolls her eyes. Born in Alabama, she traces her ancestry back to slaves active in the Underground Railroad. Her refined features and copper-colored skin are overshadowed by fierce amber eyes that light up when she's excited.

"A collection plate is missing?" I ask to confirm what she signed.

"Yes, the gold one!"

She signals for me to follow her. We go to the cabinet where we store the collection plates, and Opal points to the spot where our gold-plated collection plate should be. "Gone!" she signs.

I stare at the vacant spot, dumbfounded. The missing collection plate has been a part of Miller Memorial Church for well over a hundred years. It is a cherished artifact, and I'm stunned that it is not in its usual place. We had purchased lighter brass plates, so we haven't passed the gold one in years.

Opal is apoplectic. If she signs any harder, she'll dislocate a shoulder. "We need to call the police this minute!"

"We're not calling the police, Opal. I'm sure it will turn up."

Opal's Ginsu knives are back at it. "Turn up? We've been *robbed!*"

"I don't believe that."

"Take your head out of your rump! It's gone, isn't it!"

"Maybe someone borrowed it."

"Borrowed it?" Opal rolls her eyes again and marches out of the room.

I take a moment to collect my thoughts. There must be an innocent explanation for the missing collection plate. When I walk back into the chapel, Opal is looking up at Jesus on the cross, signing to Him in a fury. When I frustrate her, Opal turns to Jesus, and for that, I'm grateful.

Virgil walks through a row of pews, picking up cups and leftover bulletins. He looks up at me and joins me at the back of the chapel. He rubs his beard for a moment as we both watch Opal talk to God. Then he says, "We don't have enough kids in youth ministry for the Christmas show, Pastor."

"Yes, I know. We have dwindled in that area."

"Jesus loves the little children," he says, his voice clear and commanding.

"All the children of the world," I respond.

I feel the weight of it all pushing down on me. Our church is aging, a collection plate is missing, and Virgil has *ipso facto* made me the casting director of this year's Christmas play.

God help us all.

My house is three blocks from the church. My knees ache, and my one arm grows tired from pulling Moses along behind me. I pause to switch hands and remember when this walk felt like a breeze. Now I trudge along, pressed against the wind in an aging body. I am blessed, as my beloved Matty used to say, "to have my original parts." Despite this, today's walk has exposed a need to sit less and spend more time getting about. As Gladys often professes, "We are to walk with the Lord, not sit on our lard."

I breathe in the sweet aroma of honeysuckle and continue on my way. My cottage rests amidst a beautiful garden, and in the waning colors of dusk, I'm reminded of paintings by the artist Thomas Kinkade. This scene brings me back to those summer nights when Ellen sought to count the stars and Harpey would remind us of the miracle of creation.

"God breathed everything into being," Harpey said one night as we sat on the cul-de-sac just before it was time to go inside.

"I wonder if He has bad breath," Billy asked.

This was Billy. He wondered about things nobody else ever thought of.

I arrive at my walkway. A line of gray cobblestone leads to my porch, and the wheels of Moses's trunk thump along until I reach the porch steps. I pause a moment to catch my breath and then pull the trunk up onto the porch. I don't leave Moses at the church because I worry my longtime sidekick might become the victim of a fire. The church is old and wooden, just like Moses, and despite the sprinkler system, I can't risk losing him. Moses has been with me for most of my life, and with the help of the Lord, we have saved many souls. We are a team.

I stand on the porch, kiss my fingers, and touch the tile Matty had painted and affixed next to the door with lettering that said, "God in our thoughts." I ring the doorbell, knowing I will not hear the shuffling of Matty's slippers across the tile as she comes to answer the door. I imagine her opening the door and saying, "Oh, it's you again," before we embrace and share a kiss. Ringing the doorbell when I get home became a tradition after Matty became ill. Frequently, while asleep during the day, I would come in the house and, in her words, "scare the wits out of me" by coming in unannounced. "Ring the bell," she said one day, "It'll force me to get off my duff and answer the door." I thought it was a silly idea but went along. The next day, I rang the bell when I came home, and she answered it just as she did from that point forward, "Oh, it's you again."

It became our tradition, and I could not stop myself from ringing the doorbell ever since. It's been almost a year since Matty's passing, and as I enter the house, the emptiness I feel is overwhelming. Still, I am grateful for the years we had together and content to know she is her old self again, free from pain and awaiting my arrival. I smile and wonder if she might have had a doorbell installed at the pearly gates so I can ring it and she can answer and say, "Oh, it's you again." That would be my Matty; that would be my heaven.

Like so many things I learned from Harpey Mendelson, the importance of connecting the present to the past remains a staple of my life. I set the trunk containing Moses in its place beside my living room couch, walk to the kitchen, and begin making my lunch. Hot dogs. Hebrew National.

Harpey would insist.

Chapter 8

Sunday, June 14, 2020
Summer Sermon Series: Week Two

I peek into the chapel. The church is standing room only. It has been a blessing that the story of Harpey Mendelson has spread through word of mouth, which is ironic when you consider its pedigree to ventriloquism. I kneel in my office and speak my prayer in a whisper. "Dear God, may my words be yours. Grace me with your wisdom. Open their hearts and minds and let my sermon honor you in all ways. Amen."

Gladys plays the opening medley of "The Old Rugged Cross" and segues into her special version of "Amazing Grace." She told me during Wednesday night rehearsal that she "put a little spice into it." Gladys was quite the hell-raiser in her day.

According to her husband Stanley who she met in Haight-Ashbury in '67 during the Summer of Love, Gladys was never a part of the status quo. "She's always been a rebellious soul," Stanley said to me one afternoon at a church picnic. He leaned in toward me to be sure no one else could hear. "In that mini dress with knee-high boots, flowers in her hair, playing her guitar, singing 'Where Have All the Flowers Gone?' What chance did I have?"

"What chance indeed," I said.

"She looked like Peggy Lipton. Remember her?"

"Who could forget Peggy Lipton? *The Mod Squad* was a favorite of mine."

"Back in the day, Gladys could be her twin. Whenever she says she will put a little spice in something, I can still see the hippie in her eyes. Melts me like butta," he says, emphasizing the colloquial pronunciation of "butter."

If there is such a thing as a match made in heaven, Gladys and Stanley are it. They still gaze at one another with adoring eyes, still hold hands, and still say "I love you" at least once a day.

"It's a miracle we're alive," Stanley said. "We tuned in, turned on, and dropped acid. We followed the world. We were in it, of it, and totally out of it. Then we met a wild-looking, modern-day John the Baptist. He had a crop of untamed hair, a thick beard, and piercing blue eyes. He stood at river's edge at Woodstock, bare-chested in hip-hugger jeans, and spoke of the ultimate radical—Jesus Christ. 'Follow the one who changed the world!' he bellowed. And we did. Have ever since."

We each come to God in our own way. For me, it was through an encounter one strange summer with a boy named Harpey Mendelson. I enter the chapel with Moses in tow, lead the congregation in prayer, and continue my sermon.

Chapter 9

---∽---

A t witnessing the strange ritual in the Mendelson's window, Mr. Pepsin's creepy voice echoed in my brain. "Grow, my little children! Grow!"

But Mr. Finley's rage at Billy made me forget Mr. Pepsin. On summer nights, everyone kept their windows open, so when Mr. Finley yelled at Billy, everyone heard. "What did I tell you about cleaning up this room? It looks like a pigsty!"

I recoiled.

Izzy's door swung open. "In the name of Pete, are the men in this neighborhood losing their minds?"

The yelling frightened me. Billy was my friend, and I wanted to help him, but what could I do?

I lay down on my bed and looked up at the glow-in-the-dark stars I had pasted to my ceiling. I was afraid of the dark, and like my dad who read the Buy, Sell, Trade section to hide his curiosity about the neighbors, I put up stars so I wouldn't have to ask for a night-light and admit my fear. I thought about the Blob, how it consumed people, and in my mind's eye, Rory Pitts became the Blob. It had his gap-toothed smile and that feral look Rory got when he locked in on a victim. *It wouldn't be so bad if Rory was the Blob*, I thought. The Blob didn't have fists. I patted my jaw and knew how easy it would be for Rory to knock my jaw off its hinges. I looked at the bright side. If he broke my jaw, it would be wired shut, and I'd be forced to practice throwing my voice without moving my lips.

Ellen's laughter interrupted my thoughts. I went to my window and peered through the screen. It was dusk, and the sky, painted in swaths of orange, pink and red, hung over the neighborhood like an artist's canvass. Ellen was in her pajamas chasing fireflies on her front lawn. She looked like an angel as she leaped about with the elusive bugs dancing all around her. Ellen's parents sat on their porch and watched Ellen play. They clapped and swooned. Mr. Yancey leaped to his feet and joined her, lifting her into the air and spinning her until they both collapsed to the ground in a fit of laughter. I wondered if these were moments fathers saved for their daughters. Mr. Yancey got up and bent forward, putting his hands on his knees so Ellen could jump on his back.

"Giddy up!" Ellen commanded, and Mr. Yancey did his best imitation of a horse as he galloped toward the front door.

"Open the gate, Mom!" Ellen yelled. Mrs. Yancey opened the front door, and they entered the house, letting the screen door close behind them.

I knew Ellen's dad was an executive with a beer company, so he didn't have to endure sweltering days in a factory like my dad, but this did little to quell the longing I had to do something fun with my dad. I grabbed Mr. Mercury and practiced throwing my voice.

"Some kids have all the luck," I said.

"Stop whining. It's embarrassing."

"Yes, sir," I said and went to sleep.

On Sunday morning, everyone was up early getting ready for church. My mother ran late putting her face on. Izzy, in the throes of teenage rebellion, refused to wear any dress below the knee. My mother asked Izzy to wear a longer skirt, but Izzy refused. "Eve wore a fig leaf. I think I'm good."

The more I studied voices, the more I realized how powerful they could be. Izzy spoke in directives, as if whatever she said was so obvious only a moron would disagree. It was genius.

My mother wore a green dress and pillbox hat. Jackie Kennedy was the trendsetter back then, and my mother did her best on the wages of a waitress and a factory worker to match the First Lady's style. She looked fabulous. My father was a different story. His suit didn't look too bad, but his wide tie ended just below his breastbone. It looked like a bib.

"Are we going to church or The Crab House?" Izzy asked, pointing at the tie.

My mother stared at Izzy with the same intensity Superman displays when he deploys his X-ray vision. "Church. And since God rested on the seventh day, perhaps you could rest your sarcasm."

"I'm not tying it again," my father said.

My mother tapped his shoulder. "It's fine, Walter."

We walked outside, and my mother glanced at the new kid in his wheelchair in front of the Kelly's old house. "That's so sad."

My father never went over ten miles an hour on our street, and as we passed the boy, he waved as if we were on a float in a parade. My mother smiled and waved back. "How sweet. Did you meet him yet, Nix?"

"No. Billy said they go to church on Saturdays and don't celebrate Christmas. They're Jews."

"Did you hear that, Walter? They're Jews."

This was another mysterious practice that went on between married people. My mother constantly asked my father if he heard this or heard that. If you didn't know better, you'd think he was deaf.

"I expect you to welcome him to the neighborhood," my mother said.

"But Billy said—"

"Did you hear me?"

"Yes, ma'am."

When we got to the church, Ellen was on the church steps being greeted by Reverend Malty. She wore a blue polka-dot dress and saddle shoes. She had daisies in her hair and a silver bracelet on her wrist. I was stunned. She was unrecognizable from the reliable centerfielder who liked to spit in her glove and rub it in with the heel of her hand. Ellen had never worn a dress to church before, and she looked, well...beautiful. Izzy noticed Ellen when I did.

"Uh-oh. Looks like your pal discovered she's a girl. She just joined a different league, and guess what? You're not in it."

"Shut up."

"See that posture? That's the classic 'Step right up, boys, and eat your hearts out.' For a first-timer, she's a natural."

"You're a jerk, Izzy!"

My mother glowered at us. "Stop it this minute! For goodness sake, we're at church."

We got in line and made our way up the brick steps that led to the chapel. As my mother and father shook hands with Reverend Malty, I looked behind me as Rory Pitts walked up the sidewalk with his parents. My jaw dropped. I didn't recognize him at first because he wore a suit that was so tight he looked like a flabby arm constricted in a blood-pressure cuff. His black hair was slicked back and parted in the middle, and the knot in his tie was the size of a grapefruit. He was scowling. I had never seen him at church and wondered if it might be a part of his penance for stealing from the 7-Eleven. If so, I was in double trouble. My first prayer was that God would strike Rory blind or make me invisible, whichever was easier. Rory had already violated the "thou shalt not steal" commandment. If he saw me, I was sure "thou shalt not kill" would be next.

The chapel was packed. We had to search for an open pew. Billy said they called them pews because church stank. "It's actually *p-u*'s," he said. Billy hated church because his mother made him get up early every Sunday morning to polish his shoes. "How stupid is that? You think Jesus made the apostles polish their sandals? Think he said, 'Hey, Mark, you've got a scuff on your strap. Whip out the Kiwi and give it a shine.'" I knew Billy would be late. He always came in after the music because Billy's father said it gave him a headache.

Izzy spotted a seat by Margaret Ann and split from the family before my mother could protest. We found three spots, second pew center. I was hoping to sit near Ellen, but she and her family were in a full row near the back of the church. My mother and father sat beside one another, and I ended up sitting next to Mantis, whose bug eyes gave me her infamous prolonged look of indifference.

"Hi," I said and glanced away. Mantis's ability to stare kids down was legendary. Trying to outstare her was like trying to beat Wild Bill Hickock in a gunfight. Even Harvey Shillberger, who had a neurological disorder and only blinked when he remembered to, lost to Mantis.

The service began with several old hymns. My mother sang with gusto. She did this to make up for my dad, who mouthed the words without making a sound. I wasn't a big fan of church, but the Reverend Malty's sermons became a weekly lesson in the art of vocalization. Reverend Malty, otherwise known as "The Rev," was an amalgam of Abe Lincoln and Ichabod Crane. At six feet, five inches, he was a towering figure with a salt-and-pepper beard, a crop of rust-colored hair, and the awkward gait of a man on stilts. His appearance aside, it was his voice that captured my attention, the way he breathed more air into some words and less into others, how he raised and lowered his voice and altered his tone for effect. Today, he talked about how Jesus instructed the faithful to turn the other cheek.

"And Jesus said to them, 'You've heard it was said, an eye for an eye, and a tooth for a tooth. But I tell you, do not resist an evil person. If anyone slaps you on the right cheek, turn to them the other cheek also.'"

Mantis whispered, "Amen," and someone poked me on the shoulder.

I turned and came eye to eye with the devil himself. Rory leaned toward me and said, "Too bad you don't have an extra nose to offer."

Rory's father grabbed Rory's shoulder and pulled him back into his seat. Fear washed over me. Rory was going to punch me, and Jesus said I should let him do it and turn the other cheek so he could do it again. How would giving Rory two shots at my face help anything? The Rev said we should love our enemies and pray for those who persecute us. Great. What was his next piece of advice going to be, that I should draw a bullseye on each cheek to improve Rory's aim?

When the kids were released for Sunday school, I was out of my seat and through the side exit before Rory had a chance to stand. I stepped on an old lady's foot on the way out, and she mumbled, "Jesus Christ Almighty," even after I said I was sorry. I should have asked her to offer her other foot so I could step on that one too, but

I needed to get to Sunday school before Rory ambushed me in the hall.

When I reached the Sunday school room, Mr. Waycrest stood in the doorway. I breathed a sigh of relief. He wore a toupee that wouldn't stay put, and his dentures were always slipping, and his shoulder went out a lot. It made me wonder if he had other body parts that weren't securely fastened. You'd think he'd avoid shaking hands, but he insisted on greeting every Sunday school attendee with a vigorous handshake. It gave Rory time to catch up, and he got in line behind me and wasted no time letting me know he was there.

"Think Waycrest's teeth move around? Just wait till I get done with you. Your teeth are gonna scatter on the ground like loose Chicklets." He took his knuckle and ground it into my spine.

"Cut it!" I yelled, swatting his hand away.

Waycrest looked toward us. "Is there a problem?"

"I accidently bumped into him," Rory said, and then he looked at me with pious eyes. "Sorry, friend, please forgive me."

Waycrest smiled. "To forgive is divine."

Man, was I in trouble. I thought about that movie, *The Hunchback of Notre Dame*. The hunchback was the bell-ringer at the church, and you never saw a guy happier to ring a bell in your life. Apparently, the bell-ringer at this church would be Rory Pitts, and the bell he would ring was mine. I gently shook Mr. Waycrest's clammy hand to avoid making his shoulder pop out and walked into the classroom. I needed a miracle and silently prayed to Jesus to protect me from Rory. I promised Him I'd be good to the new boy, even though he went to church on Saturdays and didn't celebrate Christmas. Our chairs were positioned in a semi-circle, and Rory sat directly across from me. Mr. Waycrest folded his hands.

"Let us pray."

We all followed suit, except Rory, who retrieved a pack of candy-cigarettes from his shirt pocket. He removed the cellophane while Mr. Waycrest thanked God for the sunny morning, good friends, his health, his Aunt Ann's successful surgery for her bowel obstruction, world peace, the church potluck, and a special prayer that Hank Casper's new prosthetic leg, set to arrive on Tuesday, would be a perfect fit. Rory proceeded to "smoke" and glare at me. He wedged the candy cigarette into the cleft between his teeth and held up his hands as if to say "ta-da!" Then he slid his finger across his throat, letting me know I was about to suffer the consequences of not keeping my mouth shut at the 7-Eleven.

After Mr. Waycrest said, "Amen," Ellen walked into the room and took the seat between Rory and Marsha Boyle. Marsha was so skinny it made you wonder how all the standard internal organs fit inside her body. Kids at school called her Olive Boyle because she looked like Olive Oil, Popeye's skinny girlfriend. Marsha was awkward in social situations, especially around boys. Whenever a boy said something, she laughed even if it wasn't funny and said things like "Isn't that a hoot?" and "What a riot!" But Marsha had her limits, so when Rory put the fake cigarette between his teeth and made faces during prayer time, she didn't laugh or say a word.

Mr. Waycrest welcomed Ellen into the room. "Ellen Yancey, I didn't recognize you. You look very pretty this morning."

Mr. Waycrest proceeded with the lesson of the day, the story of David and Goliath. As the story unfolded, I imagined Rory as Goliath and me as David. I had a slingshot and a rock and soon, Rory, the Philistine, would fall dead at my hand, and then I'd cut his head off! Well, maybe I wouldn't cut his head off. That was gross. But I'd put a knot in the center of his forehead the size of a grapefruit, and all the kids in school would fall at my feet and yell, "Hail, Nixon!"

Like I said earlier, we all had big imaginations back then.

Chapter 10

2020

I raise my arm to emphasize my proclamation and stand like some perverse version of the Statue of Liberty. Moses swivels his head toward me and arches his thick brows. The congregation laughs. His expression gets them every time. "Hail, Nixon?"

"I got carried away."

"By who? Attendants from the funny farm?"

Gladys plays *ba-da-da-dum* on the organ to emphasize the joke. Moses winks at her. In her rearview mirror, Gladys winks back. I lower my arm. "Five-minute warning," Gladys announces.

"So did you get socked or not?" Moses asks.

My gaze shifts to the stained-glass window where an image of Jesus in a boat calming the sea radiates a majestic aura. "No. Just as Mr. Waycrest was finishing up the lesson, Rory's face broke out in nasty red blotches. He started itching, rubbing his eyes and then wheezed and yanked at the knot in his tie. Something was wrong with him. Mr. Waycrest panicked and almost coughed up his teeth. Marsha Boyle looked over at him. 'It's anaphylaxis!' She pointed at me and screamed, 'Get Dr. Howard!'"

I ran into the chapel and yelled, "We need Dr. Howard, stat!" which was an odd thing to scream in church. But Izzy, who thought Dr. Kildare was a dreamboat, was constantly fainting on her bed and yelling, "Get Dr. Kildare, stat!" So that's what I yelled. Everybody froze for a moment; and then Dr. Howard followed me into the room where Rory was fighting to breathe. In a calm, stern voice, Dr.

Howard instructed Mr. Waycrest to summon an ambulance. Rory's parents rushed to his side and followed the ambulance to the hospital.

"And?" Moses asks.

"Rory was allergic to rose water, and Ellen had doused herself in it before church. It was her mother's favorite perfume. You might call it a coincidence. I call it an answered prayer."

"Ding!" goes the egg timer.

I come in right under the bell. The congregation groans. They'll have to wait until next Sunday for more of the story.

As I place Moses back into his trunk, Gladys, who serves as treasurer in addition to her responsibilities as organist and choir director, informs me we did well with tithes and offerings, but continue to come up short in the building fund. The church needs a new roof, and the heating system, an archaic boiler that makes sounds Gladys deems demonic, is on its way out. Add to this our recent capital expense of ridding ourselves of old appliances in the kitchen, and our building fund is near defunct.

"I'm not sure what we will do about Beelzebub if giving doesn't pick up," she says. "Wally's done all he can patching things. Says the demon won't spit a single flame come winter."

Beelzebub is the name Gladys gave our boiler. Gladys likes to personalize things. She's the one who named the organ, Buster; the boiler, Beelzebub; and the steps leading up to the chapel, Jacob's ladder. Her car, a bright yellow 1968 Volkswagen bus, otherwise known as Mr. Bumble, is the only vehicle she's ever owned, not counting Jezebel, her Buzzabout X-3000 scooter, which is the envy of everyone at the senior center.

"Darn thing's practically street capable," Stanley said, the day he watched the woman he calls his "bride and joy" take it for a spin around the church parking lot the day he bought it.

"I'm not in a panic yet," Gladys says, "but when the average age of your congregation is Social Security eligible, the temperature in the church needs to be at least seventy-eight come winter."

"We'll get there," I say. "Have faith. More prayers, a few more bake sales. Seems we always get a windfall just at the right time. The Lord provides."

"Guess that's so. We've made it this far. Great sermon today, Pastor. Gave me the willies even though I knew what was coming."

"It's a gift to reminisce."

"Oh, I quite agree. Stanley's waiting. See you at Thursday rehearsal?"

"I'll be there." I watch as Gladys makes her way out of the church.

I am a worrier by nature, and Gladys's reminder of our financial shortfall adds a concern. I have the roof issue, the boiler problem, the missing collection plate mystery, and casting the church Christmas play to fret about. That doesn't include the bigger issue of getting more young families to join our congregation. I remind myself of Jesus's words, "Come to Me, all you who labor and are heavy laden, and I will give you rest."

Pastors wear many hats. We are Bible teachers, accountants, prayer warriors, marriage counselors, grief counselors, fundraisers, mentors, strategists, public speakers, and more. Now, on this otherwise fine Sunday morning, Opal and Virgil enter my office with more bad news, and Opal adds armchair detective to my list. My hope that the missing collection plate would show up has proven to be a bust, a mystery now heightened because there is no evidence anyone broke into the church. Opal checked every window and door for signs of forced entry and found nothing to indicate a breach. She even had Virgil check just to be sure.

"Tight as a miser's checkbook, Pastor," Virgil says, confirming Opal's assessment.

Opal signs, "It's an inside job," her communication unequivocal. "We need to call Poke. The perp has probably fenced it by now."

"Tight as a miser with a solar battery in his hearing aid," Virgil adds.

"The perp? You're watching too much crime TV," I say.

Opal rolls her eyes.

"Tight as a miser who counts his fingers after he shakes your hand," Virgil says. "So tight he throws money like—"

Opal waves a stop sign at Virgil, but he finishes in rapid fire. "A man with no arms." Once Virgil gets on a roll, there's no stopping him.

Opal glares at him.

"I'm done," Virgil says.

"Virgil said he'll go to the pawnshop and ask Barter Bill if anyone tried to fence a hot collection plate," Opal signs.

"Lord, have mercy. We're making a mountain out of a molehill."

Opal waves me off and marches out of the room.

"Can't hurt nothing to have a visit with Barter," Virgil says.

I ask Virgil, "How could it be an inside job? The only people with keys to the church are you, me, Gladys, and Opal."

Virgil removes his cap, the one with the John Deere logo on it, and scratches his head. Then, as if the scratching caused a winning combination to appear on an instant lottery ticket, Virgil says, "The perp could've done it during Bible study!" He says this as if he just discovered who the killer was in an Agatha Christie mystery.

I have an odd urge to scratch my own head but tap my chin instead. "I just don't see it. During a Bible study?"

Virgil removes his hat and scratches again, because the first scratch caused an itch. He places the cap back on his head, taps it in place, hitches up his jeans by the belt buckle, and says, "This dilemma got my brain tied in one of those knots you need a woman's fingernails to undo."

"Mine too," I say.

"But Opal's right about calling Poke. If we wanna recoup the plate's value with an insurance claim, we'll need a police report to provide to the insurance company."

Poke Stevens is the local police chief.

Fortunately, Winnie had worked in the insurance industry and made sure the church and its contents were covered. I was surprised by the collection plate's value, which was listed at an amount just north of two-thousand dollars. We could use the money. We had Beelzebub to contend with and our failing roof, but I had no desire to have anyone who set foot in the church arrested, at least not until I knew their story and circumstances.

"We'll see," I say.

Virgil leaves to visit Barter Bill, and I take a moment to calm myself. I straighten the portrait of "Laughing Jesus" that hangs on my office wall. Beneath the portrait of Jesus laughing is the verse, "Blessed are you who weep now, for you shall laugh," from the Beatitudes. It reminds me of Billy, who once asked Mr. Waycrest if Jesus ever laughed. "Can you tell us a story where God laughs? If he was human, you'd think he'd laugh sometimes, right?"

Mr. Waycrest had little patience for Billy's questions and told Billy the Bible had no references to Jesus laughing.

"Are you sure about that?" Billy asked.

"Quite."

"But it says he was fully human, right?"

"It does."

"Do you ever laugh?"

"I do."

"Have you ever met a fully human person who never laughed, not even once?"

"I have not," Waycrest said, doing his best to display the virtue of patience, but Billy was testing whatever Waycrest had left in the tank.

Fortunately for Waycrest, the church organist played the first notes of the final hymn, signaling the end of the Sunday service. Some are saved by the bell; Waycrest was saved by the organ.

I am comforted by the sight of my Savior laughing. I think Billy was right. Jesus loved children, and I can't imagine him remaining stoic as they laughed and played in His presence. When I told Harpey about Billy's question to Mr. Waycrest, he swiveled to me and proclaimed, "Oy vey, are you kidding? You want funny? How about the Tower of Babel? Now that's funny! Imagine your classroom if God suddenly made everybody speak a different language. Ha! How about turning Lot's wife into a pillar of salt? He could've turned her into anything, but one minute she's a woman, and *poof!* The next, she's a condiment!"

Harpey Mendelson knew more about the Hebrew Bible than anyone I ever met. He was my rabbi. I say a prayer for my friend, a remembrance that brings me a sense of peace and connection. I look down at my desk and see that Virgil has left me the cast list for this year's Christmas show that read, "Just five months, Pastor. Chop, chop."

As my friend and rabbi would say, "Oye vey."

I pack Moses into his trunk and begin my walk home. On each fifth cutout of the sidewalk, I pause and count a blessing, another tradition born of the romance between Matty and me. One day, when I was feeling down, Matty stopped me in the middle of my walk and gave me what for.

"You have been blessed beyond words, Nixon Bliss, and I find your moping to be most unattractive!"

When I think back to that moment, to those words, I smile. Matty didn't correct me often, but when she did, her love shone through her words. She wanted the best for me, and if I veered from the straight and narrow, she wouldn't hesitate to intervene. Matty and I met when I was in seminary in Mooresville, Alabama. She went to the same church I did and sang in the choir, but it wasn't her singing voice nor her radiant green eyes nor the disarming smile that caused me to fall in love with her. It was rather the cadence of her voice, the tone, the way she added a splash of southern twang the way chef might add a dash of spice to a favorite dish. She spoke lyrically, which was music not only to my ears but to my soul. For me, it was love at first listen, for Matty, well, it took a bit longer.

"Count a blessing this minute Nixon Bliss," she said.

"I have you."

Her expression softens. "That's a start. From now on, on our walk home on the block between Washington Street and Franklin, we will each count a blessing on each fifth cutout of sidewalk."

"Agreed," I said.

The last thing I ever wanted to be was "most unattractive" to Matty. So I stand on a single sidewalk cutout and thank God for the years of love I enjoyed with Matty Bliss. According to Jewish tradition, forty days before a male baby is born, a heavenly voice shouts out whom he shall marry. I think of this often and imagine that heavenly voice shouting, "Matilda Harley Kirkland!" on November 20, 1951.

Harpey told me the only truly dead are those that are forgotten. Just as Jesus provided a way of remembrance, Judaism's beliefs and practices are tied to the gift of memory. It feeds the soul to recall the past. It reminds us that God exists outside the boundaries of time. Some moments in our lives, seismic and impactful, go unnoticed, but upon reflection, we realize these were fragments of time that changed us. Moments where if we dust of the incremental moments of life, we discover the fingerprints of God.

I arrive home, eat my lunch, and to my great surprise, take a nap that turns into an afternoon of hibernation. I have learned that with age, what weighs on your mind also weighs on your body and realize I have not done a very good job of giving my worries to God. I decide to spend the week in scripture, to rest and give the house a good cleaning. Before I know it, a new Sunday has arrived, and I am once again standing before my congregation. They are eager, and I am reenergized. This is the Sunday I tell of my first meeting with Harpey Mendelson.

Chapter 11

———— ⁂ ————

I woke up late on Friday morning. Mr. Cappy said it would be more like fry day than Friday. "So get out the Coppertone and turn for an even burn!" My father was in the kitchen. He snapped the morning paper open and shook his head in disgust. He hated Mr. Cappy.

"Hey, Dad," I said.

"What's today?" he asked, his head buried in the paper.

"Fry... Day."

"Don't get smart," he said, which is an odd thing for a parent to say to their kid. I never talked back, because I'd be getting smart again and hear questions like, "How would you like to stay in for the day?" or "How would you like a week of additional chores, young man?"

Unlike me, Izzy was fearless and invited confrontation. When my mother told Izzy she didn't like the look on Izzy's face, Izzy replied, "Me either. But since I got the look on my face from you and dad, I hardly feel responsible for it."

"Are you getting smart with me, Izzy?"

"No, I'm going it alone," she replied and was out of the door before my mother could respond.

"Oh, I know," I said to my dad. "I need to bring the cans up from the curb."

"Right."

"I will. Have a good day at work."

"Will do," he said, not looking up from his paper.

I ran outside into a carnival of sounds. Screen doors slamming, kids laughing, and Connie Francis singing "If My Pillow Could Talk," her voice blaring through Izzy's transistor radio. Izzy was on a beach recliner in her bikini writing out her entry into the "If My Pillow Could Talk, What Would It Say?" deejay contest. If she won, she'd get a one-hundred-dollar savings bond, a phone call from Connie Francis, and a complete library of Connie's albums.

I looked for Billy and saw he was cutting his lawn. The new kid watched Billy from his wheelchair across the street. I was still spooked by the ritual we witnessed the night before, but it seemed less scary during the day. I went over and introduced myself. Billy would be mad, but my mother said if I didn't, she would march me over there and introduce me herself. Talk about embarrassing. Besides, I promised Jesus I would be nice to the new kid if He protected me from Rory, and a deal was a deal. I walked down the sidewalk and waited for the kid to look my way. He focused on Billy. He wore a black suit, red bowtie, and a skullcap.

"Hey," I said.

His gaze swept toward me. "Hi."

"I'm Nixon. I live right over there." I pointed at my house.

"My name's Isaac, but people call me Harpey. Isaac Harpey Mendelson. Because when I was a baby, I wouldn't sleep until my mother played harp music."

"Oh."

"It's the instrument of angels. In Genesis, it tells us Jubal, the first musician, invented the harp and the flute. I let you know because I wouldn't want you to think they named me after harpies, which are ugly women with wings from Greek mythology."

"Oh," I repeated.

Harpey's head swerved toward my front lawn. He moved as if driven by remote control. "Is that your sister?"

"Yeah. Izzy."

"She's a hot tamale. I feel like King David on the roof. I'm going to try not to look at her."

"Okay," I said. He flicked his gaze back and forth between her and me.

"Oy vey, I did it again! The flesh is weak!"

Billy was right. Jews were weird. He was acting like Izzy was a solar eclipse, and he'd go blind if he looked at her. Izzy rolled off the recliner and went inside.

"She's my Bathsheba," Harpey said.

"Who?"

"It's in the Bible." He held up the book resting in his lap. "The sight of the sensuous and beautiful Bathsheba seduced King David when he saw her bathing on the roof. I get the sweats just thinking about it. Have you read the Bible?"

"No."

"You should! It's full of magnificent battles and miracles and sinful behavior!"

"It is?"

"Best stories ever. That's what I love about God. He doesn't cover things up like they do in *True Detective*."

True Detective magazine showed pictures of women with black bars hiding intimate parts of their partially clad bodies. It was full of lurid, true-crime fiction. Billy's dad had a subscription, and Billy and I would sneak into his parent's bedroom when they weren't home to look through the latest issue. What can I say? We were boys.

"I have a muscle disease," Harpey said.

"Gee, sorry."

Harpey sighed and said, "*Yeder mentsh hot zikh pekl.*"

"What?"

"It's Yiddish. It means everyone has his own burden."

Harpey filled his lungs with air between sentences, creating an erratic rhythm to his speech, and his voice was unnaturally high. Beneath his yarmulke, his black hair, slicked down and parted, contrasted with his pallid skin. The way he looked and talked captured my attention. "Who's the kid across the street?"

"Billy."

"His father's an anti-Semite. I can spot an anti-Semite a mile away."

"What's that?"

"Someone who hates Jews. Have you ever met a Jew?"

"Not that I can say."

"Well, you have now!"

Izzy came out of the house, letting the screen door slam behind her. As Harpey spoke, he continued glancing at her.

Billy spotted me standing by Harpey. His eyes bore into mine. I didn't enjoy disappointing my friend, but it didn't seem right to hate someone because they didn't go to church the same day you did. "We're going to run under the sprinkler later, so if you want, you can come over." I was sure he couldn't run under the sprinkler with us, so I thought it was fine to ask.

His eyes widened. "If it's okay with my parents. Thanks!"

"Sure thing," I said. My ploy had backfired.

I was right about Billy being mad. "He'll stab you in the back, just wait and see. Jews always stab their friends in the back."

"I don't have a choice. My mom said I had to be nice to him," I said.

I positioned the sprinkler in the center of the lawn. Izzy was back in her recliner reading *Teen Magazine*. She had her transistor radio next to her. Murray the K played "Chantilly Lace," and Izzy had cranked up the volume. Ellen was wearing a yellow bathing suit and had her hair tied in a ponytail. She was the traitor. Why did she suddenly dress up for church and act all girly-girly? I was sorry I came up with the sprinkler idea. I should have stayed with baseball to see if she'd show up in a dress or her baseball cap with a wad of Bazooka in her mouth. I was about to turn on the sprinkler when Harpey came out of his house. Harpey had changed out of his suit and bowtie and into bathing trunks, a red shirt, and a giant floppy hat. When he got closer, you could see that his shirt had LIFEGUARD written across it. His pale, straw-thin legs were almost translucent, and his bony kneecaps stretched against his skin.

"What he's doing?" Billy asked.

"I invited him over. Don't have a cow," I said.

"Yeah, Billy," Ellen said, "don't have a cow."

"You guys are jerks!"

"Just give him a chance," I said.

"Your funeral," Billy said.

Harpey struggled when his wheelchair rolled off the sidewalk onto the grass.

"I'll help," Ellen said. She ran over and pushed his wheelchair, leaning into it with all her might.

"Thanks, you're a *mensch*," Harpey said.

A smile blossomed on Ellen's face. "Thanks. What's a mensch?"

"A really nice person."

Ellen positioned Harpey's wheelchair a safe distance from the sprinkler. Harpey pulled a pair of lady's cat-eye sunglasses from the pocket of his wheelchair and put them on. They were way too big for his face.

"You look stupid," Billy said.

"Shut up, Billy," Izzy said, inserting herself into the conversation. She slipped her own fashionable sunglasses down on her nose and smiled at Harpey. "You look marvelous, darling—truly."

"Yes, marvelous," Ellen agreed.

Harpey's smile was so big that his face almost disappeared. "Thanks!"

"What's your name?" Izzy asked.

"Isaac. But my friends call me Harpey. Harpey Mendelson."

"Welcome to the neighborhood, Harpey," Izzy said. "Love the shades." Then she pushed her sunglasses back up on her nose and stuck her face back into *Teen Magazine*.

"Turn on the water, Nix!" Ellen said. "Let's play!"

"I'll be lifeguard," Harpey said.

"That's an excellent idea, because if anyone could drown in a sprinkler, it'd be these dweebs," Izzy said.

Ellen put her hand on the arm of his wheelchair. "You can't walk at all?"

"No. My legs don't work, but don't worry, I get around like a *yenta* at a bar mitzvah." Harpey blew his whistle. "Everybody into the pool! No roughhousing or splashing the lifeguard!"

I turned on the sprinkler, and the magic of summer came to life. Izzy's radio played "Pretty Little Angel Eyes" as water from my dad's high-powered sprinkler arched into the air. The image of a rainbow briefly appeared. I stood on one side of the sprinkler and pretended to hold a red cape. Ellen pitched forward, put her pointer fingers to the side of her head to create horns, and scratched her bare foot on the grass.

"Charge already," Billy said.

Ellen charged through the water and screamed in delight. We laughed and played, and as the afternoon progressed, Billy let his guard down and forgot about Harpey being a Jew. We invented games, imagining the sprinkler had come alive.

"It's a dragon spitting fire!" Billy yelled.

"It's a giant at home plate spitting between pitches!" Ellen said.

We danced, leaped, and rolled around in the grass. Mrs. Mendelson came out of the house and slathered additional layers of suntan lotion on Harpey's face. She was a bird-like woman with delicate features. She doted on Harpey, and you could see how much she adored him.

"Mom, stop. You can't interrupt the lifeguard while on duty. I'm saving lives here."

"The lifeguard can't save lives if he lets the sun turn him into a lobster." Mrs. Mendelson adjusted Harpey's sunglasses and pulled up his socks.

"This is my mom."

"Hey," Izzy said. "Nice to meet you."

We all waved to Mrs. Mendelson, except Billy, who continued jumping through the sprinkler.

"Don't let me interrupt." She waved again and walked back to her house.

Izzy went inside. No boys had showed up yet, so she went to make some phone calls.

We continued to play until lunchtime, and then Ellen announced her plan to mind bust clouds on the cul-de-sac after she finished eating.

"Can I do it?" Harpey asked.

"It's private," Billy said.

"Is not," Ellen said. She pointed to the cul-de-sac and told Harpey, "It's right there, and you can come." Ellen knelt down in front of Harpey. "I can push you if you want." She pointed at Harpey's lifeguard whistle. "Just whistle when you want help."

Harpey's eyelids flapped open and shut in mechanical fashion. It reminded me of Ellen's creepy Chatty Cathy doll. She had a string in her back, and when you pulled it, Chatty would say stuff without moving her lips. Ellen hated dolls, but her mother kept buying her girl things. The day Ellen's mother bought her a Barbie doll, Ellen brought Barbie over to my house and insisted I have one of my toy soldiers take her as a prisoner of war. "I don't want her shot. I just don't want her at my house."

Billy glared at Ellen. He mocked her by imitating her voice. "Just whistle whenever you want me to help. Ellen and Jew boy sitting in a tree, K-I-S-S..."

Before he could finish, Ellen stood up, whirled around, and marched over to Billy.

"Take it back!"

"If the shoe fits, Jew lover."

Ellen socked him in the eye. Billy stumbled backward and fell on the ground. Billy's father had just arrived home for lunch and saw Ellen punch Billy. Mr. Finley got out of his car and walked toward us. He wobbled and slurred his words. It was lunchtime, and Mr. Finley was already drunk.

"Billy. Get over here, boy!" he screamed.

Billy cowered. I'm sure he was afraid, but his face flushed in shame. Billy idolized his dad, and now the man he looked up to was drunk in the middle of the day for all to see. Billy's lips quivered.

Ellen ran to my side and gripped my wrist.

"Get home, na...na...now!" his father yelled. He swayed in the street in front of our yard. Billy stood up.

"Never thought a boy o' mine could get beat up by a girl. You embar...embar...barr...ass me, boy."

A stern voice rang out. "You embarrass yourself." Mrs. Mendelson was on her porch. She had heard the commotion and came out to check on Harpey.

67

Mr. Pepsin opened his screen door and peered out.

Mr. Finley staggered and gazed at Mrs. Mendelson, his blood-shot eyes blinking. "Filthy Jew," he sneered. "If God chose you people, He chose damn wrong!"

Mrs. Mendelson twitched. It was as if the words had gathered into a hand and slapped her face.

Mrs. Finley came running out of her house, the screen door slamming behind her. "Tucker, what are you doing?"

Izzy flew out of the house as if shot from a cannon.

Mr. Finley turned and stumbled back toward his house.

"For cripe's sake," Izzy said.

Mrs. Finley lifted her hand to her mouth, horrified.

Billy strode by me. "Told you they were trouble," he said and sulked back to his house.

Harpey turned to me and Ellen, his big eyes wet with tears. "Sorry," he said. His mother came and helped him navigate his wheelchair out of the wet grass.

Ellen released her grip from my wrist and cried. "What's happening?"

"I don't know," I replied. And truly, I didn't.

Chapter 12

1963

I walked Ellen home. She took my hand in hers and squeezed it so tightly that when we got to her front door, it was numb. The washer rattled and banged in her garage, which was why Mrs. Yancey didn't hear the commotion outside. Ellen turned to me, chin trembling. "Maybe people really are being invaded?"

"It'll be okay," I said. "Mr. Finley, he's just being a jerk, that's all."

We stood on her stoop for a moment, holding hands. My heart throttled in my chest. I would have been happy to stand there with her hand in mine for the rest of my life, but as the door opened and her mother entered the garage, Ellen yanked her hand from mine.

"Thanks for walking me back," she said and hurried inside.

Things would never be the same between Ellen and me. We would never again have another day of just playing ball or riding bikes or comparing prizes pulled from a half-eaten box of Cracker Jacks.

I ran home. Izzy was still standing in the front yard, shaking a bottle of hot pink nail polish. She wouldn't admit it, but I knew she was watching out for me. Once in my yard, I said, "Man, that was bad."

"What do you expect from a knuckle-dragging Neanderthal with the brains of a bowling ball?"

"Do you know anything about Jews?"

Izzy shrugged. "Jesus was a Jew. Then He wasn't. He fought against the fallacies, and they had this big conspiracy with a pilot to kill Him, and there was a ta-do about the pilot needing to wash his hands. I'm not exactly an aficionado of the Bible, but I'm in the ball-park. It's not like I'm sitting on the edge of my seat in church." Izzy held up her bottle of nail polish as if she were looking at a test tube. "Anything else you wanna know, get out the Britannica."

"Harpey said there's a lot of violence and sinful behavior in the Bible."

Izzy's brows tugged together. "That tiny kid said that?"

"Yup. He kept trying not to look at you, but he couldn't help himself. He was imagining you taking a bath on the roof. He thinks you're a hot tamale."

Izzy smiled and placed her sunglasses back on her nose. "Boys," she said, and then she went back to her recliner and lathered on the Coppertone.

I fixed myself a glass of Tang and took it back to my room, where I spent the afternoon reading *Alien Invaders*. I thought Billy was right about his dad. Mr. Finley could be mean, but the spittle that flew from his lips as he sneered at Mrs. Mendelson didn't seem like Mr. Finley to me.

I had a lot to think about. Harpey seemed harmless enough, but the ritual we saw when we peered in the Mendelson's window creeped me out. And what about the pods in Pepsin's greenhouse? I thought about what Harpey said about Izzy, how he tried to stop looking at her but couldn't help himself. It reminded me of the day Mr. Waycrest caught Billy telling the boys in Sunday school class he had a nightmare about playing spin-the-bottle with Ellie May Clampett from *The Beverly Hillbillies*. He said every time he went to kiss her, she turned into Mrs. Hathaway. I thought Mr. Waycrest would have a stroke. I saw Mr. Waycrest before Billy did. I tried to warn Billy, but he was too far into the story to notice.

"There I am ready to swap spit with Ellie May, and she keeps turning into that hag, Miss. Hathaway," Billy said.

"William Baxter Finley!" Waycrest said, "I am disgusted!"

"Who wouldn't be? It'd be like swapping spit with your grandma."

The skin around Waycrest's face tightened, and the thin vein that reached out from beneath his toupee looked like a pulsing tree root. "Sinful! Just sinful!" Waycrest said, but his teeth shifted, and the words came out as, "Thinful. 'Ust thinful!"

After church, Waycrest told Mr. Finley that impure thoughts were not proper in church. Mr. Finley told Waycrest to get a grip and suggested a few extra dabs of denture adhesive would be an excellent start. "A boy dreams about kissing a girl? Big deal. I'll let him know to keep normal thoughts to himself in church."

Not one to be intimidated, Mr. Waycrest responded with, "It's a thlippery thlope, Mr. Tinley."

I knew about the consequences of impure thoughts. The Rev got us boys together one day and said, "It's like this, fellas, think of *Combat!* You all watch *Combat!*, don't you?"

We nodded. *Combat!* was on Tuesday nights at seven thirty. It was a favorite show for most of us.

"Your mind is a war zone, boys. You've got an army led by the flesh in a fierce battle against godly thoughts. Looking at girls impurely is like looping your finger into the pin of a hand grenade, pulling it, and *blammo*! The shrapnel of sin is everywhere, cutting at your heart, severing your soul." I've always remembered that brief talk. When the Rev explained things, they stuck with you.

My thoughts drifted back to my first encounter with Harpey Mendelson. He was such an oddity. I was sure of one thing. Harpey might move like a puppet and be the spitting image of Jerry, but Harpey was a real boy. Now it came to the basics. Was he friend or foe? I considered this equation when my mother called me for dinner. Things got off on the wrong foot the moment my mother dropped three Swedish meatballs onto Izzy's plate.

"What is that?" Izzy asked, pointing at her dinner plate.

"Swedish meatballs," my mother said.

Izzy shook her head. "Nope."

"Izzy—"

"Italians do meatballs. Swedes do snowballs."

"Just try it. You're so picky."

Izzy pushed her plate away and leaned back in her chair, acting as if the meatballs contained radioactive material. "I did a report on Swedes. They eat pea soup with pancakes."

"Ew," I said and skeptically peered at my Swedish meatballs.

"Taste them. If you don't like them, you can have a peanut butter and jelly sandwich," my mother said.

"On one slice of bread? That's how the Swede's make a sandwich. Next time you look for a recipe, pick a country that's known for more than Vikings, meatballs, and herring."

"Vikings?" I asked, intrigued.

"That's right. Add pillaging and wanton slaughter to the meatballs and herring."

"Izzy Bliss! For goodness' sake, they're meatballs." My mother plucked the meatballs off Izzy's plate with a fork and gave them to my father. "Every molehill a mountain."

I couldn't imagine a gang of Vikings sitting around a fire eating Swedish meatballs, but I ate them anyway. Izzy had corn and a peanut butter and jelly sandwich, which to me, wasn't far off from pea soup and pancakes, but I kept quiet.

After dinner, I went to my room. When you're a kid, you exist in two distinct worlds—day and night—and the two couldn't be more different. During the day, you see things rationally. But the cloak of darkness covers the day like a shroud, and the adolescent mind becomes a playground of the macabre. Shadows come alive, mundane noises morph into bumps in the night, and the closet and space under your bed become caves where monsters hide. During the day, Harpey Mendelson was strange but harmless. At night, I wasn't so sure, not after watching his participation in the ritual where his mother recited incantations and dabbed her eyes with wine.

"The wine represents blood, like the grape juice in church," Billy said.

Even Mr. Pepsin seemed like an all-right guy when his shadow wasn't hovering over him like a disembodied spirit. Today was different. Billy's dad had broken through the day/night continuum and frightened us in the middle of the afternoon. It was as if vampires had suddenly become immune to the sun, giving no respite to the living. As I sat in my room that night, I wondered about my dad. On an ordinary night, Izzy's behavior would have generated a forceful admonition, but Izzy's Swedish meatball rant didn't draw a word from him. I wondered if he was retreating even deeper into his shell, or worse, if an invading alien had crawled into his shell with him. Something bad was about to happen. I just knew it.

Chapter 13

————— ⟡ —————

I finish the sermon and turn to Moses, who wipes some invisible sweat from his brow.

"You okay?" I ask.

I swivel his large wooden head in my direction. "And I thought the burning bush was scary," he says.

Gladys presses her hands down on the keys, and Buster breathes an ominous cord, its aged pipes adding a resounding death rattle.

"Lord Almighty," Ms. Nellie whispers.

We finish the service with Gladys playing a spiced-up version of "I'll Fly Away." It's one of my favorites, and the congregation belts it out with abandon.

I am putting Moses back in his trunk, and when I turn around, I see that Poke Stevens is still in the chapel. Poke is a burly man, over six feet, three inches with a burgeoning belly and puffy cheeks. He looks like an overweight chipmunk hoarding nuts for winter. Despite this, he is an imposing figure, but it's Poke's deep bass voice that sets him apart. He has the voice of a country singer when he speaks, but for reasons no one understands, including Poke, his voice climbs several octaves when he sings. It puzzles Gladys. "He speaks bass but sings soprano. Practically a high C."

"Wonderful sermon, Pastor," Poke says. His words echo in the empty chapel. "I understand you've been robbed."

I sigh. "Opal?"

She thinks it might be an inside job is what she said. "Well, you know…" Poke waves his arms in his best attempt to replicate the signing Opal presented to him. "Something like that. That woman flat amazes me. I can hardly remember the alphabet, and here she is, clearly communicating without saying a word."

"She is a wonder but a tad overzealous about this. It's missing. That is not in dispute. But missing and stolen can be two different things."

"Can for sure. But Opal thinks—"

I hold up my hand. "Give me a week. If we don't find it, I'll file a report."

Poke thinks this through, rolling his thick tongue from one side of his mouth to the other, poking at his cheeks from the inside out as was his custom when considering something, hence the nickname "Poke." Polk is his legal name. Polk Stevens. "Okay, Pastor. But you need to talk to Opal. If she finds out I'm not investigating this, she'll sign my head off and roll it down the alley like a bowling ball."

"I'll tell her. If she knows there's a firm timeline, she'll be fine."

"But the more time that goes by, the more witnesses forget things, and evidence is destroyed."

"Duly noted."

I let Opal know of my agreement with Poke. She doesn't sign a word, which isn't a good sign, and goes back into the chapel to give her troubles to Jesus.

I begin my short walk home in the company of the twins, Francis and Winnie Dern. They have just completed changing the saying on our outdoor announcement board. The Dern sisters have been in charge of that role since 1962. Last week's sign said, *"Don't Give Up! Remember, Moses Was Once a Basket Case!"* This week's read, *"If God Had a Refrigerator, Your Picture Would Be on It."*

"One of my favorites," I say.

The Dern sisters live two blocks from the church, and despite the heat, they do what they have done since they were children; they walk to and from Miller Memorial every Sunday morning, pausing at least once to admire an aspect of God's creation. As we amble from the town square and down the block, I pull Moses's trunk behind me. Its wheels produce a steady *clickity-clack, clickity-clack* as they rumble over the cracks in the sidewalk. We pause in front of a gigantic oak that provides an umbrella of shade. Francis smiles.

"Our dad would often stop here when we were kids and repeat the parable of the mustard seed. 'What is the kingdom of God like? To what shall I compare it?'"

Winnie answers, "It's like the grain of the mustard seed, which a man took and put in his own garden."

They turn to me and smile. We complete the parable together. "It grew and became a gigantic tree, and the birds of the sky lodged in its branches."

We walk. Francis and Winnie shuffle along, sliding one foot in front of the other, as if the ground is a thin patch of ice.

"It's a glorious morning," Winnie says. "Dr. Kildare could leave his slippers under my bed any day," recalling the part of my previous sermon and my mention of the popular TV doctor.

"Winnie Dern!" Francis snaps playfully.

"Talk about God's masterpieces," Winnie says.

"Sinful," Francis says. "Act your age."

Winnie waves her sister off. "Humph. Such a silly saying." Winnie turns to me and speaks conspiratorially. "At bingo, she curses the caller."

"I don't curse!" Francis says, appalled that such behavior was exposed in front of her pastor.

I feign shock. "You go to bingo? With the Catholics?"

They giggle like schoolgirls. This is an ongoing joke between us.

"We can both be quite naughty," Winnie adds.

We stop in front of their house, a perfectly maintained Folk Victorian, its intricate spindle work and jigsaw-cut bargeboards of blue and white the envy of the neighborhood. It is the home of their childhood. I imagine them as young girls, laughing as they play in their yard.

"Here we are," Winnie says.

"Home," Francis says, and her voice echoes a sense of profound contentment.

Francis and Winnie have had their challenges over the years. Both lost husbands early in their marriages. Both survived serious illnesses. Yet through it all, their faith has remained steadfast, and their love for life (and bingo) has never wavered.

"Next Sunday then?" Winnie asks.

"Yes," I say.

"The fourth week is one of my favorites," Francis says.

"Mine too," I reply and continue my walk home.

I stop at my blessing steps and count my blessings. I smile to myself. It's an activity more of us could enjoy. When I counsel people, it's one of the first questions I ask. "How often do you smile to yourself?" Blessing counters know the joy of a smile shared between just them and God. The affirmation that we are blessed is one of life's greatest gifts. It pains me that so many of us dwell on what we want instead of what we have. As a natural worrier, Matty knew how important it would be for me to be one of the blessing counters, and one that I always count is Matty Bliss.

After counting what is good, I can once again consider the challenges before me. I make my way toward my gate and mull over our aging congregation. I think it might be time to bring on a youth pastor, someone who could assume the pulpit when I retire. We need new blood. I resist the notion of retirement, but as it says in Ecclesiastes, "To everything there is a season, a time to every purpose under heaven."

I will have lunch and pray about it.

Feeling a cold coming on, I forego my weekly visit to the hospital. I spend the afternoon piddling around the house. It unnerved Matty. I am a creature of habit, and my comfort zone is my routine. Sundays are particularly regimented. Rise at five o'clock. Make a cup of black coffee and sit in my study to review my sermon. Do my stretches. Eat a light breakfast and walk to the church. After services, eat lunch and spend the afternoon at the hospital. Eat dinner. Spend the evening in prayer. Read a beloved C. S. Lewis novel for the fifth or sixth time, a habit that perplexed Matty. One night as we sat at the table playing Parcheesi, she said, "How can you keep rereading the book when you know perfectly well what the ending is?"

"I enjoy them more on subsequent reads. I discover things unnoted in my first read, which is purely for plot and character. And might I add, my love, that you watch reruns of *Law & Order* and

Murder, She Wrote all the time. I think you've seen the same episodes multiple times."

"You know full well I watch *Law & Order* because I have a crush on Bobby and *Murder, She Wrote* because I'm in love with Cabot Cove."

This is an exchange we had often. I loved teasing her about her "crush" on Bobby.

"I can understand your crush on Bobby, but why you would be in love with a small town that, by capita, must have the highest murder rate in the world?"

Matty glared at me. "Are you trying to ruin my fantasy?"

"Of meeting Bobby in Cabot Cove where the two of you would settle down in a cottage by the sea and live happily ever after between murders?"

Matty rolled the dice and moved toward home. "Yes, that very one."

"I'm just trying to point out certain realities will need to be dealt with."

"In my fantasy?"

"Yes."

"Then what should we make of your crush on Priscilla Presley and woolgathering on the possibility of moving into Graceland where the two of you watch old Elvis flicks in the Jungle Room? Shall we discuss the realities of that?"

"Point taken," I said.

With prayer and care, my cold subsides. I walk to church on Sunday morning and read this week's announcement board, which says *"The World Has Fallen, and It Can't Get Up. Without Jesus."* I laugh heartily. That's a good one.

I ready Moses, say a prayer, and walk into the chapel. Once again, we are at capacity, praise God.

Chapter 14

———— ✦ ————

Sunday, June 28, 2020
Summer Sermon Series: Week Four

The next morning, when I went outside, Billy was sitting on the curb popping tar bubbles with a stick. His eyes were red and puffy. I wasn't sure what to do, so I sat down next to him and watched as he destroyed the last tar bubble within his reach.

"My dad moved into the garage," he said. He tossed the tar-stained stick into the street. "He's not the same person. You saw that, right?"

I nodded. "Yeah. I saw."

"He might lose his job. That's what my mom told him. She went over to the Jew's last night and apologized. I wish they'd go back where they came from, don't you?"

"I don't know. Maybe."

Billy picked up a stone and threw it. "My mom said I have to be nice to that kid or else. I'd tell her about what we saw going on in their house the other night, but I'd have to admit we were spying, and she'd have a fit. She wouldn't believe me, anyway. Adults never believe kids."

The screen door squeaked as it opened and Harpey and his father came out of their house. I turned to Billy. "If we act like we're friends with him, maybe we could get into his house. It's what Frank and Joe Hardy would do," I said to add credence to my plan.

When I made a plan, Billy felt better. In the short term, it gave me a way to get to know more about Harpey. "Is it a plan?" I asked.

Billy nodded. "It's a plan."

Mr. Mendelson rolled Harpey out onto the middle of their lawn, kissed him on the head, and walked back inside. Harpey turned to us, his head rotating mechanically as if someone else had the controls. He waved.

"We should go over," I said.

Billy wavered. "I dunno, maybe."

"Do you want to get in his house tonight or not?"

Ellen came out of her house wearing her baseball cap. She skipped across her lawn into the street, hopped the hopscotch board, and met us by the curb.

"Hey," she said. "You okay, Billy?"

"Not so much."

"His dad moved into the garage," I said.

"Oh." She sat down next to Billy on the curb and put her arm on his shoulder.

Then something strange happened. Addy Wolf came out of her house in her housecoat, walked to her mailbox to get the mail, saw us, nodded, and walked back inside.

"Holy smokes," Ellen whispered.

"That was weird," I added.

Addy never came out of her house when anyone was around, and when she did, she'd be waving her arms and screaming or arguing with someone that wasn't there. She'd push down her crop of hair in frustration, point her finger, all as if she were having it out with an actual person.

"Victim number 2," Billy said, referring to the alien body invaders.

"I don't think so. That's the most normal she's ever acted," I said.

"And normal for Addy is weird for everybody else. She might be one of them now. We need to find out."

Billy's theory reminded me of Mr. Waycrest's Sunday school lesson about the Holy Spirit. He said people act differently when they invite the Holy Spirit into their lives. It made the notion that an alien could invade a person's body more believable.

A white van pulled onto our street and into the Mendelson's driveway. It had a picture of a hammer ready to pound a nail on the side panel with the words "SOLLY'S HOME IMPROVEMENTS" painted above it. The back-panel doors were open to accommodate the two by fours in back of the van. The windows were open. As music blared, the man seated inside sang in a deep, boisterous voice. He stepped out of the driver's side of the van, and with the music still blaring from the van's open windows, danced his way over to Harpey's wheelchair. Dressed in white coveralls with a hammer slapping at his leg like a gunslinger's six-gun and his corpulent belly bouncing like a bowl of Jell-O, the man sang and pumped his fists in the air to the beat of the song. Mrs. Mendelson appeared at the door and did her best to get the man's attention, but it was futile. The man was in a world of his own. His head was shaved, and he sported a thick, untended beard. Like Mr. Mendelson and Harpey, he wore a skullcap, and it was a wonder it stayed on his head. As he danced, he spun and stood on his tippy toes like a ballerina. He clapped and snapped his fingers as the music played, which mesmerized us. We had never witnessed an adult caught up in such unbridled joy.

"Solly!" Mrs. Mendelson screamed.

Solly halted and turned his palms upward. "What'd I do?"

"You're impossible," Mrs. Mendelson said. She smiled and ambled to him. They embraced as if they hadn't seen one another in years. The greeting was interrupted at the cranking of Billy's garage door opening. Mrs. Mendelson stiffened and stepped away from Solly.

"Uh-oh," Billy said.

Mr. Finley's powerful arms extended over his head as he finished opening the garage door. He gave it a shove on its rollers until it banged against the frame. He watched Mrs. Mendelson. At the bang of the garage door, Mrs. Finley stepped out of the house, coffee cup in hand, and raised it.

"Good morning!" she said, calling out to Mrs. Mendelson. Then she looked at Harpey. "And good morning to you too, young man!"

Harpey waved to Billy's mom.

Mr. Finley didn't say a word. He went to his car, got in, and drove off.

After he left, Mrs. Mendelson waved to Billy's mom, who lifted her coffee cup a second time, and went back inside.

"What a mess," Billy said.

"Your dad wasn't very nice," Ellen said.

"It isn't my dad!" Billy yelled.

Ellen turned her attention to the man in Harpey's yard. "That guy acts like Santa Claus without the suit."

"I told you already," Billy said, "they don't believe in Santa Claus."

Solly looked over at Billy, Ellen and me. He raised an arm above his head, swept it across his belly, and bowed. Then he called out to us. "I need helpers! The pay is good. Five shekels! You need shekels, yes?"

We weren't sure what to say since we had no idea what a shekel was. Despite this, Ellen turned to us and said, "I'd like some shekels."

Mrs. Mendelson said something to Solly. He feigned surprise and turned back to us.

"I've been informed you may not understand the value of Solly's shekels!" He placed a palm on his forehead. "Such a *chamoole*!" Then he called out, "Five shekels equals one ice cream sundae at Dairy Queen!"

That's all it took. Going to Dairy Queen for something as pedestrian as a cone was a triumph. But a sundae? That was the holy grail. Suddenly, we all wanted shekels.

Mr. Pepsin had left for vacation the day before, so we ran across his yard without fear of reprisal. We stood by Harpey as Solly removed a cloth from the back pocket of his coveralls and patted the beads of sweat that had gathered on his brow. "Who do we have here?"

Ellen stepped forward the way she did when we played Mother May I. "Ellen, sir," she said.

"'Ellen-sir?' Ha! A wonderful name. Very unique, Ellen-sir, and how should I refer to you?" Solly asked, pointing at Billy.

"Billy, sir."

Solly feigned a look of confusion. "Are you related to Ellen-sir?"

"No, sir."

"Are you also a sir?" Solly asked, pointing to me.

"No, sir. Nixon."

"I see. So we have Ellen-sir, Billy-sir, and No-sir, Nixon. Do I have that right?"

"Solly, you're confusing them. Just Ellen, Billy, and Nixon," Mrs. Mendelson said.

"My apologies. I'm old and feeble." Solly turned to Harpey. "Time to get to work, yes? Lazy hands make a man poor, but diligent hands bring a man wealth. Who said this, Isaac?"

"Solomon. In Proverbs."

Solly turned to Mrs. Mendelson. "The boy knows his Bible, Nina. This is why he's my favorite nephew."

"He's your only nephew, Solly."

Solly acted like this was news to him. He turned to Harpey. "Is this true?"

"Yes. We go over this all the time."

For the rest of the afternoon, we helped Uncle Solly build the frame for a playhouse Solly was constructing for Harpey.

"Uncle Solly's a master carpenter," Harpey said.

"Yes, tell them, nephew. Watch and learn. If God creates another flood, together, we will build an ark!"

We sang, laughed, and cheered as each new section of the playhouse was complete. Solly taught us how to dance the *hora*, a Jewish dance of celebration, showing the simple steps with enthusiasm. To Solly, everything was a blessing. Billy, Ellen, and I placed our hands on one another's shoulders and moved in a circle, doing our best not to step on each other's feet. Harpey clapped as Solly tapped his hammer to create the proper rhythm. Throughout the afternoon, Solly peppered Harpey with questions about Jewish life.

"Nephew, why is amen said at the end of every prayer?"

"That's easy. Because in ancient times, many people couldn't read, so the people would listen to the prayer and then respond by saying, 'Amen.'"

"That's right. Very good, but the questions get harder. Wait." Solly wiped his sopping wet brow. "Have you ever seen a man leak like this? I'm ready now. If you get this right, I will add three of Solly's shekels to your pay. Eight shekels means banana splits all around."

"You can do it, Harpey!" I said.

Even Billy got involved. "Don't say the first thing that pops into your noggin. That's what I do in math, and I'm always wrong."

"I'm double-crossing my fingers," Ellen said.

"Here goes," Solly said. "Why does the groom break a wineglass at the end of a Jewish wedding ceremony, eh?"

We held our breath. Ellen put her crossed fingers to her forehead and whispered, "Please, please, please…"

Harpey smiled. "Because in the olden days, people believed noise warded off evil spirits. That's why church bells ring and why a bottle of champagne is cracked against the hull of a ship before its maiden voyage and why a groom at a Jewish wedding breaks a glass—it's to ward off evil spirits."

We all looked at Solly. While we focused on him, Mr. Mendelson had come out of the house and was standing behind us.

"Well, Solly, it appears you've gained another debt."

"That's a lot of shekels," Solly said.

"Thirty-two, to be exact, Uncle," Harpey said.

"You see this? He will be a rabbi one day. You mark my words."

"Does that mean we're going?" Ellen asked.

Before Solly could answer, the blare of a siren assaulted our ears as an ambulance made a hairpin turn onto our street. We dashed to the front yard as the ambulance raced past Harpey's house and then Ellen's and Billy's. Izzy was in the street, waving her arms and guiding the ambulance into our driveway.

"I gotta go!" I ran so fast I tripped over myself and fell. Izzy directed the men from the ambulance inside. She grabbed me before I could follow them in.

"What's going on?"

"It's Dad. We need to stay out of the way so they can help him."

"I want to see him!" I cried.

"Not now."

Izzy wrapped her arms around me, pulled me close, and kissed me on the head. "It'll be okay." Her heart hammered in her chest as she held me.

We stood aside as the men from the ambulance wheeled my father by us on a stretcher. His eyes were open but vacant. My mother came out of the house, car keys in hand.

"Izzy, you stay here with Nixon. I need you to call Grandma and let her know what's going on. Stay by the phone."

We wanted to go, but hospitals in those days restricted kids from visits.

The Mendelsons and Uncle Solly stood in our yard with Billy and Ellen. Mrs. Mendelson said, "We will watch over them, anything you need."

My mother smiled. "Thank you."

As my mother drove off behind the ambulance, fear swept through me.

"Let's pray," Mr. Mendelson said, and we joined hands. Harpey led the prayer.

"Dear God, we pray for the healing of Nixon's dad and ask that you swiftly send him a complete renewal of body and spirit. Amen."

I couldn't get the image of my father's vacant eyes out of my mind. Was it a medical issue or something more sinister? Billy's eyes met mine. We were both thinking the same thing—alien invaders. I ran to the side of my house, grabbed a soda bottle from the garbage can, and smashed it with my foot. It wasn't the last Jewish ritual I would perform.

Chapter 15

⸺ ⌘ ⸺

After the sermon, we take communion in remembrance of the one who sacrificed Himself to give us eternal life. The act of remembering is a precious gift. God knows the human heart, knows how easily we get caught up in the trivial, so He created communion to remember Him and to enshrine the blessing of memory. I remind my congregation of this simple but powerful truth: that the act of remembering gives us dominion over time, which is itself a miracle.

In Jewish life, after a loved one passes away, a *shivah* candle is lit in the home, and on every anniversary of the loved one's passing, a *yahrzeit* candle is lit to symbolize the spirit and soul of the deceased. When we reach back each year to remember a loved one, we interrupt the linear passage of time, and we merge the past with the present. To remember is a sacred act. After communion, with the closing prayer complete and just before dismissing the congregation, I turn the floor over to Moses.

"If you want to share a memory, raise your hand. Like this," Moses says, and I raise his hand above his head.

"Not too high!" he complains. "I have arthritis."

"You can't have arthritis. You're made of wood."

"Fine. I have sawdust in that shoulder. Happy now?"

Ms. Nellie raises her hand. "I have a memory. When I was a little girl, if one can imagine it, my father would insist we dance in the rain. It gave my mother fits, but father insisted. On one particular morning, it showered when we were having breakfast, and my father—mid-bite of our breakfast, mind you—took my hand and ran out onto the front lawn." Ms. Nellie's eyes grew wide as the picture in her mind gained clarity. "There we were, father and daughter, dancing in the rain in our pajamas! Can you imagine? He put me on his shoulders, and said, 'Turn off the faucet, Nellie!' and my arms"—Ms. Nellie extended her arms up in the air, replicating the moment—"reached up as high as they could. I turned my wrists, and wouldn't you know it, the showers stopped!"

I take a moment to enjoy the childlike wonder in Ms. Nellie's voice. We all do. Tears well in her eyes.

I raise Moses's hand. "I have one!"

"Maybe next week," I say.

I flap Moses's eyelids. "You're gonna make me wait? Me? Moses? I parted the Red Sea!"

"God parted the Red Sea. But fine. Make it quick."

"Picture it. I'm walking up Mount Sinai for the second time. Oy, what a hike. And I'm wearing sandals. Not like all of you with your no-slip bottom sneakers with Velcro straps. Or Birkenstocks. We didn't have Birkenstocks back then."

"No?" I say, feigning surprise.

"And I had plantar fasciitis."

"That must have been tough."

"And my plumbing got backed up, if you get my drift."

"Too much information, Moses."

"I took Wormwood on the way up. Things loosened up on the way down."

"This is the memory you pick?"

"It's one I'll never forget."

"I feel your pain," Ms. Nellie says, and the congregation breaks out in a fit of laughter.

Oh, Lord, how I love my little church.

The service ends with several hymns, announcements, and a closing prayer. I shake hands with the congregants and return to my office. With the mystery of the missing collection plate still unsolved, and the building fund underfunded, I force myself to begrudgingly file a police report so Opal can submit a claim to the insurance company. But it feels as though I am conceding it was stolen, a notion that makes me uncomfortable. I meet Poke in my office to make it official. Opal insists on being present, and I have no reason to object.

Poke likes the pomp and circumstance of the job and reminds me that filing a false police report is a crime.

"It's protocol that I tell you that, Pastor. No offense."

"None taken."

Poke takes a pencil from his shirt pocket and licks the point. "On what date did you discover the item was stolen?"

"Missing," I say.

Opal grunts and signs, "It was stolen! Don't be a horse's rump-roast!"

I am amazed at Opal's ability to call me, without cussing, the hind end of almost every animal that gained entry to Noah's Ark.

"What'd she say?" Poke asks.

"Never mind," I say. "Let's get this over with. I need to make hospital visits today."

"Date?"

"We noticed it missing a week ago, Sunday," I say.

"Any sign of a break-in?"

"No."

"Anyone suddenly missing from Sunday service?"

"Why?" I ask. "I thought people like to return to the scene of a crime."

"That's for murders. This here's a run-a-the-mill theft."

Opal's arms go into overdrive. "Robbery!"

"What'd she say?" Poke asks.

"She says it's a robbery."

"Not robbery. Robbery involves force. More like larceny," Poke says.

Opal reads Poke's lips, and her eyes circle like marbles on a roulette wheel.

"Well, Poke, I'm not sure I know of anyone who hasn't been to church since the plate went missing, but I'll think about it," I say.

"Be my first suspect if you did, since I'd think guilt would run amuck in a case like this, being it's a church and all."

I'm not being honest with Poke. I know of someone who hadn't been to church in a few weeks, but I think it's best to keep it to myself, especially with Opal as wound up as she is.

Poke sighs dramatically. "Well, it would've helped had you reported the crime sooner. Seems a waste of fingerprinting powder to dust the crime scene since a week has gone by."

"Well, Poke, I'd just rather make the claim and be done with it. So if you could give a copy of your police report to Opal, she can send it in, and all will be well."

Opal is signing away at me, but I keep my eyes trained on Poke.

"One last thing, Pastor. What was the value of the item?" Poke asks.

"Just north of two thousand."

"Dollars?"

"Yes."

"Holy mackerel! That's a whole different can o' fish, Pastor. That's grand larceny—a felony."

Opal pounds her fist on the table and signs, "Bingo!"

Poke lifts the gun belt over his belly and turns to walk out the door.

"Are we done?" I ask.

"Whole other can o' fish," he repeats. "Be back in a minute with my fingerprint kit."

"Oh, Lord," I mutter.

If Poke thinks he'll dust for prints and leave, he's mistaken. And if I think the case of the missing collection plate will take a back seat to other church business, I am as mistaken as Poke. There is no way Opal will let either of us off the hook. The moment Poke packs up his fingerprint kit and heads for the door, Opal intercepts him with the precision of a heat-seeking missile, making it clear he isn't to leave without cleaning up his mess.

"What's she signing?" he asks.

"She says you're not leaving until you clean up the scene of the grime," I say.

"Funny," Poke says and then begrudgingly obliges. While he cleans, Opal sits at her desk, compiles a list, and hands it to him.

"What's this?" he asks.

"Suspects," Opal signs.

"Suspects? This is getting out of hand," I say. "Frankly, Poke, I don't want to know who took it. We'll make our claim to the insurance company and be done with it. If someone took it, then they were in need."

Opal's eyes practically eject themselves from the sockets. "In need? So if I rob a bank it's okay because I'm in need?"

"We're not a bank. We're a church," I say.

"I'm not sure you can file a police report but instruct the police not to investigate the crime," Poke says. "That'd be a new one on me."

"Jesus forgave the thief on the cross," I say. "I won't press charges."

"Well, you could have told me that before I dusted for prints and then dusted the dust I used to dust for prints."

"I apologize. I've felt off-kilter with this from the beginning. I'd just like to make our claim to the insurance company and move on."

I wait for Opal to mount a protest, but the disappointment in her eyes is much worse. She lowers her chin to her chest and walks out of the office.

"I know it may not be my place, Pastor, but I think you might be making a mistake on this one. Seems to me that collection plate belonged to the congregation, and maybe they feel like the forgiving part should come after the repentance part. Anyway, not my business." Poke grabs his fingerprint kit and walks out of my office.

"Good grief," I whisper.

I visit the hospital that afternoon. I put Moses in the passenger seat for what Virgil would describe as craps and giggles. I drive the same car I've had for the past twenty-seven years, a 1993 Chevy Caprice Station Wagon with eighty-seven thousand gentle miles on the engine.

"Wonder how many you have on your feet?" Virgil once asked. "Seems you like walking more than driving."

About this, Virgil is on point. I drive only when my destination requires and walk when possible. I live within the bounds of my zip code and travel beyond it only when I must. Prior to becoming the pastor at Miller Memorial, I was a missionary, and despite my aversion to unfamiliar surroundings, my calling sent me to Haiti, Mexico, and the Philippines. This was out of my comfort zone. I am, by nature, a homebody, and those years gave me a greater understanding of the cost to following Jesus.

As I moved from one place to the other, nervous and unsettled, I recalled the words Jesus spoke to the man who told Jesus he would follow Him wherever he went. "Foxes have dens and birds have nests," Jesus replied, "but the Son of Man has no place to lay his head." I would not take back the years I spent in those countries, but I was happy to be back in the States after recovering from a bout of malaria I contracted in Haiti. Aside from the nausea and vomiting, I remember little and have recovered, at least physically. I now have an intense fear of mosquitoes and have slapped myself in the head at the faintest buzz, twice causing an affliction known in boxing as cauliflower ear. When out and about, I apply enough bug spray to put down a plague of locusts. My missionary work behind me, it was a joy to be hired as pastor of Miller Memorial, and I have kept travel to a minimum.

I visit the sick at least once a week, and if a parishioner is ill, more often as necessary. Malaria aside, I have been blessed with good health. Matty said my visits to the sick had built up my immunity, and I agree. When the older among us grew up, our parents allowed us to play in the dirt and drink straight from the garden hose. Nowadays, a parent risks a visit from Child Protective Services for such allowances. Every generation laments the practices of the one before it, but if cleanliness is next to godliness, I believe we can do with less cleanliness and more godliness.

A memory of a moment with Ellen and our garden hose brings a smile. Ellen wanted a drink from the hose, and I wiped the dirt off the nozzle with my sleeve before handing it to her. It was the first time her blue eyes lifted to mine, not as a tomboy, but as a sweet adolescent girl that made my heart ache. I reach back in time more often these days and hold on to the special moments of my life. There is an old Jewish saying. "When the time comes for you to live, there aren't enough years." As I grow older, I gain a greater appreciation for this wisdom.

My ride to the hospital is uneventful, and for this, I praise the Lord. The week prior, I was pulled over by a policewoman for failing to secure a passenger in a motor vehicle. She didn't inspect my passenger and scolded me for not buckling the child in.

"He's a dummy," I said, to which this young policewoman—and I would find out later, mother of two—took great offense.

"Unbelievable," she muttered. "Wait here," she instructed and walked back to her squad car with my driving credentials in hand.

She commanded me to remain inside the car with the engine turned off. Moments later, a second patrol car pulled up. A burly officer stepped out and spoke to the officer I assumed was writing me a ticket. It was sweltering out, and because she made me turn off the engine, I was sweating profusely. I leaned my head out of the driver's side window and called to the officer that had just arrived.

"Sir, if I could have a moment?"

"In a minute."

"The passenger is a dummy," I said.

This piqued the officer's interest. He walked to my car and peered inside. I pointed to Moses. He looked at me with hoisted brows, and his eyes, at first all business, became a beacon of mischief. He glanced back at the female officer then turned his attention back to me. "Okay, here's the plan."

"The plan?"

He pointed to the female officer. "That's Officer Becca. It's her first week on the job, and you—oh, thank the gods of the universe—are her first traffic stop."

"There's only one God," I said and pointed to the small sticker on my windshield that identified me as clergy. I noted the nametag on his uniform pocket. Officer Bennett.

"Oh. Right." He smiled. "This will be good. I'm gonna send this dash-cam footage into *America's Funniest Home Videos*. If we win, I'll donate my cut to the church. How's that?"

"Officer Bennett, I'm on my way to make my weekly hospital visit and—"

"I'm gonna tell her it's a potential kidnapping."

"What!"

Before I could protest, he pulled open my door and commanded, "Step out of the car, sir! Now!"

"But—"

"Now!"

I stepped out as Officer Becca leaped out of her patrol car. "What is it?"

"Kidnapping!" Officer Bennett said, "Get the boy!"

Officer Becca ran to the passenger side door, yanked it open, and pulled Moses from the passenger seat. A moment later, her jaw dropped as she held the dummy in her hands.

"Holy Moses!" Officer Bennett bellowed. He had his hands on his knees, laughing so hard he could hardly breathe.

Officer Becca glared at me then put Moses back in the passenger seat. She buckled him in and slammed the door. With a hint of a smile, she said, "I'll get you for this, Bennett," then walked back to her patrol car, got in, and drove off.

"Made my day, Pastor," Officer Bennett said. "You have a pleasant one, now." Then he got in his car and followed Officer Becca.

Now, when I'm on my way to the hospital, I drive the speed limit while watching for Officer Becca's patrol car.

My heart breaks every time I enter the children's wing of the hospital. This is the place where my faith is tested. Parishioners believe a pastor's faith never wavers, but at moments, like Jacob, I wrestle with God. It was Harpey who let us know about the miraculous match between God and Jacob. I remember the wonder in Harpey's eyes as he recounted the most momentous wrestling match in history.

"They wrestled all night!" Harpey said.

"What moves did they use?" Billy asked.

"I don't know," Harpey said.

"Maybe the Iron Claw!" Billy said, "Especially Killer Kowalski's!" Billy squeezed the top of Harpey's tiny head in one hand. Killer Kowalski was a famous wrestler back then. The Iron Claw was his most treacherous move.

"Hey, that hurts!" Harpey said and pushed Billy's Iron Claw from his head.

"And mine isn't even iron. How about the Sleeper Hold?" Billy asked. "Turn around, Nix, so I can show him."

"No way! The Sleeper Hold's dangerous!"

Billy's insistence that Harpey name a wrestling hold got under Harpey's skin. "Killer Kowalski ripped a guy's ear off. A genuine wrestling match always has moves, so it wasn't a genuine match."

Harpey was indignant. His eyelids stretched so wide I thought his eyeballs might fall out. "Of course, it was a genuine match! It's in the Bible!"

"You'd think a guy as powerful as God would have a signature move," Billy said. "Who won?"

"Nobody. It was a tie," Harpey said.

"Because there weren't any moves," Billy said.

Harpey became so frustrated by Billy's relentless inquisition, he blurted out, "God had a move!"

"What was it called?" Billy asked.

"The Socket Touch!" Harpey said in frustration.

"The Socket Touch? What the heck?"

"That doesn't sound right," Ellen said.

"But it is!" Harpey insisted. "God touched the socket of Jacob's hip and wrenched it. And after the match, Jacob had a limp because of his wrenched hip. To this day, Jews do not eat the tendon attached to the socket of the hip because Jacob's hip was touched by God."

Ellen's reaction was priceless. She looked like she had just sucked a lemon. "Ew, gross! I wouldn't eat a tendon if God used the Socket Touch or not!"

I smile to myself and realize how much Harpey Mendelson taught us all about God. He made the stories in the Bible come alive.

As I carry Moses down the hospital hallway, I ask God to bless these children and that His Spirit guide me to the child in greatest need. "Let me bring a moment of solace, summon a smile, and lighten a heart. Amen." A moment later, a boy being swallowed by his wheelchair emerges from his room. His sullen eyes, pasty white skin, and bald head beneath his yarmulke speak of his illness. Sometimes God works in mysterious ways, but other times, His hand is obvious.

I look at the action figure in the boy's arms and know this moment is meant to be.

"Good morning," I say. "I see you have a *golem*."

The boy's weary eyes brighten in surprise. Non-Jews are rarely aware of the golem, but during the summer of '63, when Billy and I idolized Superman, the Hulk, and Batman, Harpey introduced us to his own superhero—the mystical Golem of Prague.

"What's your name?" I ask.

"Israel. But everyone calls me Benny. Benny Penzik. Are you Jewish?"

"No. I'm a pastor, but my best friend when I was your age was Jewish, and he told me all about the Golem of Prague."

Benny is twelve. Like Harpey, he is small for his age, but he doesn't have Harpey's puppet-like movements.

"I have cancer."

"I'm sorry for that."

"Oh well, yeder mentsh hot zikh pekl."

My jaw drops as Benny repeats the same words Harpey Mendelson shared with me the day I met him. "Everyone has their own burden," I say. Again, Benny's eyes light up.

"That's right!" he says, amazed that I know the Yiddish saying. Then he turns his attention to Moses. "That dummy looks like Moses."

Benny pulls back when I throw my voice as Moses responds. "I am Moses, and who are you calling a dummy?"

Then it happens—a child's laughter. The music of God. I tear up and do my best to control my emotions. I am a crier by nature. Matty said I have a loose faucet, and she loved me all the more for my tears. There is not enough joy in the world and far too little in the children's ward of a hospital.

Benny smiles. "I don't think you're the real Moses."

I flip Moses's eyelids then swivel his head toward me. "Oy, look at this. Another non-believer." I turn Moses back toward Benny. "Test me."

"Okay. What was your mother's name?"

"Yocheved. What's yours?"

A woman's voice calls out from behind me. "Leah."

I turn. The woman's resemblance to Benny is not immediate, but after a moment, I pick up on the curious eyes and decisive manner she shares with her son.

"Hey, Mom," Benny says.

I sense her protective nature. I stand and introduce myself. "I'm Pastor Bliss."

Her eyes narrow. "Pastor?"

"Yes. I was just telling Benny about my friend from my childhood, Harpey Mendelson, who told me all about the Golem of Prague."

"He can make that dummy talk," Benny says.

I turn Moses's attention back to Benny. "We'll see who the dummy is," Moses says.

Benny's laughter tempers his mother's suspicion. Her smile blooms as if it had been waiting a season to open and receive the sun. I surmise Benny hadn't laughed in some time. Her expression softens.

"I have more questions," Benny says.

"Benny isn't sure Moses is the real deal," I explain to Mrs. Penzik.

"Ah. Well, Moses will find my son to be quite the scholar regarding the Torah."

If déjà vu is a real thing, I felt as if I were experiencing it. Sometimes life, like history, repeats itself, leaving us to wonder if what we are experiencing is a coincidence or meant to be, something with a purpose.

"How many times did you refuse God's command to confront Pharaoh?" Benny asks Moses.

"Five. Let's talk about the Red Sea. The movie had it all wrong. The sea didn't split right away."

Benny's jaw drops. "That's right." His eyes lift to meet his mother's intent gaze. "The sea parted overnight, not in an instant."

"But I did look like Charlton Heston back then."

"Be careful," I say to Moses. "Remember what happened to Pinocchio's nose."

"Okay, okay, I didn't have those abs. But it wasn't my fault. Manna's full of carbs."

This time, even Mrs. Penzik laughs.

Benny, a shy boy, now seems more comfortable with himself, which often happens when Moses gets into the act. I point at Benny's golem. "He is a powerful creature. Protector of the Jewish people."

"Benny knows all there is to know about the golem," Mrs. Penzik says.

The rattle of wheels echoes down the hall and Benny turns toward the sound. A girl emerges from her room, pulling an IV pole. One of its four wheels spins and wobbles, making a distinctive clanking. She appears to be Benny's age with freckles sprinkled on her nose, pale blue eyes, and shoulder-length blond hair. Benny is smitten. She takes a few steps toward us then turns and walks the other way. Benny tries to hide his disappointment but looks at the floor. He shifts the golem in his lap, and his shoulders slump. The boy who had smiled and laughed just moments before was gone, replaced by a sullen boy with a terrible disease. "I'm tired."

"I understand. Perhaps, if you're here next week, I will see you again?"

"Okay," he says in a colorless tone. He rolls himself back into his room, retracting like a turtle finding shelter in its shell.

"The children here have not been kind," Mrs. Penzik says. "Benny was a shy boy even before the cancer, but now..." her voice trails off. "Thank you for spending time with him. He hasn't laughed like that in a while."

"He reminds me of my friend. You don't mind if I visit him again?"

"No, of course not."

"And don't worry, if he tries to convert me, I'll resist." I want to reassure her that I was not there to challenge the boy's faith.

She smiles. "Jews don't convert people."

"Yes. Rabbis have it easy. Well, yeder mentsh hot zikh pekl, right?"

Her smile blossoms once again. "Yes. We each have our own burdens."

97

As I walk toward the hospital exit, I'm reminded of Einstein's quote: "God does not play dice with the universe."

Certainly not this time, I think.

I arrive for church the following Sunday and find Gladys and Stanley pulling into the parking lot riding Jezebel. They both wear helmets, and Stanley hugs Gladys's waist as they arrive on her prized Buzzabout X-3000 scooter. They live just a block away from the church and ride Jezebel whenever the day promises sunshine. Gladys navigates Jezebel into her reserved spot, and the long-married couple step off their ride.

"Morning, Pastor!" Stanley says.

"Morning, Stanley. How's she running?"

"You mean Jezebel or my bride?"

Gladys elbows Stanley. It's a tap, but Stanley buckles over in dramatic fashion. "Zip it!" she says and then turns to him and lifts her chin so he can undo the strap of her helmet. He obliges and then lifts the helmet from her head with care. She smiles at him and taps his chest with her palm. "Thank you, dear."

I catch myself breathing in as if the love between them could fill my lungs as much as it fills my heart. This is what God intended for each of us, to be loved and cared for, that we wouldn't lose our sense of wonder or forget the power of a simple touch or a kind word. Theirs has been a life well lived.

"I wish I'd known you two back in the sixties," I say.

"Goodness, don't get him waxing nostalgic," Gladys says.

"Neither of us," Stanley says. "We're so old, when we get nostalgic, we see cave paintings."

"Get me inside. I need to get Buster ready," Gladys says.

I follow Gladys and Stanley into the church, wheeling Moses behind me. An hour later, I am once again standing before the congregation with Moses by my side. The chapel is standing room only. We're on.

"Good morning," I say and begin.

Chapter 16

Sunday, July 5, 2020
Summer Sermon Series: Week Five

Izzy and I sat on the plastic-covered seat cushions of our living room couch as my mother told us my father would need to remain in the hospital for several more days. "He had a stroke. It means he wasn't getting enough blood to his brain."

It amazed me how calm my mother was that day. She must have known we needed a steady hand in a crisis.

"Why did it happen?" Izzy asked.

"They don't know exactly, but your father's been under a lot of stress lately. His blood-pressure was high when they brought him in, so he'll be on medication for that. He's lost some control on the left side of his face, but the doctors say there's an excellent chance it will improve. In the meantime, I need both of you to be on your best behavior. When your dad comes home, the last thing he needs is to hear you two fighting."

"Is he still going to be Exhausted Ruler?" I asked, wondering if his illness got me off the hook for the Talent Show.

"Exalted, not exhausted, knucklehead," Izzy said.

My mother stared at Izzy.

"Sorry, Kay, it's a habit."

My mother placed her hand on Izzy's cheek. "Your dad and I love you both so much. We'll get through this. And to answer your question, Nix, your father is very proud of being Exalted Ruler, and that won't change. In fact, it's more important than ever that the talent show be a success."

The doorbell rang, and my mother went to answer it. Mr. and Mrs. Mendelson, Harpey, and Solly stood on our porch. Mrs. Mendelson handed a casserole to my mom. "A little something."

"It's tuna, not gefilte," Harpey said.

My mother took the dish and asked the Mendelsons if they'd like to come inside. "We can't stay. How is he?" Mrs. Mendelson asked.

"He had a stroke," my mother said. "Thankfully, they caught it in time. He'll have a long recovery, but the doctors are optimistic."

Mrs. Mendelson's eyes softened. "You're in our prayers. God be with you all."

Harpey was still fighting the temptation to stare at Izzy. He kept looking at her and then yanked his eyes away as if he expected to be struck by lightning.

Solly put his hand on Harpey's shoulder. "We will keep building the playhouse. I owe banana splits to the workers," he explained to my mother.

"That's nice," my mother said. "I think the quicker we get back to our routines, the better. Thank you for your kindness."

Later that afternoon, I met Billy on the island.

"I'm telling you, Nix, it's the alien invaders, and now one is trying to take control of your dad. We need to find those pods before it's too late. If this goes on much longer, they'll have control of both our dads."

Billy's assessment seemed not only possible but probable. The mix of *Creature Features*, an adolescent boy's imagination, and the ritual we had witnessed in the Mendelson's window convinced me something horrible was happening right on our street. I imagined my dad in the struggle of his life, fighting back with all his might against an alien invader. He was buying time, and it was up to me to save him. "Pepsin's on vacation. I say we get in his greenhouse tonight while he's away."

After dinner, I met Billy in front of my house. It was a moonless night. As spies, that was an advantage. It was easier to complete a mission undetected in the dark, but it sent our imaginations into overdrive. The wind swept across our faces like fiery breath, and the lone streetlight on our block cast an eerie glow over Ellen's hopscotch board, its pink chalk outline effervescing on the macadam. In my mind's eye, a goblin skipped across the hopscotch board, its guttural laughter echoing down the block. It was too quiet. Something wasn't right, but this was a mission like no other—a mission to save our dads.

"Ready?" Billy asked.

"Yeah, ready."

"When we get to the greenhouse, we use the flashlight, not the overhead bulb," Billy said.

"Got it."

Billy adjusted his spy belt. He got it for Christmas, and it came equipped with a flashlight, plastic binoculars, a screwdriver, and a pen with disappearing ink.

"What's the disappearing ink for?" I asked.

"Secret messages," he said as if it were the dumbest question ever. "Like if we get caught and we have to send messages back and forth."

"What are we going to write on?"

"I don't know. Am I supposed to think of everything?"

"Okay, but if we have to use it, let me write the message. Then whoever finds it will have a chance to figure out what it says before the words disappear. You misspelled so many words the last time—"

"I wrote 'x-scape.' It was plain as day. Don't blame me if you can't decode the obvious."

"I got 'x-scape.' It said 'burn' instead of 'berm.' 'X-scape to the burn.' I didn't know where the—"

"Geez, it's old news! Just let it go!"

We used the berm as cover and positioned ourselves behind Mr. Pepsin's backyard. Pepsin left a bulb lit in the greenhouse. Billy took the binoculars from his spy belt and surveyed the target area.

"Look at that," Billy whispered. "Pepsin left a nightlight on for his children."

A chill swept through me. I made a joke of it. "Yeah, I guess Margery, Victoria, and Rosie are afraid of the dark."

The wind lashed across the berm. One leg of the swing set in the Mendelson's backyard lifted out of the ground like a stumped leg and slammed back down into its hole. The swings clanged and twisted, and the glider swayed.

"It's just the stupid wind," Billy said, doing his best to relieve the tension. "We army crawl just like they do in combat, got it?"

"Got it."

Billy unclipped his spy belt. We got on our stomachs and did the army crawl to the greenhouse. Billy reached up to open the greenhouse door. It was locked.

"Dang, something's definitely up. Why would he lock a greenhouse? Who'd want to steal his stupid plants?"

Billy slipped the screwdriver out of his spy belt and worked it against the door's locking mechanism. After several tries, the door latch released. The door, caught in a wicked gust of wind, whipped open and slammed against the cement block Pepsin used as a doorstop. Before either of us could react, the door's thin metal frame twisted, shattering the glass in the upper windowpane. I saw it before Billy did. A section of glass was slipping from the frame just as Billy reached for the door to pull it back. I yanked Billy from under it just as the sheet of broken glass released like a guillotine blade right where Billy's neck would have been. The glass shattered on the brick walkway. We raced back to the berm, and when Billy realized how close he had come to having his head cut off, he wet himself.

"Jesus, Mary, and Joseph. I wet my pants," he said matter-of-factly.

"I almost crapped mine," I said, and in the strange way that happens when we're not sure how to react, we both began rolling around in fits of laughter.

We calmed ourselves and sat behind the berm for a few minutes to see if anyone heard the breaking glass, but no one did. It was Thursday night. Izzy was watching *Dr. Kildare*, and everyone else was entranced by the latest case on *Perry Mason*. Billy looked down at his wet pants and realized he didn't have his spy belt.

"We need to go back. My spy belt's there. Pepsin will know it was us!"

"Oh, man, Billy," I moaned.

"You go, and I'll be the lookout."

"No way! You're the one who left it."

"My pants are wet."

"So?"

"Geez, some friend. I'd never make you crawl around if you wet your pants. If my dad finds out, I'm dead. Last time this happened, he made me wear a diaper all day just to teach me a lesson."

"When was that?"

"Who cares when it was? It was his fault. He wanted to see a movie, and they couldn't find a babysitter, so they took me with them."

"And you wet your pants?"

"It was *The Tingler*! Of course, I wet my pants!"

"I don't get it. We've seen *The Tingler* at my house plenty of times, and you never wet your pants."

"Right. On TV. In the theatre, they had the Percepto! And... I was only nine years old. I'm sure grown men wet their pants because of the Percepto!"

The Tingler starred Vincent Price and was about a centipede-like creature that fed on human fear. The Percepto was a device the producers installed in the theatre that made your movie seat vibrate whenever the Tingler latched onto a victim.

"The Percepto made all the difference," Billy said. "And they bought me a large drink before the movie started. What kind of parents buy their nine-year-old kid a large drink with the Percepto attached to the seat?"

I relented. "Okay, I'll go. But keep your eyes peeled."

I crawled back to the broken door. I was careful not to cut myself on the shards of glass that scattered over the bricks when the door broke. The wind howled, and the swing set chains rattled in the dark. I had visions of Marley's ghost showing up and telling me he wished he hadn't forged so many chains in life and how godawful it was to be dead. I grabbed Billy's spy belt, but his flashlight had rolled inside the greenhouse. It was still lit and cast a ghoulish glow over the rows of empty pots and gardening tools. The prongs of a pitchfork projected against the plastic wall looked like fingers reaching up out of a grave, and when a gust of wind shook the plastic, the fingers moved as if beckoning me in. It didn't help that Billy just brought up *The Tingler*. Where else would a centipede-like creature be crawling around, if not a greenhouse? My heart pounded against my ribcage. I couldn't get to the flashlight without putting my hands and knees on glass, so I had to stand, hunch over, and do my best to keep my PF Flyers from getting cut up from the glass.

Billy called out to me. "Hurry, will ya?"

I leaped over the bricks into the greenhouse, grabbed the flashlight off the floor, and dashed back to the berm with the flashlight and spy belt in hand.

"Did you get a look at the plants?" he asked.

"No! I was too busy getting the evidence you left behind."

"It's okay. I have another plan. We get up tomorrow morning and tell Ellen we're going on another spy mission. We bring her back here and tell her we need to spy on Pepsin's greenhouse because we think that's where the pods are hidden. She sees the door busted and wa-la! We act surprised and go check it out. Plan?"

"Plan," I said, and we both ran home.

No one noticed when I walked into the house. My mother was in her bedroom, and Izzy was watching *Dr. Kildare* with Margaret Ann. The night before, they watched *Ben Casey*. They were both gaga over the shows two stars, Richard Chamberlain and Vince Edwards. They debated which doctor they would rather get a serious disease for. "Who cares what disease?" Margaret Ann said one night when I was listening in with my drinking glass pressed against my closet wall. "I'd take Ben over James every time."

"Don't be an ignoramus, Margaret Ann," Izzy argued.

"I'm not!"

"Are you telling me you'd want to meet Ben with a bunch of molten, puss-laden sores all over you?"

"Well, no."

"Of course, no. You'd want something internal that wouldn't mess with Maybelline and Max Factor."

"How about kidney failure?"

"Not bad, but I'd go for something respiratory. That way he'd have to get in close to listen to my lungs."

"Or a heart problem!" Margaret Ann said, excited that she'd come up with such an outstanding idea.

"With it beating out of your chest? No way. You don't want a guy to hear your heart going all wild like a schoolgirl."

"Oh," Margaret Ann said, deflated. "I guess you're right. You think of everything, Izzy."

"Yeah, if school had anything to do with life, I'd be valedictorian."

I went to my room and grabbed Mr. Mercury. I needed to get serious about practicing my ventriloquism. It was one thing to do it alone but something else entirely to do it in front of other people. I was nervous about performing, but now that my dad was sick, winning the talent show was the least I could do for him. I took several books out of the library during the school year to learn all I could about ventriloquism. I didn't know that humans use their eyes to locate sounds, and if you do a good job of not moving your lips, the audience's attention focuses on the dummy. To perform in front of an audience, I'd have to practice in front of a mirror, which meant spending time in one of two places—the bathroom or my parent's bedroom. Since my mother was in the bedroom, and Izzy and Margaret Ann were focused on Dr. Kildare, I took Mr. Mercury into the bathroom to practice. I would make my dad proud and maybe even get him to learn how to be a ventriloquist too. Then maybe we could talk to each other all the time, even if neither of us ever moved our lips.

I got up the next morning to The Crystals singing "Then He Kissed Me." Izzy and Margaret Ann had what they referred to as their "mood records." If things were going well with their boyfriends, "So Much in Love" by The Tymes was a favorite. If Izzy broke up with a guy, which happened every other week, she played "The End of the World" by Skeeter Davis. For Margaret Ann, if she and Harry broke up, it was "Judy's Turn to Cry" by Leslie Gore. Outside my window screen, Ellen was skipping through the boxes of her hopscotch board. The next record on Izzy's turntable to play was The Everly Brothers singing "Let It Be Me." As Ellen skipped from one box to the next, I watched her and understood what it meant to have a mood song.

Chapter 17

I look out over the congregation and know that many are reflecting on their childhood adventures, games, and first loves. Before they return from their reverie, Gladys plays, and I sing the opening stanza of "Let It Be Me."

I swivel Moses's head toward me.

"That's some mushy stuff there, Pastor."

"I know."

"So…you and this Ellen girl, you ever get together?"

"Maybe. We haven't reached that point in the story yet. But that song became the song I thought of whenever I looked at Ellen."

"But he never told her," Ms. Nellie says, her voice echoing in the chapel.

"No," I say, "I never did."

"Why not? Scared?"

"I was twelve."

"So what? I was eighty when I led my people out of Egypt."

"It's not the same thing. I wanted to tell her more than anything in the world. Reflecting, I think God was putting something on my heart that day."

"How so?" Ms. Nellie asks.

I smile at Ms. Nellie. She loves to participate in this sermon, and I'm happy to have her as a foil.

"Because it made me think of my father, about how hard it is to say the things you want to say, so hard you feel as if you're choking when you can't get the words out."

"I would've told her," Moses says.

"You never got cold feet?"

"Not in the desert."

"I would think you of all people would understand. You told God you weren't good with words and got tongue-tied, and your words got tangled all the time."

"I wasn't like that around women."

"Really?"

"Did I stutter?"

"Actually, many Bible scholars believe you did. Didn't God allow your older brother, Aaron, to speak for you?"

"The first time. Then I took over," Moses says.

"That first time you spoke, how was it?"

"Are you kidding? I was a basket case."

The congregation howls.

"I can relate to Billy losing his bowels," Moses says. "I felt things loosen up in the pipes when I saw the burning bush."

"Seems to be a pattern. Didn't you have the same issue on Mount Sinai?"

I swivel Moses toward the congregation. "I was eighty, so my stopgaps had some mileage on them. But I held on. They didn't list every miracle that occurred in the Good Book."

"Speak it, brother!" Virgil says. "Sometimes it's better when the truth doesn't set things free!"

These are the moments that invigorate my soul. I allow the laughter to resonate. We are too quick to move on from expressions of joy these days. Laughter, much like words of love and encouragement, need time to effervesce. This world of information overload and instant gratification are the devil's playground. Like a Judas goat, it leads us away from the bountiful table that feeds the soul to the troth where we gorge ourselves on clickbait and soundbites. We become less discriminating, less patient, and in our haste, less human. I take issue with my fellow New Jersey native, Mr. Springsteen. We are not born to run; we are born to stroll, to meander, to be still.

"That's why God created the Sabbath," Harpey once told us.

When Swanson came out with TV dinners, Harpey was beside himself. He didn't have a TV, a fact Ellen, Billy, and I found hard to fathom.

"You should share your meal at a table," he told us. "It's sacred."

Sometimes the Mendelsons seemed more alien to us than alien invaders, but I have come to accept what Harpey so fervently believed—that our rituals are sacrosanct. They bind us to God and to each other. I have seen the pain and heartbreak that results when people abandon the ties of tradition, only to find themselves unmoored from anything truly meaningful.

"How would the Last Supper have worked if all the disciples were sitting around, eating TV dinners?" Harpey said.

In a Jewish household, the dinner table is the center of the home, and the home is a consecrated place. When we take a moment to sit at the table and give thanks, we feed not just our stomachs but our souls.

I say a closing prayer and dismiss the congregation. Poke meets me in my office to give me an update on the mystery of the missing collection plate. Opal made sure she was front and center.

"I'm sorry to report that I've got squat, Pastor. Plenty of fingerprints are at the crime scene, but none were usable. Just a bunch of smudges and such. I talked to Virgil since he cleans the place, trying to reduce the window of opportunity, but he couldn't remember the last time he saw the item in question."

Opal signs.

"What'd she say?" Poke asks.

"She wants to know if you talked to everyone on the suspect list."

"Not yet. Spoke to Virgil, like I said. Spoke to Gladys and Stanley. Nothing stood out."

Opal hands Poke papers she had stapled together.

"What's this?"

Opal taps the top page.

"Oh…your statement," Poke says and rifles through the pages. "This start when you were born?"

Opal's hands sweep to her hips. She glares at Poke. I fight to suppress a laugh.

"I'll read it later," Poke says and then turns his attention to me. "Did you submit the claim to the insurance company?"

"Yes. It's being reviewed."

Poke takes off his hat and rubs his bald pate. "Well, I hope we solve this. Hate to put it in the cold case file alongside that darn denture case."

Opal signs, "What case?"

"It was a long time ago, Opal, before you moved into town," I say.

"I bet I could solve it," she signs.

"She bets she could solve it," I say.

Now it's Poke's turn to roll his eyes. "It's police business, Opal. Thanks anyway."

After Poke left, Opal goes straight to the computer. I know she'll spend the rest of the afternoon trying to find the story about the missing dentures.

Poke's visit reminds me of the one person I haven't seen in church since the collection plate went missing—Virgil's grandson, Earl. He's recently fallen on hard times. After serving two tours in Afghanistan, he came back suffering from PTSD, an affliction that resulted in a roller coaster of addiction, rehab, and relapse. Earl's past drug issues and the ease of accessibility to Virgil's keys makes me wonder if he might have succumbed in a weak moment and taken the plate. I hate to think anything bad about anyone, and set my conjecture and suspicion aside. Virgil loves his grandson deeply. It will devastate him if we discover Earl is the guilty party.

I walk home, stopping to count three blessings just as Earl passes by, driving his father's truck. He beeps the horn, smiles, and waves. "Afternoon, Pastor!" he says.

I wave and recall that childhood summer when suspicions ran high and we discovered how wrong we were when the truth was revealed.

The rest of the week is spent praying and fretting. I am a good pastor but a terrible administrator. Despite being surrounded by a wonderful team of people to help me, I get nervous when too many problems present themselves at the same time. I love the King James Version and turn to Psalm 55:22, "Cast thy burden upon the Lord, and he shall sustain thee: he shall never suffer the righteous to be moved." It saddens me to realize how many people have never read the most beloved book in the world. Of all the gifts presented to me by Harpey Mendelson, my love of the Bible is the one I cherish most. Harpey's passion for the stories and teachings were infectious. As much as you might want to ignore one of his recitations, his voice, mannerisms, and excitement were impossible to ignore. One night, as we sat in the middle of the cul-de-sac, he captivated us as he described Moses's encounter with the burning bush.

"Moses is just a regular guy tending Jethro's flock when God confronts him as a fiery bush."

"What the heck?" Billy said. His chin was covered in chocolate from the Ho-Ho he was eating.

"But the bush isn't consumed by the fire. It just keeps burning as God speaks to Moses, instructing him to take off his sandals because he's standing on holy ground."

"I wouldn't go barefoot near a burning bush," Ellen said.

"Why did God want to be a bush in the first place?" Billy asked. "What the heck?" he repeated.

"To show us that there is nowhere on earth that God isn't present," Harpey said.

"So he's in the bush and it's on fire, and he's just talking to Moses like a regular guy?" Billy asked.

"Moses is the regular guy. God is God!" Harpey's eyes lit up as he told us these stories, and despite Billy's interruptions, I was always enraptured as he talked.

"Not being burned by a fire, that's a superpower," Billy said. "Does He have a magic ring like the Green Lantern?"

"No, God speaks things into being," Harpey said.

"So talking is His superpower?"

Harpey gave in. "Yes. Talking is God's superpower."

"What if He doesn't mean it? Does it still happen? People are always saying things they don't mean. My dad said he wishes his boss's head would turn into a speed bag so he could punch it until the stuffing comes out," Billy said.

"God always says what He means and means what He says," Harpey said.

"Like when he turned that guy's wife into a salt shaker? Do you think he ever thought, 'Uh-oh, it actually happened?'"

"Not a shaker, a pillar," Harpey said.

When I reflect on these encounters, I realize the one with the superpower was Harpey. He had the patience to listen to Billy's constant interruptions and still keep Ellen and I fixated on the stories.

On Thursday morning, I walk to Main Street and enjoy the parade. It's the Fourth of July, America's birthday, and Winslow, with its small-town charm and love of country, puts on a host of festivities that include many of my parishioners. Just as they have since they were children, the Dern sisters make their legendary lemonade and sell it at a stand, donating the profits to the local VFW. Gladys rides Jezebel dressed as Rosie the Riveter, in honor of her mother who worked at a Naval Air station during World War II. Virgil works the cotton candy machine, and Opal stands on the float decked out in American Flags, signing patriotic songs that blast from the float's enormous speakers. I miss Matty's arm in mine but do my best to live in the moment and appreciate living in a country that allows us to freely practice our faith. As "God Bless America" plays, I tear up and place my hand on my heart. I love this holiday, the parade, and this town.

On Saturday evening, I take my walk. As the sun begins its descent, I soak in the beauty, noting what I see as I stroll down the street. I miss Matty's eye for detail but do my best to draw out the distinctions in the world around me as she did when we took our after-dinner walks. "Stop a moment," she'd say, and we'd both pause wherever we were so she could observe details most people would overlook. To Matty, the world was God's gallery of fine art, and she had an eye for the tiniest brush strokes. "Look at the wisp of pink in the horizon. Just magnificent," or "Look at that redbird inching out on that branch, shuffling over like a lone sock trying to sneak its way out of the dryer." Matty loved the great works, both God's and those of lesser masters like Di Vinci and Michelangelo. We have a wonderful painting of "The Last Supper" in our living room, and Matty, who minored in Art/History in college, gave me a quick education on the iconic work of art.

"Look here," she said, pointing at the saltshaker spilled before Judas. "Did you know this is why spilled salt is a sign of bad luck?"

"I had no idea," I said.

"Or look at Thomas, how his finger is pointed in the air. Some believe it represents the finger that would later probe Jesus's wounds to help him believe."

I'm a big picture guy. Matty taught me to look for the intricacies. "God is in the details, my love," she'd say.

I listen to the birdsong and the leaves rustling in the breeze and watch a squirrel scurry up the giant oak on the corner of Oak and Elm. What I miss are the children. On summer nights not so long ago, the streets and yards were filled with laughter as children played. Now they spend their time in virtual worlds at the expense of the real one. We all lose. They miss out on physically interacting with the world around them, and adults miss out on the joy of seeing them play.

I am about to follow my usual route when I'm drawn in a different direction. I have never heard God's voice aloud as some claim they have. For me, it's a whisper, a nudging, a feeling that won't let go. As I walk, I feel compelled to take a detour down the street. A young girl is playing hopscotch, alone but very much enjoying herself. She reminds me of Ellen. Her blond hair is braided, and she wears sneakers with pink sparkles on them. She counts aloud as she hops across the board.

> Hurry Scurry had a worry
> No one liked his chicken curry
> Stuck his finger in the pot
> Chicken curry way too hot

She skips from one foot to two and back to one again. An idea comes to me. God sent me on a mission tonight. This Sunday's service will be a special one.

I arrive at the church early the following morning and share my idea with Virgil.

"I'll block off the parking lot, Pastor," he says. "It's a fine idea!"

The pews are packed. I'm excited to begin. Gladys plays "Amazing Grace," and the choir leads the collective voice of the congregation. There are more new faces. The song ends, and I begin.

Chapter 18

———— ❦ ————

L ater that morning, my mother got dressed to go to the hospital
to visit my dad. Izzy and I wanted to go, but my mother thought
it was best to give him another day of complete rest.

"Maybe tomorrow. We'll see."

My mother hugged Izzy and kissed her head. "Watch your
brother. There's a can of Dinty Moore in the cupboard. I'll be back
to make dinner."

After she left, Billy came over, and we put our plan to cover for
Pepsin's broken greenhouse door in motion. Ellen was still playing on
her hopscotch board.

"Hey, Ellen," Billy said.

Ellen kept hopping and skipping. "Can't talk now."

"We need you for a spy mission," Billy said.

"Okay." She reached down to pick up the pebble in box six.
"But not when it's too dark."

"We're going now," Billy said. "After seeing what happened to
Nixon's dad, we have to move fast."

Ellen stood there a moment, balancing on one leg like a fla-
mingo. "Okay. But make it quick. My mom's taking me to the five-
and-ten to get me Uncle Wiggly. I told Harpey I'd teach him how to
play."

"Awesome!" Billy said. "Maybe we can all play the game together
this afternoon!"

"I thought you didn't like him," Ellen said.

"Maybe I was wrong. I helped with the playhouse, didn't I? Come on, we need to get back there before Pepsin returns from his vacation."

We hurried to the berm behind my house.

"Check to see if it's an all-clear," Billy said, assuring Ellen would be the first to discover Pepsin's broken door.

Ellen crawled to the top of the berm and peered over. "I don't see anybody."

Billy and I looked at one another.

"Nobody right by the greenhouse? That's where we're going," Billy said.

"Nope." Ellen scooched herself back down between Billy and me. "But hurry up. I have to get home in a few minutes."

"You see anything strange?" Billy asked.

"Like what?"

"Not normal, out of the ordinary."

"I'm a lookout for people, and I didn't see any."

"Not just people. Is there anything unusual about the scene?"

"Like what?"

Billy blew a cork. "Like anything!"

Harpey's voice rang out from his backyard. "Hey, is that you guys back there? It looks like something happened to that guy's greenhouse."

Ellen crawled back to the top of the berm and looked at the greenhouse. "He's right. The door's twisted, and the window's smashed."

Billy stood up. "Hey, Harpey," he said, waving from atop the berm. Then he looked toward the greenhouse. "Whoa! What the heck happened there? Looks like the wind smashed the door. Perhaps we should check. Mr. Pepsin's not around, and we should be good neighbors!" Billy's authoritative proclamation for everyone in the neighborhood to hear made perfect sense.

"Why are you talking like that?" Ellen asked.

"Like what?"

"Like you're on stage in a play or something."

Harpey wheeled himself closer to Pepsin's lawn. "I heard a crash last night."

Ellen's mother called out to her.

"I gotta go," Ellen said.

"Let's check it out," Billy said.

We went to the greenhouse and looked at the damage we caused. The doorframe was twisted, and glass was everywhere. Billy stepped over the glass and went inside to check out the plants. "These are too small to be alien pods," he whispered.

"Fine, let's go before Pepsin gets back."

"His house next," Billy said, nodding toward Harpey.

"How's it looking in there?" Harpey asked.

Billy leaped over the glass and headed straight to Harpey.

"The door's a wreck. I'm thinking Mr. Pepsin didn't secure the latch. Loose latch, big wind, crash! Am I right?"

I walked over and joined them, happy to be off Pepsin's lawn. I glanced at the playhouse. "When's your uncle coming back to finish the playhouse?"

"And get us our banana splits?" Billy added.

"He's coming today so he can share in the Sabbath tonight. He'll work on the playhouse and then pick a day to get banana splits. Don't worry. Solly always pays his shekels."

"Nix and I thought we could come over and see your room. Maybe we could play a game or something," Billy said.

"Sure!" Harpey said. "We need to go in around front."

When we got to the front door, Harpey kissed the fingers on his right hand and touched a tiny box affixed to the doorjamb.

"What's that?" Billy asked.

"A *mezuzah*. It signifies that this is a Jewish home. It comes from Deuteronomy."

"Oh," Billy said as if he knew what Deuteronomy was.

"We don't have to kiss our fingers, do we?" Billy asked.

"No," Harpey replied. And we went inside.

Mrs. Mendelson came out of her bedroom and smiled. "Hello, boys."

"They want to see my room," Harpey said.

"Good. Welcome. I have cookies to nosh if you'd like."

"Not now, Mom."

"Okay. I'll bring them in later. Have fun." Mrs. Mendelson turned and walked toward the kitchen.

"This way," Harpey said, and we followed him toward the master bedroom. Since Harpey had the master, he had his own bathroom too. Not only that, it was the biggest room, so he had plenty of space to move around in his wheelchair. He had a twin bed, a dresser, a desk, and—

"Is that a pinball machine?" Billy asked, his eyes as wide as dinner plates.

"Yeah," Harpey said. "My parents got it for me so I could work on my eye-hand coordination and keep my muscles moving."

This was unprecedented. No kid we had ever known had their own real pinball machine. Prior to this, Marsha Boyle's RCA color TV was the standout because she could watch NBC on "color days" when the station ran most of their programs in "living color." Marsha was one of the first kids to see *Munchkinland* in color when she watched *The Wizard of Oz*. Color TV was cool, but a pinball machine in your bedroom was primo. The only modification to Harpey's pinball machine was the legs. They were shortened so Harpey could play it sitting in his wheelchair. It was called the "Thing," and it was the coolest pinball machine ever! It had dual flippers, and you could flip the ball to the top of the playfield with either flipper. Five bumpers across the top each had a letter and spelled out T-H-I-N-G. T and G were pop bumpers; H, I and G were static.

"Can I play it?" Billy asked.

"Sure. Just plug it in," Harpey said.

Billy plugged in the machine and the bumpers rang out, and the lights flashed.

As Billy played pinball, I spotted the model of a ship sitting on Harpey's dresser. I enjoyed building monster models and knew that this model was something special. Constructed of wood, it took up the entire length of Harpey's dresser and was made with such intricate detail that I couldn't take my eyes off it.

"Who made this?" I asked.

"My Uncle Solly. It was a present for my birthday," Harpey said.

"Was it a kit?"

"No. But it's made to scale. It's Noah's Ark. Noah is Solly's favorite hero of the Talmud."

"He didn't have instructions?" I asked, amazed that anyone could build something this complex and in such detail without a blueprint.

"The original ark was three hundred cubits long, fifty cubits wide, and thirty cubits high. That's about one-third the size of the Titanic. I helped Uncle Solly reduce it to scale."

I continued to admire the ark as Billy played his pinball game when another sound startled Billy. The rev of his father's engine. Billy's head jerked toward Harpey's bedroom window. His dad turned onto the street. Mr. Finley had a 1959 Ford Galaxy 500 with dual exhausts that roared distinctively when he shifted gears.

"I gotta go!" Billy dashed out of Harpey's house as fast as his PF Flyers would take him.

Chapter 19

———— ⟨∽⟩ ————

Gladys's bell rings. I turn Moses toward me.

"That Thing, thing. We have it in our house," he says.

"Yes, we do. It's a classic." I turn to the congregation. "As most of you are aware, your pastor is a pinball wizard."

"He used to be," Moses says. "Now, like many of us who have aged, he tilts."

"Yes, but pinball kept me young at heart." I turn back to the congregation. "What games did you all play as children? Call it out."

"Mother, May I!" Ms. Nellie announces.

"Hopscotch!" Gladys says.

Other members join in, "Freeze tag!" "Red rover!" "Jump rope!"

"Blind man's bluff!" Moses says.

"Wonderful!" I say. "In Matthew 18:3, Jesus says, 'Assuredly, I say to you, unless you are converted, and become as little children, you will by no means enter the kingdom of heaven.' We have to guard our hearts from the pride and arrogance of adulthood." I pull a box of colored chalk from the shelf under the lectern, the large kind used to draw on driveways and sidewalks. "So today, we will end our service early and reconnect with our childhood."

It takes time for everyone to gather in the parking lot, but even Ms. Nellie, despite her difficulty walking, insists on staying to watch what newfangled activity her pastor had in mind. Before the service began, I had Virgil block off a section of our parking lot for the festivities. As everyone gathers around me, I hold up the box of chalk.

"Who knows how to draw a hopscotch box?"

Winnie's hand flies up. "Back in the day, Francis and I played hopscotch until the streetlights came on. I can draw that box like it was yesterday."

"Have at it," I say. "What color would you like?"

"We always used pink back then," Winnie says.

"Pink it is. Will you be okay getting down to draw it? If not, Opal says she's more than happy to help."

"I can do it," Winnie says.

Winnie draws the box, numbering the boxes one through eight, with one being the first box and eight being the last. Box one and two were single boxes. Three and four were side by side. Five was a single box, six and seven were side by side, and eight was last.

"We need a few stones or—"

"Bottle caps!" Francis says. "Bottle caps were what we always used."

"I don't think we have bottle caps," I say.

"Francis, you have bingo chips in your purse. They will work for now," Winnie says.

Francis unclips her purse, retrieves several green bingo chips, and hands them to Winnie. "We're ready, Pastor," Winnie says.

The families across the street stroll over to watch. I smile and wave. "Good morning! Just having some fun here after our morning service!"

There are three girls and a boy, all I guess to be between the ages of five and eight, standing beside their parents.

"Who will go first?" I ask.

Virgil speaks up. "I'll do it, if you do it first, Pastor."

"Oh, this I have to see," Ms. Nellie says.

I want to protest and say it's a girl's game, but Opal, as if she can read my mind, gives me her don't-you-dare look.

"Tell you what, Pastor," Ms. Nellie says, "I'll donate fifty dollars to the church building fund for every box you attain without a foul. That's four hundred there and four hundred back."

After a moment, Winnie exclaims, "My Lord, that could be eight hundred dollars!"

"I know how much it is," Ms. Nellie says. "The Spirit has moved me."

"I'll add ten dollars a box," Gladys announces.

"I want in on this," Otis says. "A dollar a box, doubled if you make it all the way to the end. Five dollars a box for Virgil, same terms."

Several other church members join in. I look over at our visitors as the parents smile and laugh. One of the moms says, "I'll add a dollar a box."

Then the mom next to her says, "Me too."

When I see these new young families appear at the event, I know it is God's handiwork. Our new friends have added to the hopscotch wager fund.

Now every box I attain without a foul is worth ninety dollars. And that doesn't count Virgil's pledges, which amount to twenty-five dollars a box. All in, if both Virgil and I make it to the end of the hopscotch board and back again, the building fund will reap $2,300! That would help replace the stove, refrigerator, and dishwasher for our new kitchen.

"Okay, it's a deal," I say. "Remind me of the rules."

"Easy as pie," Winnie says. "You hop through the squares but skip the one you have your marker on. Each square gets one foot, and you can't have two feet on the ground at a time."

"Unless there are two number squares right next to each other," one of the visiting girls says.

Winnie smiles. "That is correct! In that case, you can put down both feet with one in each square. If you step on a line, hop on the wrong square, or step out of the square, you lose your turn."

"And some money," Ms. Nellie says.

The girl who spoke up raises her hand and waves it. Her mother whispers to her, and the girl frowns and puts down her hand. I point to her and say, "Perhaps you can show me how it's done?"

The girl looks up at her mother, who smiles and nods her approval.

Winnie hands a bingo chip to the girl. "What's your name?"

"Gracie," the girl says, and then, with the entire congregation cheering her on, she moves through the hopscotch board with ease.

"That's how you do it," she says to me and hands me the bingo chip.

"Well, you are a professional, Gracie, and I am most appreciative of your flawless demonstration."

Gracie runs back to her proud mother as I stand at the threshold of the gauntlet. The last time I tried to hop on one foot was when I stubbed my toe on the couch, and that didn't go so well. I almost fell over the coffee table.

"You can do it, Pastor!" Opal signs.

The congregation joins in with words of encouragement and advice.

"Don't overthink it!" Virgil says.

"Rest at boxes three and four!" Gladys says.

I toss my chip, which lands in the center of box two. I skip onto box one and leap over box two, landing with both feet inside boxes three and four. Cheers erupt. Little Gracie runs up alongside boxes five and six and gives me a thumbs up. Hopping to one foot on box five, I falter, but regain my balance and hop to both feet again into boxes six and seven. Little Gracie is coaching me as I go.

"Use your arms to balance!" she says and extends hers to demonstrate.

I hop into box eight, turn on one foot, and feel my calf muscle tighten. I wince, hop around to face the other way, and head back. I've got two squares to go when my calf spasms. "Gracie," I yell, "take over!" I extend my hand. She slaps it, hops into my spot, and finishes for me.

I fall to the ground, clutching my calf. The muscle is in full spasm, and the pain is excruciating. A moment later, Gracie's mother is at my side giving me instructions, stretching my leg and working the muscle until the spasm subsides. Gracie's mother is a physical therapist. God is good.

For the next half hour, members of the congregation and our newfound friends play hopscotch, mother may I? and red rover as I sit by the tree next to Moses. My heart is filled with warmth. I savor the laughter of childhood, not from the mouths of babes, but from octogenarians freed from the shackles of propriety. In heaven, I believe we will all be children again.

When the festivities are over, the participants are richer for the experience, and the capital fund gains too. Ms. Nellie happily honors Gracie's finish on the hopscotch board, and Virgil, despite a back spasm, was victorious in his skip from one to eight and back again.

As I make my way back home with Moses's trunk clattering behind me, I remember Harpey's Uncle Solly. He found the joy of childhood in work and play. I realize the events of this day, like the path I would walk for the rest of my life, were born back in that strange summer of 1963. That Friday night at the Mendelson's after Billy ran home would change everything and taught me that seeing shouldn't always be believing.

The "Thing" is in my study. I have not played a single game on my prized pinball machine since Matty passed. Moments before she left this world, she smiled at me and said, "You can turn that blasted sound on now, my love," and then she was gone. Who could imagine those would be the last words shared between us? Matty was doing what she always did, which was trying her very best to lighten my burden, but I hold a grudge against the Thing now, something I know Matty would find "patently absurd." I smile at the thought as I replay her words in my mind. "Goodness me, Nixon Bliss, that is patently absurd, and you well know it."

"Yes, Matty dear, I know it, but I'm having trouble letting it go, and even more letting you go."

Matty disliked the Thing, but she knew it gave me moments of solace, so she tolerated having it in the house as long as I turned the sound off. When I had trouble sleeping, I would go into my office with the lights off and play pinball. There's something wonderful about seeing all those flashing lights as I engaged the flippers and sent the pinballs flying at the bumpers. Playing pinball in the dark, even with the sound off, was my version of letting go.

I have lunch. A fluffernutter sandwich and a glass of Grape Kool-Aid. This is what I do during my sixties summer sermons—remember the past and indulge in the classics. When I finish, I put Moses in the car and head for the hospital. God has put Benny Penzik on my heart. I drive carefully. I have no desire to reconnect with Officer Becca. Afternoon clouds drift low in the sky, the purple kind that darken and, unlike the fluffy white ones, seem heavy—like they're straining to hold back buckets of water. I get inside the hospital just in time. As the automatic doors close behind me, a deluge begins.

I make my way down the hall with Moses in my arms. When I reach Benny's hospital room, he sits once again in his doorway, half in and half out of his shell.

"Hello there," I say.

Benny turns. "Hello."

"I wondered if you might be up for a visit."

Benny's face is drawn and pale. His yarmulke rests awkwardly on the crown of his head. The chemo and radiation are taking a toll. He shrugs. "Okay."

He has the golem in his lap. I say, "My friend told me the most famous golem was the Golem of Prague, created out of clay from the banks of the Vltava River through rituals and incantations."

Benny's eyes brighten, my question providing a power surge to his weakened spirit.

"Yes," he says and points to the golem. "He is my Golem of Prague. He has mystical powers."

"That's how I understand it. The Jewish people needed protection from the pogroms, and this rabbi had special powers of his own."

"It's true!" Benny says. "Rabbi Loew. He was a Jewish mystic, the one who brought the golem to life." Benny hugs the golem close to his chest. "And now, the golem protects me."

I sit in a chair positioned in the hallway beside Benny. "I am very glad you have him. My friend had a golem and swore by his powers."

The rattling of wheels comes down the hall. Benny stiffens. The same girl who had turned away a week ago watches us. Like Benny, she's pale and thin. Benny holds her gaze for a moment and then looks down as if he needs permission to look at a girl so pretty. I turn

Moses's attention to the girl. She holds onto the IV pole, its wheels rattling every time she steps closer to us.

I engage Moses before she turns away again. "That's an interesting feed bag you have there," Moses says. "Maybe Balaam should have rewarded his donkey with such a gift after beating the poor animal for trying to talk sense into him."

The girl laughs. "It's not a feed bag. It's an IV."

I turn Moses toward Benny. "Tell her, Benny, if you know, what special talent Balaam's donkey had."

"He could talk."

"No way," the girl says.

"Yes, way. Balaam's donkey and the serpent in the garden of Eden are the only two animals to speak in the Bible."

"Give the boy a shekel!" I have Moses say.

The girl shuffles forward, pulling her IV pole along with her. Benny steals another glance at her. I decide to help them get to know one another. I let Moses take the lead.

"Benny, I bet I can guess this girl's name before you can. I will ask some questions." I turn Moses's attention to the girl. I put Moses's palm to his forehead. "I'm getting some vibes. It might be a flower. Is it Rose?"

"No."

"Petunia?"

She laughs. "No, it's not a flower."

"Your turn, Benny. Name a category."

Benny shrugs. "I dunno."

"We don't have a clue, so we need one," Moses says.

"It's a place," the girl says.

"Chicago?" Moses says.

The girl laughs, and the beauty of it echoes in the hallway. "No."

"I know, I know, I know!" Moses says. "Benny, say hello to… Charlotte!"

The girl's laughter is free and boisterous now. Benny joins in. "No, not Charlotte."

I widen Moses's eyes. "Egypt?"

Now the girl's eyes widen. "No, but I like it!"

"I give up," Moses says.

The girl glances from Moses to Benny to me and then settles her gaze back on Moses.

"Brooklyn," she says.

I widened Moses's eyes. "Brooklyn! Oy vey, I should have known. I bet it was a toss-up between Brooklyn and Queens, yes?"

Brooklyn smiles. "No."

"The Bronx?"

"No."

"Staten Island?"

Now both Brooklyn and Benny laugh. Several other children come out of their rooms and move toward us. This is the magic of ventriloquism. There's something disarming about a dummy that talks. I turn Moses to Benny.

"Benny, what do you think of that name?" Moses asks.

"Which one? Brooklyn or Staten Island?"

"Brooklyn."

Benny hesitates. For a moment, I fear he may roll back into the safety of his hospital room. Then he says, "I like it. It's...different and...has a nice...it's a nice name."

Brooklyn smiles at Benny. "Thanks."

"You're welcome," Benny says, and the burden of isolation falls away from him.

A boy, older, maybe fourteen, stands at the door to his room across the hall and points at Benny. "What's with the doll?" His tone is snide and demeaning.

Before Benny can retreat, Brooklyn comes to his defense. "Who asked you, Kyle?"

"The golem is a superhero," Benny says. "He's a protector."

I turn to Benny with the most serious look I can muster. "Are you sure you want to share the secret of the Golem of Prague with strangers? It's a mystery held for centuries."

"I wanna hear it," Brooklyn says.

"Me too," another child says.

Benny straightens his back and tells the children about the Legend of the Golem of Prague. He is in his wheelhouse now. It enraptures the young crowd. Even Kyle listens intently. Benny leans in, and his eyes seem to go light and dark as he speaks of the Kabbalist and alchemist, Judah Loew, the Jewish mystic who brought the golem to life. Before long, several nurses stop to listen, and if only for a little while, the children forget about their sickness.

Down the hall, Benny's mom walks toward us with another parent. She stops in her tracks. At first panicked at the sight of all the people in the hallway around Benny's room, her nervous expression turns to wonder as she realizes her shy Benny is holding court. We exchange a smile. I excuse myself from the group and make my way home.

It is a busy week. On Tuesday, I meet with the building committee—Otis, Stanley, Virgil, Opal, and me—to discuss our needed repairs. We decide to tackle the roof first and vote to forego repairs and have a new roof put on. Our next project will be to have Beelzebub repaired in late September. Virgil suggests we might consider a new heating system altogether, but we settle on getting a professional opinion before making a final decision. If one can have affection for a boiler, I sense that we all harbor an affinity for Beelzebub. As we grow older, we gain an attachment to things that have been around as long as we have, and Beelzebub has heated Miller Memorial since 1948.

After the meeting, I help Opal add flowers to the flower boxes and head home. It's been a productive week, and I'm looking forward to Sunday morning.

Chapter 20

———— ✦ ————

I stand at the entrance to the church and spot Gracie skipping toward me with her parents on either side of her.

"Welcome! It's wonderful to see you here!" I say.

"Gracie insisted," her mother says. "I'm Nicole, and this is my husband Ray. How's the leg?"

I tap it. "Good as old."

Virgil leads the family to an open pew and then returns to express the hope we always have: that new families will connect with our little church and feel the presence of the Lord. "That Gracie's a sweet one," he says. "She'd make a great lamb on stage, Pastor. Hope they find this to be their church home."

"From your mouth to God's ear," I say.

I remove Moses from his trunk and say a quick prayer. I think of Harpey Mendelson and thank God for placing him in my path. The older I get, the greater the appreciation I have for the impact Harpey had on my life. Gladys plays her spiced up version of "A Crown with Many Thorns," one of my personal favorites. I enter the chapel with Moses beside me. I set him on the lectern and look out across the congregation. The pews are full. I spot little Gracie and smile. She has a cherub's face, and I imagine little wings on her back as she sits on a cloud. I am fascinated by the role of the cherubim in Scripture. They are angels, and Gracie fills that bill. She sits between her parents and waves to me.

"Good morning," I say and receive the same calming response I have received for the past forty years.

"Good morning."

I let the words resonate in my soul. It *is* a good morning. We are alive. We are here. And the Good Shepard is with us. I turn Moses toward our new visitors and make his eyes go wide.

"It's Graceeee!" I have Moses say. I swing Moses toward me. "She's as cute as a button on a Birkenstock."

"Birkenstocks don't have buttons."

"No?"

"Cute as a Kewpie doll?"

"That and more."

"And she's some scotch-hopper."

"Hopscotcher," I say.

Gracie's laughter is its own kind of song.

"Welcome to our church," I say to Gracie and her parents, "we are so happy that you're here. We are in the middle of a sermon series that recounts my summer in 1963 when I met an unusual Jewish boy named Harpey Mendelson."

Ms. Nellie stands. "I'll catch them up after today's service, Pastor."

"That would be splendid, Ms. Nellie," I say and continue with the sermon.

Chapter 21

————— ❧ —————

After Billy ran home, I played pinball with Harpey and thought about how I could get him to show me his garage. The way Harpey navigated the flippers was evidence of his disability. If a pinball came at the flippers after rocketing off a bumper, he couldn't react quickly enough to avoid losing the ball.

"Oy *gevalt*!" he'd yell in frustration.

As Harpey struggled at pinball, I looked around his room to see what kind of stuff he had. That was when I saw the golem. Harpey had a poster of one on his wall and a golem action figure on the pillow of his bed.

"What is that?" I asked, right after Harpey lost his last pinball.

"The Golem of Prague. The *Goyim* have Frankenstein, the Jews have the golem."

"The Goyim?"

"People who aren't Jewish."

I pointed at the golem. "He's a monster?"

"Most golem are. But the Golem of Prague is a superhero."

"What powers does he have?" The golem looked like the Hulk, but unfinished, as if his transformation was incomplete.

"No physical element can harm him. He can grow to enormous size with the might of armies! He was brought to life to protect Jews from the blood libels."

"What's that?"

"A false accusation of murder against the Jews. They said Jews used Christian blood in Jewish rituals to bake the Passover *matzoh*."

I thought of the ritual Billy and I had witnessed several nights before when we peered through the Mendelson's window.

Harpey's modulating voice took on a breathless quality when speaking about the golem. "Rabbi Loew molded the golem out of clay and brought him to life in 1580. The Rabbi was a wonderworker who knew the Jews needed protection, so he used his mystical powers to create the monster."

"How come he isn't in any comics?"

"Because he's real. The golem was brought to life and then reduced to a pile of dirt in the attic of a synagogue in Prague when his mission was complete. Before he died, Rabbi Loew decreed that no one should ascend to the attic where—to this day—a red pile of dirt remains under old and tattered prayer shawls."

I wanted to know more about the golem, but the thing about Jews murdering Christians and using their blood to bake things had me creeped out. Mrs. Mendelson came in the room with two butter knives, a plate of cream cheese, and a box with the word "matzoh" written on it. That was the same thing they accused the Jews of baking with blood.

"A little nosh before dinner," she said and set the plate down on Harpey's desk.

"Thanks, Mom."

"I heard your father is doing better," Mrs. Mendelson said. "Each evening, we pray the *mi sheberach* for him."

I didn't know what the mi sheberach was, but knowing their family took time out each day to pray for my dad was nice to hear. She left the room.

Harpey spun his wheelchair around from the pinball machine, went right for the box of matzoh, and pulled one out of the box. It looked a like a monster-size Saltine cracker. He broke it into four pieces, spread cream cheese on it, and tried to hand it to me.

"No thanks," I said.

Harpey turned to the Golem of Prague on his bed. "Why doesn't he want it?" he asked and then paused a moment. "Oh," Harpey said, answering as if the golem had informed him of something. He turned back to me. "The baking in blood thing is made up. We couldn't bake anything like that. It wouldn't be kosher. Besides"—Harpey handed me the box and pointed to the brand—"it's Manischewitz. Store-bought. I don't think Manischewitz is murdering people to make matzoh."

That sounded reasonable. Besides, I was hungry. Harpey handed me a piece of matzoh with cream cheese on it, and I took a bite. I love cream cheese, and the matzoh wasn't bad. I ate another piece and thought about how I could get Harpey to show me his garage.

"This is a cool house," I said. "Our house is set up just like it. Our garage doesn't have much in it. How about yours?"

"Just stuff," Harpey said.

I wasn't getting anywhere. Then I got an idea Billy would be proud of. "It might have a secret door."

Harpey rotated his head toward me. Everything he did with his body seemed to be connected to gears and wires. "A secret door?"

"It's been a rumor forever. A kid at school said he found one in his garage with a baseball card collection hidden inside. One was a Ted Williams rookie card."

Harpey's eyes widened. "Maybe we'll find one of the Hebrew Hammer. That would be something."

"Who?"

"Al Rosen. He played for the Cleveland Indians and refused to play on the high holy days. Rabbi Feldman talks about him all the time."

"Oh."

"Or Sandy Koufax!"

"We should check. You never know, right?"

"Not for another week or two. There are boxes in there now, and I can't get around."

"I could check. Let you know."

"No. My parents won't let you in there with all those boxes piled up."

My plan foiled, I let it go. Mrs. Mendelson came and got me. Izzy was at the front door. My mom had stayed late at the hospital, and Mrs. Mendelson invited both Izzy and me to stay for dinner. Izzy thought it was a grand idea for me, but she had plans.

"Nixon would love to stay, I'm sure," she said and gave me a hard stare. "Wouldn't you, Nix?"

The last thing I wanted was be in the Mendelson's house after dark, but I couldn't think fast enough to get out of it.

"Yeah, I guess," I said.

"I'll be back to get him around nine," Izzy said and left.

Solly's van pulled into the driveway, and we both went out to meet him. The moment he stepped out of the van, he began dancing, snapping his fingers and singing "Hava Nagila."

Solly danced and sang until he ran out of breath. Then he put his hands on his knees to get his wind back. When he stood, he placed his hands on his hips and smiled.

"Harpey! My favorite nephew!"

"I'm your only nephew, Uncle."

Uncle Solly looked at me and shrugged. "I can't fool this boy. Wise as Solomon. And you, Nixon, sir, how is your father?"

"Getting better."

"God be with him," Solly said and wiped his clammy forehead with a hankie he drew from his pocket. "Let's go inside. I'm leaking out here."

Once inside, Mr. and Mrs. Mendelson embraced Solly, and an hour later, the Shabbat meal was underway.

We gathered around the dining room table. Mrs. Mendelson lit the candles. "Isaac, shut the lights off, please."

"Not tonight, we have a shabbos goy!" Solly said.

Solly told me that a shabbos goy was a non-Jew who could perform duties on the Sabbath that Jews were forbidden to perform. "And here you are! A miracle is Nixon-sir! Please do us the honor of turning out the light."

I did, and the Sabbath dinner began.

Two wine glasses were on a tray and two loaves of bread covered with cloth. Mrs. Mendelson covered her eyes with her hands and chanted, "Bah-ROOKH ah-TAH ah-doh-NOY eh-loh-HAY-noo meh-LEKH hah-oh-LAHM, ah-SHER keed-SHAH-noo b'meetz-VOH-tahv v'tzee-VAH-noo, l'HAD-leek nair shel SHAH-bat-KOH-desh."

This was the ritual Billy and I witnessed the night we peered in their window. My throat tightened.

Mrs. Mendelson poured wine into each of the wine glasses, and some wine spilled over. When the chanting finished, she put her fingers into the wine and dabbed her eyes with it. "Good Shabbos," she said.

Harpey, Mr. Mendelson, and Solly all repeated, "Good Shabbos."

"It means 'Good Sabbath,'" Harpey explained.

"Oh," I replied.

We ate, and Solly acted as if the table were an amusement park. "What a beautiful table, Nina! Harpey, my favorite nephew, tell me, for the sake of the education of our shabbos goy, why women are required to light the Sabbath candles."

"Let the boy eat, Solly," Mr. Mendelson said.

Solly ignored Mr. Mendelson and looked at me. "Are your ears open, shabbos goy?"

I nodded.

Harpey answered. "The Talmud tells us that since it was a woman who caused man's downfall—"

Solly tapped Mrs. Mendelson's arm. "Are you listening, Nina?" Before she could answer, he winked and smiled.

"She caused the light of the world to be dimmed. So it's a woman's obligation to light the candles and bring light back into the world."

"This boy of yours, Immanuel, God has blessed him with a quick mind and the memory of an elephant!" Solly said. "Try the gefilte fish," he said to me, extending the plate as an offering. "No one makes it better than Harpey's lovely mother. She's the Liberace of gefilte fish! Nina, have some havdalah wine, eh?"

Harpey laughed. "Yeah, Mom, have a few sips."

Mrs. Mendelson suppressed a smile. "You're incorrigible, Solly." She looked at Mr. Mendelson, who had a napkin to his mouth that did little to hide his laughter. "You find this amusing?" she asked playfully.

"No," he replied, but he could not keep his composure. "Yes! I can't get the image out of my mind!"

Suddenly everyone was laughing. "What is it?" I asked. "What's so funny?"

"It's a superstition," Harpey said, "that if a woman drinks from the havdalah glass, she will grow an immense beard!"

"Don't worry, Nina—you'll look good. Like Rabbi Rabinowitz but cuter," Solly said.

"And you know what, Solly?" she replied, pointing at him with her fork. "*Loyfn zolstu in beys-hakise yede dray khadoshim!*"

Solly turned to Harpey, feigning shock. "Can you believe this, nephew? What your sweet mother cursed me with? It's already working." Solly stood up to leave the table.

"Sit, Solly," Mrs. Mendelson said. "I take it back. Finish your meal."

"What happened?" I asked.

"You don't speak Yiddish?" Solly asked.

"No."

"She said I should run to the toilet every three minutes or every three months!"

Dinner at the Mendelsons was filled with periods of solemn prayer, joyful song, and boisterous laughter. For them, dinner was an event, a time to shut out the world, to be with one another and with God. I didn't understand the meaning of the tradition back then, but I envied the meal because it was so much more than just eating. Before I knew it, Izzy came and got me.

"What did you have for dinner?" she asked.

"The felt-a-fish."

"What's that like?"

"Sort of like SPAM but with fish. It was okay. But I really liked the potato kugel. It tasted like tater tots. Is mom home?"

"Yeah. And Dad's counting on you for that talent show, so you'd better get practicing. Mom said he asked about it twice."

Chapter 22

⸙

The choir stands, but before they begin, Gladys leans over and whispers to them. Otis, who is hard of hearing, lifts his ear trumpet and places it in his ear. Otis refuses to invest in new-fangled hearing-aids, favoring ear trumpets instead. His wife Augie, now long deceased, bought him one as a joke when he lost some of his hearing, and to her dismay, Otis found it suited him just fine.

"Say again?" Otis says, turning the ear trumpet toward Gladys, almost hitting Winnie in the head with it as he does.

Winnie scowls. I mouth, "Patience," to her.

Gladys stands, walks over to Otis, and whispers into the ear trumpet.

"That'll be fine," Otis says.

Despite Otis's hearing impairment, his baritone voice is beautiful. Gladys changed the first song selection to "Jesus Loves the Little Children" in honor of Gracie. Gladys plays the opening bars, and everyone recognizes the old favorite. Buster's pipes sound resplendent this morning, and I see that Gracie's mother, Nicole, is singing along with gusto. Her vigorous soprano is a welcome addition to the collective chorus of the congregation. Gracie's appearance and that of her parents make it clear how wonderful it would be to add more young people to our church family.

After the service, I commend Nicole on her wonderful voice and tell her I hope she will return.

"Oh, we will. And I'll invite some friends. We just moved into the new development, and plenty of young families are moving in."

"More music to my ears!" I say.

Otis shuffles by and taps Nicole's shoulder. She turns and smiles. Otis shows his teeth. Not in a menacing way, more to display his new dentures. They gleam. He showed them to me the first day he got them. "Newest of the newfangled," he said. "Metal-free, slightly flexible and they fit like a glove." Why Otis got the latest technology in dentures but insists on using an ear trumpet is beyond me, but as Matty often said, "To each his own."

"You've got the voice of an angel," Otis tells Nicole. "Could use some young blood in the choir. You're able and we're willing."

I think it too forward, but Nicole appreciates the offer.

"I'll consider that, sir. Thank you for asking."

As I put Moses in his trunk, Virgil walks into the office with something on his mind. He paces. Sighs. Takes a deep breath.

"I'm worried about Earl, Pastor," he finally says.

"Why? What's wrong?"

"I'm an actor, so I know acting when I see it, especially bad acting, and he's acting as if he hasn't got a care in the world. But he's forcing it, not feeling it. Remember the year you played one of the wise men?"

"Yes. Unfortunately."

"Do you remember what I told you?"

"That I wasn't feeling it. I was…"

"Emoting. The great Russian acting theorist, Stanislavsky, said we shouldn't emote. We should pursue a goal. Earl's emoting all over the place. Something's weighing heavy on him. I can see it plain as day."

I wonder if what weighs on Earl is our missing collection plate but keep the notion to myself.

Virgil rubs his chin. "I asked Earl if he had a weak moment and started with the drugs again, but he denied it. He saw some terrible things over there in Iraq. Hell's preamble is how I see it."

"Yes, a terrible thing," I say and put my hand on my friend's shoulder. "We'll put his name on the prayer list."

"Thanks, Pastor, he could use it."

I go to my office, lean back in my chair, and consider the timing of Earl's behavior. The matter weighs heavy on my heart. If Virgil discovers Earl stole from the church, it will devastate him. I consider my options. Maybe I can connect with Earl on the premise of not seeing him in church the past few weeks and he'll be moved to tell me his addiction got the best of him.

Opal walks into my office.

"I think it might have been an insurance scam," she signs.

"I'm not following."

Opal sets a paper down on my desk, a chart with names filled in boxes and arrows going this way and that.

"I don't understand. What am I looking at?"

"Those are people who had their dentures stolen," Opal signs.

Ah, the cold case. Poke will regret bringing this up in front of Opal. "And?"

Opal points to the three names, one in each box and signs, "They knew one another. They were in the—" Opal signs so fast I couldn't keep up.

"Slow down. They were in the what?"

"The...same...bridge...club," she signed.

Opal explains her theory about the missing dentures. One of the names on the list is Augie Oliver, Otis's deceased wife. Based on newspaper stories and local gossip, Opal believes Augie was in cahoots with the two other women whose names I don't recognize in an insurance scam. I'm beside myself.

"This is crazy," I say. "We need to stick to church business. You have nothing to base this on but loose conjecture."

I realize the only guilty party here is me. To get Opal to stop obsessing over the missing collection plate, I encouraged her to pursue the case of the missing dentures. But I never expected her to come up with a theory that would include a former parishioner of scamming an insurance company by making a false claim about false teeth.

"They knew one another, and they were the only victims," Opal signs. "Augie admitted in *The Corner Post* that her new dentures fit like a glove and her old ones were giving her gums fits. All three made insurance claims and were reimbursed."

The Corner Post is the local newspaper, and back in 1991, when the dentures went missing, they personalized the stories. That's how Opal knew all the victims were in the bridge club together and made insurance claims.

"Look," Opal says and points to all three ladies posing for the camera, displaying their new sets of false teeth.

Augie proudly displays her new dentures between two other ladies, and I remember how Otis displayed his teeth to Nicole. It gives me pause. Was it synchronicity or just happenstance? The psychologist Carl Jung believed that some coincidences were meaningful. I couple this with Jung's belief in God and often think of synchronicity as one way God speaks to us. Nonetheless, I am convinced Opal's suggestion is poppycock, and I tell her so.

"Leave police work to the police. We have more important things to worry about."

"Why would anyone break in someone's home to steal dentures?" Opal asks. "You want poppycock? Believing that is poppycock! This makes more sense than that."

"Maybe so, but this crime—be it fraud or theft—is well beyond the statute of limitations, and I want you to let it be."

Opal stiffens at my tone. It's unlike me to be that stern but the whole mess—the stolen teeth and missing collection plate—has me at my wits end.

"I'm sorry. Maybe I'm getting too old and tired for this, and retirement is past due."

We are both surprised. In all my years as a pastor, I have never hinted that it might be time to retire from the pulpit.

Opal locks her eyes on mine and signs, "You're not serious."

I shrug. The notion pops out of my head like a clown from a jack-in-the-box. "I *am* on in years."

Tears well in her eyes, and Opal dashes out of the office.

"Oh, my Lord," I whisper. "Oh. My. Lord."

I walk home. As Mr. Rogers often sang, it is a beautiful day in the neighborhood. Despite this—the sunshine, the cloudless sky, and birdsong—I trudge along, dragging Moses's trunk behind me. I'm in a fog. My outburst at Opal left me unsettled. I pass two of my blessing stops without taking notice. I stop at the third, feeling a tug from behind as if Matty has grabbed me by the shirt. And then, right there on the sidewalk, I weep. My chest bellows, heaves like an old accordion. I sit on Moses's trunk and work to suppress the tsunami of emotion. I fail. The dam has given way, and the waters will not be denied.

"Help...me, God," I whisper, and the words escape on truncated bursts of air. My chest quakes with disjointed hydraulics. My encounter with Opal has released a year's worth of grief, and I'm forced to recognize that my stiff upper lip is no match for my broken heart. Matty left me a year ago tomorrow. I have cried but like a miser hording coins, I have rationed my tears in fear that, one day, they would be gone and leave me without enough for my beloved Matty and that would somehow be...be what? It is as if, despite knowing better, I believe Matty would be disappointed in me if I couldn't produce enough tears for her.

Prior to Matty's illness, we rarely discussed my retirement. Matty loved the church. She believed being a pastor's wife was her calling. Pastor's wives are the unsung heroes of Christianity. The spouse of every pastor I know is a pillar of strength. Few people understand how difficult it is. It is lonely, and the weight of living under a microscope can be debilitating. It takes a woman of profound faith and commitment to choose such a path, and Matty had both in spades. I am unmoored. My earthly anchor, my lighthouse and love, who steadied me in rough waters, is no longer by my side. I miss her terribly.

I hear a voice. It sounds distant at first and then comes closer. I look up at Stanley and Gladys on Jezebel, both wearing their helmets, out on their Sunday drive on the Buzzabout X-3000.

"Pastor? Pastor, are you okay?" Stanley asks.

Gladys navigates Jezebel to the curb. She steps off the scooter and hurries to me. "What's wrong? Do you need an ambulance?" she asks in a steady, concerned tone. "Is it your heart?"

"Matty will have died a year ago tomorrow," I say. I take in a deep breath and let it out.

"You poor dear," Gladys says, wrestling with her helmet mid-sentence.

"I'm okay. It just…came over me."

"Well, of course it did." Gladys's words are muffled when the helmet gets stuck midway as she fights to remove it. "Stanley…"

Stanley steps off the scooter and spreads the sides of the helmet before slipping it the rest of the way off Gladys's head.

"Sticks to me like a barnacle," Gladys says. The helmet leaves her beehive hairdo looking like someone stepped on it. She uses the palms of her hands to resurrect the hive.

My face, heated by the flush of embarrassment, breaks out in beads of sweat that collect on my forehead. Stanley reaches into a lunch carrier strapped to the back of the scooter and retrieves a cold bottle of water. "Here, this will do you."

"Thank you," I say. "Look at me. I've become a sideshow on the sidewalk." I stand, take a drink of water, and brush myself off. Such an odd reaction. It's not like I was rolling around in the grass. "Wearing my heart on my sleeve this way," I mutter.

"Well, you just wear it wherever you darn well please," Gladys says. "My Stanley is as dependable as they come, but as God is my judge, if he doesn't break down more than my old scooter after I'm gone, he'll get what's for and then some."

"Don't I know it," Stanley says.

"I'm good now, just had a moment, I guess. Water helped," I say.

"We'll follow you home," Gladys says.

"No need. I missed some blessing steps, and I'd like to take my time. You folks go along."

Gladys eyes me suspiciously. "You're sure?"

"The air and the walk will do me good."

"Very well," Gladys says.

Stanley helps her get her helmet back on, and they continue their Sunday ride.

I retreat to my missed blessing steps and thank God for the life I had with Matty, friends like Gladys and Stanley, and for discernment regarding this sudden thought of retirement. I lumber along, as Harpey would say, schlepping Moses in my wake. I tug Moses's trunk onto my porch, touch the tile, ring the doorbell, and listen for Matty's voice. "Oh, it's you again," I hear her say, and go inside.

I fix my lunch. Bean soup and tuna on toast. I say a prayer and imagine Matty seated at the table across from me. She has a weightless quality that makes me believe she might levitate. Her silver hair falls across her shoulders. Her eyes, radiant green, fix on me.

"What?" I ask.

"It's okay to be sad, and it's okay to be happy. For everything there is a season."

"Yes."

She subtly tilts her head. Matty's body language is transient, almost imperceptible. Unlike Harpey, whose spasmodic movements mirrored a conductor directing an unseen orchestra, Matty's tics appeared and vanished like Billy's disappearing ink, ephemeral fine print that demanded your attention. I listen for her voice, my birdsong. "And Jesus said to them, 'Do not worry about tomorrow—'"

"'—for tomorrow will worry about itself,'" I whisper.

Matty's eyes sparkle. "Yes, my love. Now carry on. There's work to be done."

I drive to the hospital. God is with me. I pass Officer Becca—who has her squad car positioned at a bend in the road—and check and see I am going thirty-five miles an hour, the posted limit. My mood lightens. I am victorious and have outwitted an opponent. "Sorry, Officer Becca!" I proclaim, "Not today, my dear, not today!"

I walk into the children's wing of the hospital and head toward Benny's room, pulling Moses's trunk behind me. The rubber wheels glide along the glassine tile floor. The steamer trunk is an antique, a well-traveled Louis Vuitton, black with a leather strap belt, steel corners and brass-domed rivets. A Christmas gift from Matty and customized by Virgil, who added wheels and a handle for ease of transport. It is the most stylish thing I own. I had it monogrammed—MOSES, in gold lettering—to proclaim its occupant.

Children's eyes light up, many of whom saw me and Moses with Benny when I visited last week. I smile and whisper silent prayers. My heart soars and breaks. The hospital is an emotional roller coaster.

I approach Benny's room. Benny and Brooklyn, each in a wheel-chair, both sit, oddly still. Such a strange sight. As I get closer, I see they are wearing masks and sit as still as stone, two hideous gargoyles guarding the entrance to Benny's room. Above the door is a home-made sign that reads: Old-New Synagogue.

"Well, what have we here?" I ask.

A nurse with a nametag that identifies her as Claire sees me and smiles. "Hideous, aren't they?" We gaze at the two masked chil-dren seated like statues before us. "I haven't figured out what they're doing, but in five minutes, the creatures will need their meds. So perhaps you could help."

"Gargoyles. They're guarding the golem." I point to the sign above Benny's door. "Legend has it that the body of the Golem of Prague lives in the *genizah* of the Old-New Synagogue in Prague."

"The genizah?"

"It's a storage area in a Jewish synagogue or cemetery."

"I never liked those things…those…gargoyles," Claire says.

"Chilling examples of medieval architecture. They were con-structed on churches to remind people of the horrors of hell."

"Time!" Brooklyn says, and both she and Benny remove their masks.

Claire checked her watch. "Thank goodness."

"Where on earth did you get those masks? Or was it on earth at all?" I ask.

Brooklyn's eyes are vibrant in a way I hadn't seen before. "They're Benny's! He has more at home, but his mother only brought these two. Cool, aren't they? After dinner, if we're both feeling okay, Benny will show me how—"

She stops speaking as if her sentence hit a wall. I turn as Kyle glares at her. His menacing stare reminds me of Rory Pitts.

Brooklyn glares right back at him. As Harpey often said of Ellen, Brooklyn has chutzpah. "Take a picture, it might last longer."

"Of you and the Jew? I don't think so."

Nurse Claire whirls toward Kyle. "Kyle Martin, that is quite enough!"

The boy turns his gaze to Nurse Claire's, an unrepentant stare that seeks dominance, but Nurse Claire will have none of it. "Apologize this instant, or I'll have the TV removed from your room and confiscate your phone."

"You can't do that!"

Nurse Claire walks to within a foot of him. "Try me."

Kyle's face tightens. "Sorry," he says, spitting the word from his mouth like a prune pit. He turns and storms into his room.

Benny's eyes fill with hurt. This is history's oldest hatred. Like a virus, it adapts and reemerges. Around the world, anti-Semitism is on the rise, which concerns me. I recall what Solly told us after the incident that summer. "For many, the scapegoat is their favorite pet."

Brooklyn put a hand on Benny's shoulder. "He's jealous, that's all."

"Yeah," Benny says, "I know."

I leave later that afternoon, remembering the lie we often told one another as kids: that sticks and stones might break our bones, but words would never hurt us. I know the power of words for both good and evil. I do my best to forgive Kyle, remembering he is just a boy with a terrible illness, and recall the Savior's words as He died on the cross. "Father, forgive them, for they do not know what they are doing."

Chapter 23

———— ⌬ ————

Matty passed a year ago today. I feel her presence. Like the Holy Spirit, loved ones live within us and dwell in our hearts and minds in a manner that exceeds our understanding. I sit at the kitchen table with Matty's favorite breakfast across from me. Eggs over easy, lightly buttered toast, and a cup of hot tea.

The steam rises from the teacup, ethereal as it hangs in the air. I teeter between profound sadness and feeling blessed for the life I had with Matty. I look up at the wall clock and smile. Matty bought it not long after her first bout of chemo. It has a saying imprinted on its face: "I'm awake. If you were expecting bright-eyed and bushy-tailed, go catch a squirrel." That was Matty. Amid her fear and her pain, she put all of her faith in God and did what she could to lighten my heart with her humor.

The Talmudic sage Yose be Abin taught that "The day of death is when two worlds meet with a kiss; this world going out, the future world coming in." I believe that in the future world, heaven awaits, and Matty and I will be together again. But God has left me here for a reason. One of the greatest gifts I received because of my friendship with Harpey Mendelson was his conviction that every life had a purpose.

"God assigns a divine task and sacred mission to every human soul," Harpey explained one afternoon as Billy sat on the curb popping a tar bubble and Ellen worked her way across her hopscotch board.

"Save it for Sunday," Billy would say whenever Harpey talked about God or religion.

Ellen always came to Harpey's defense. "Billy Finley, if you don't have anything nice to say, don't say anything."

To Harpey's chagrin, Ellen would sandwich childlike questions between Harpey's more profound discussions. "Lois Lane's so stupid. How could she not know Clark Kent is Superman?"

Billy, suddenly engaged, would respond. "Maybe she does but doesn't say anything. Girls do that all the time, keep secrets about stuff."

It annoyed Harpey, but he'd continue on just the same. I was different. Harpey's words and mannerisms captivated me.

As I watch the steam in Matty's teacup dissipate, I immerse myself in this moment of remembrance. This is my version of the shivah candle. A cup of tea just as Matty liked it—piping hot in her favorite teacup, one given to me by Gladys with, "Be careful what you say or you may end up in my sermon," written on it. No one would know better of this truth than Harpey Mendelson.

On Sunday morning, as Gladys plays "How Great Thou Art," I enter the chapel with Moses in tow. I begin by welcoming everyone and open with a prayer. "Dear Lord, please bless our precious little church. Bring healing to those who are sick, peace to those who may be struggling, and wisdom to us all. Amen."

I look up and struggle to hold back tears. "Where were we?" I ask.

"You had just left the Mendelson's after dinner," Nicole says.

"And Izzy reminded you about practicing for the talent show," Ms. Nellie adds.

"And you were the Shabby Guy!" Gracie says.

Laughter, oh Lord, yes, beautiful laughter fills the chapel. "You are correct, Gracie. The shabbos goy," Moses says. I turn Moses's head toward me. "I love that little Gracie."

"We all do," I say and continue with the sermon.

Chapter 24

Sunday, July 26, 2020
Summer Sermon Series: Week Eight
1963

The next morning, when I woke up, a police car sat in Harpey's driveway. A policeman stood by Mr. Mendelson, taking notes, while a second policeman took pictures of the Mendelson's car. Large words were spray-painted in green letters across the side of the Mendelson's Rambler. *Filthy Jews.* These were the words Mr. Finley had used when he sneered at Mrs. Mendelson a few days earlier. I threw on my clothes and ran outside. Ellen stood beside Harpey, who, for the first time since I'd met him, looked crestfallen.

Solly's van pulled up. When he walked up alongside Mr. Mendelson and saw the writing on the car, his round face deflated like a balloon losing air. His chin slumped to his chest. He turned and embraced Mr. Mendelson, cupping the back of his head in his enormous hand. Mrs. Mendelson stood off to the side as her husband and brother consoled one another. Across the street, Billy stood on his porch. Everyone knew who spray-painted those hateful words on the Mendelson's car. Billy looked at me and then went inside.

Harpey looked sad and withdrawn. It was as if the words caused him to wither in size. Ellen kneeled down and whispered to him. He didn't react. I walked over to Ellen and Harpey, not knowing what to say. We knew how wrong it was to write such words, but we knew nothing about anti-Semitism then, had yet to learn about the horrors inflicted upon the Jews during the Holocaust. "I bet they can get it off your car. The body shop can fix anything nowadays," I said.

Harpey shrugged.

Mrs. Finley exploded out of her front door, almost taking it off its hinges. She marched across the street. When she saw the writing on the car, her mouth fell open, and she yanked her head away as if the words had scorched her eyes. She wrapped her arms around her waist and looked at Mrs. Mendelson. "I am so, so sorry." Mrs. Mendelson lifted her arms, and Mrs. Finley reached for her. They embraced. It felt like an accident scene, a terrible crash where someone had died. I wanted to cover the words, to hide them so they couldn't hurt anyone anymore. But some images are so seared into your soul they are never forgotten.

Uncle Solly walked over to Harpey and kneeled in front of him.

"This is a terrible thing, but if we let the haters steal our joy, they win, yes? But if we continue to laugh, dance, and honor God, we are the victors. I brought you something."

Solly went to his van and came back with a small box that contained a brand new Kodak Instamatic 100 camera. "I worked for a man who owns a camera shop. He gave me this, but it's too newfangled for your uncle Solly."

Harpey took the box. "Thank you, Uncle."

"You are very welcome." Harpey hugged Solly. "Go along now and play with your friends."

The police spoke to Mrs. Finley, who shook her head. "He's at work," she said, and I knew she was talking about Mr. Finley.

Solly went to his truck, got black spray paint, and sprayed over the letters on the side of the car.

My mother came out of the house with Izzy and called me. It was time to leave to go see my dad. I smiled at Harpey.

"See you later, okay?"

On the ride to the hospital, I told my mom and Izzy what happened to the Mendelson's car.

"I told you he was a knuckle-dragging Neanderthal," Izzy said. "Did he spell it right? I'd think a word like 'filthy' would be a challenge."

"Let's not jump to conclusions, Izzy," my mother said. "Maybe it was some rowdy teenagers. Let's wait for the police to investigate before we tar and feather the man."

"Yeah. I'm sure it's a coincidence he calls our neighbors 'filthy Jews' and 'filthy Jews' ends up spray-painted on their car."

"Such a quiet block," my mother said. "If I believed in such things, I'd think someone put a hex on the neighborhood."

Or aliens showed up, I thought.

Izzy and I sat in the hospital waiting room. My mom insisted on going upstairs to check on my dad before we went up. Izzy placed her hand on my shaking leg. "Please stop it."

"I can't. I'm nervous."

"It's no big deal. He's going to look weird. Try not to stare."

"Weird how?"

"Kind of like, funhouse mirror weird like…distorted on one side of his face. Droopy." She pulled down the corner of her mouth to give me a preview. "And he's got some foot drag."

"Foot drag? You mean like…" I got up off my chair and stepped forward with my right foot and dragged my left to meet it.

"Something like that. And his speech is slurry because of the droop. Just act natural and don't stare."

Izzy was instructing herself more than me. I was upset about my dad's stroke, but Izzy was having a hard time adjusting to the new normal. I listened in one night from my closet when she discussed it with Margaret Ann.

"This is a stress bomb. I was comfortable being the teenage anti-Christ and then this happens. If I have to flip-flop back into my goody-two shoes, I could have a mental breakdown and end up like Joanne Woodward in *The Three Faces of Eve*."

My mother came to the waiting room and motioned us to follow her. We got into the elevator. On the ride up, my mother and I stood like soldiers while Izzy examined her reflection in the silver sheen of the elevator walls. "Remember what I said, no fighting. The last thing your father needs is to be stressed, understood?"

We nodded and proceeded up the hall. My father was in room 313, just one room from the end. I tripped twice when the bottom of my PF Flyers stuck to the tile floor.

My mother scowled. "Pick your feet up."

"I am," I said and lifted each foot as if stepping over trip wires.

"Nixon Bliss, stop the drama this instant!" my mother said through gritted teeth.

Then one of Izzy's flip-flops stuck, and she tripped. My mother glared at Izzy, and Izzy glared right back. Izzy slipped them off her feet just as a nurse walked out of a room and admonished her.

"You have to keep them on. Hospital rules."

My mother glared at Izzy again. "Do I not have enough to worry about?"

"Excuse me, Kay, but I'm not the one who waxed the floor into a strip of horizontal fly paper."

We made it to room 313. The moment I saw my father, the windowless room swam, and everything went black.

*****

A distant voice broke through, as if it were coming from the end of a long tunnel. "Nix-on, Nix-on." A smell assaulted my nostrils, and my eyelids flew open like spring-loaded window blinds. A nurse, her face a few inches from mine, smiled. "There you are." Her breath smelled of peppermint. I glanced around to get my bearings. "What happened?"

Izzy leaned down into my field of vision. "You passed out. She used smelling salts to revive you."

I looked up. When I saw my dad, I got light-headed again. His face drooped on the right side, and his eyes shifted toward me, peering through sunken sockets, an empty, emotionless gaze. The right side of his mouth lifted in a half smile. My stomach wrenched. I wanted to run.

I whispered, "That's not him."

"What?" the nurse asked.

I motioned for her to get closer to me. "That's not him. It's—he's—" I wanted to tell her about the alien invaders, but I knew an adult would never believe me.

My mother's eyes reflected her disappointment. The nurse turned to her. "This happens a lot. I'll take him out in the hall while you two visit."

Izzy glared at me. I looked back at my dad. A tear leaked down his collapsed cheek.

"You have to fight it!" I cried. He waved me over. I hugged him, and he patted my back. "It's o-way. Ever-e gon be oway."

Izzy hugged my dad. His eyes widened, and his jaw dropped. He had spent the last year watching Izzy drop through the teen-age wormhole and emerge so unlike the child he'd known as to be unrecognizable. It gave me time to refocus. I couldn't let the alien know I was on to it. My dad didn't talk much. Izzy went to the cafeteria to get a soda, and when my mother stepped out of the room to speak with the nurse, I was left alone with him—just me and my dad. I would have wanted this before his stroke, but his distorted face and slurred speech convinced me we weren't the only ones in the room.

My father lifted his arm and pointed to the light switch. "Off, ease," he said. I got out of my chair and tuned off the light. The room darkened, casting our faces in shadows. My pulse quickened. His gaze modulated as if his eyes were peepholes shared by two sets of eyes. A line of spittle leaked down the crevice of a smile line. He lifted his good arm and wiped at the drool. Then he winked, and the eye vanished and reappeared and seemed nothing like my dad's. My neck tightened. I couldn't breathe. I was certain I just had an encounter with an alien invader.

Chapter 25

—————— ✂ ——————

As we left the hospital and walked to our car, Izzy poked my shoulder. "You acted like Dad was a leper."

We got back just before lunch. The police car was gone. I wondered if the police had picked up Billy's dad. I was sure Billy was right; aliens were on the move in our neighborhood.

My mother made grilled cheese sandwiches for lunch. I ate on a TV tray in the living room. I watched *Truth or Consequences* and wondered about Billy. Knowing how mad Mrs. Finley was, I thought she'd kick Mr. Finley out of the house, and if the police could prove he spray-painted the Mendelson's car, he might go to jail. I felt bad for Billy and more determined than ever to find the alien invaders. I went outside where Ellen was riding her bike in front of Harpey.

"Now, Harpey, now!" she said and stood up on her pedals in a pose.

Harpey snapped a picture with his new Instamatic.

"Got it!" he said.

I ran over to them. "That's a neat camera."

"It's the first Instamatic to come on the market," Harpey said.

I sat on the curb beside him.

Ellen parked her bike and joined us. One of Harpey's shoelaces had come undone. She kneeled down and tied it. It was her way of caring for him. "There," she tapped the lace, "good as new!"

I was envious. Ellen loved Harpey. She stood up and balanced on one foot and then the other, striking poses like a ballet dancer. "We're not letting anyone steal our joy. How's your dad?"

It was hard to put into words. "He has trouble sort of…like when he talks."

Ellen sat beside me. She patted my back. "It's okay, Nix. He'll get better."

Izzy came out of the house and strutted to her lounger. She wore a black bikini, oversized sunglasses, and flip-flops. With suntan lotion and *Teen* magazine in one hand and her transistor radio in the other, she nestled into her lounge chair, a hot pink recliner with thick rubber tubes stretched over the metal frame. Harpey stiffened and did his best not to look at her, but he couldn't help himself.

Ellen got back on her bike. "Take more pictures."

Harpey held the camera up to his one eye and tried to look toward Izzy with the other. As Ellen passed in front of Harpey, the camera drifted toward Izzy. "Over here!" Ellen said.

Harpey moved the camera back toward Ellen and snapped a picture. He set the camera on his lap and glanced back at Izzy. "Oh, Bathsheba, why are you so beautiful?" he lamented. "She's my Delilah. I'd tell her all my secrets if she asked." Harpey spun his wheelchair around until his back was to Izzy. "Is she still there?"

"She'll be there all afternoon."

"Such is my luck. If I were an undertaker, people would stop dying." He rotated his head to get another look at her just as Izzy slid her sunglasses to the end of her nose. She smiled. "Is that a camera?"

Harpey's jaw fell open. He nodded before he spoke. "An Instamatic," he said and then posted an immense, mechanical smile.

"Roll over here and take mine," Izzy said.

Harpey's eyes swerved toward me before settling back on Izzy. "Okay."

Ellen circled back around on her bike. She dropped her bike on the grass and glared at Izzy. She was no longer the center of Harpey's attention.

Izzy stretched out on the recliner and winked at Harpey. The flash popped. "I think I got it," Harpey said. "I should take a few more to be sure." He reached into a pocket of his wheelchair and took out another package of flashcubes. Izzy struck a series of poses as Harpey repositioned his wheelchair to get the perfect angle.

Billy came out of his house and waved for me to come over.

"Be right back," I said to Ellen and ran to meet Billy in his front yard.

"Did you look in his garage?" Billy asked.

"No. He said his parents won't let him in there until they unpack more stuff."

"That's a crock. You saw the ritual. And my dad didn't spray paint that car. He thinks it's a set up. He told the cop, 'Do you think I'd be stupid enough to spray paint the exact thing I said? Maybe they did it to frame me.' They asked my dad if they could check the garage, and he told them they could check the entire house. I'm telling you, Nix, it wasn't my dad."

"Maybe it wasn't him. Maybe *they* did it, and he doesn't even know it."

Billy rubbed his hand over his flattop. "I guess that's possible."

"Sure, it's possible. Maybe this was the alien's plan all along, to turn us against one another. You know, divide and conquer. If we're all fighting, they can pick us off one by one."

Billy grabbed a stick and sat on the curb. "You saw your dad today, right?"

"It's happening to him," I said. I told him about his wink, the disconnected stare, and how my dad's eyes seemed like his one minute and strange the next.

"We need to find them. Get in Harpey's garage, Pepsin's, and Addy Wolf's too."

"Addy's? Geez, Billy, I don't know."

"What's not to know? Are you gonna chicken out now?"

My shoulders slumped. "No."

I feared Addy Wolf more than Pepsin or Rory Pitts. Addy's erratic behavior, which included midnight rants followed by spooky organ music, were on par with stories about the Jersey Devil and Greystone Park, the abandoned lunatic asylum. The longtime gossip was Addy's husband paid more attention to his mannequins than he did to Addy, so she murdered him with a meat cleaver and buried him on Crematory Hill, where bodies were cremated with the remains buried in the adjacent graveyard. It was located off a dirt road in

Monroe Township. Local lore about ghosts and strange occurrences made going there a teenage rite of passage.

"Until we find the pods, ask your dad questions, keep him talking," Billy said. "That will make it harder for the alien to take over his mind. The more your dad controls his own thoughts, the harder it will be for the alien to take control." Billy watched as Harpey snapped another picture of Izzy. "I think Jew Boy has the hots for your sister."

"Stop calling him that."

"Whatever. But when you find out I'm right, you'll be sorry."

A car turned onto the street. Pepsin was returning from his vacation. We froze and watched as his pea-green station wagon rolled by and turned into his driveway. Billy whispered in his creepiest voice, "Margery, Victoria—Daddy's home."

The vibration of the *Tingler* ran up my spine.

Chapter 26

G ladys adds melodrama by including spooky chords I hadn't heard before. The last eerie note echoes in the chapel.

Moses covers his eyes. "Can I look yet?"

"All clear." I lower his hands. I look out over the congregation, and my heart swells. My life affirmed, I immerse myself in the expressions of love on the faces of my parishioners. Ms. Nellie smiles—and as is her custom after this chapter of my summer sermon ends—winks. I smile and wink back. Such a subtle yet powerful connection.

Years back, when Ms. Nellie got pneumonia, I visited her at the hospital. The doctor described her condition as "touch and go," and I held her fragile hand as the rhythmic pulse of her ventilator pushed air in and out of her weary lungs. Swoosh...swoosh... swoosh. I prayed hard that day, worked to concentrate the words into something more powerful, knowing full well that God did not need the emphasis to know my heart. But we are humans who do human things, so I tried to bend God's ear the way I had seen the Amazing Kreskin bend spoons on TV in the seventies. That's when Ms. Nellie's left eye opened, spotted me, and winked, an homage to the summer sermons she loved so much. I winked back and knew my prayer had been answered.

I continue the wrap-up of my sermon. "I think now of our Father in heaven, how He offers us an invitation to open our hearts and allow the Holy Spirit to dwell within us. To give us peace, discernment, and love. To change us and help us become more like the one who endured the agony of the cross to give us everlasting life. It is an invitation, not a demand—a gift to be accepted or rejected."

When the service ends, I retire to my office to unwind. Feeling a twinge in my back, I set Moses on the chair across from my desk and rub the base of my spine. Opal walks in and notes my distress. My bad back is a recurring problem. She signals for me to pay attention to her and so begins our ritual yoga moves that often bring me relief. I nod, and we begin with "mountain pose," then move into "tree," where I balance on one leg, position the other against my inner thigh, and extend my prayer-clasped hands overhead. Eyes closed, we steady ourselves. Unbeknownst to Opal and me, Earl has entered the office, and thinking we are in a position of supplication, feels compelled to join us. When Opal and I open our eyes, Earl is doing his best to maintain his pose, his gangly arms extended, palms clasped, eyes closed. Earl maintains his center. He shares his grandfather's thicket of red hair, coarse as a scouring pad and tightly curled.

"Earl?" I say.

Earl opens his eyes. "Pastor."

"You can relax."

"Actually, I kinda like how it works my core."

Opal lifts a finger and instructs both of us to put our hands on the desk and move into a modified version of downward dog to loosen our backs. Earl joins in without hesitation, and we follow Opal's lead. We finish.

"Thank you, Opal. I'm good now," I say, and Opal leaves the office, closing the door behind her.

Earl goes to sit when he sees Moses seated in the chair. "Oh. If you don't mind my saying so, your doll creeps me out a little."

"I understand," I take a moment to return Moses to his trunk.

Earl sits. He lifts his hands like a magician getting ready to perform a card trick. "I don't know if you remember, but you taught me this when I was a boy." He performs the finger trick I have taught to many children over the years. "Here is the church, here is the steeple, open the door and"—he wiggles his fingers—"see all the people."

"I remember," I say.

"It's strange how things come back to you. I've had something weighing heavy on my mind. I was good once." He tries to stifle a cry, one of those coughed up bursts that happen when something long-buried escapes confinement.

I hand him a tissue. He takes it and taps at his eyes.

"Out of nowhere I just start doing the church, steeple, people thing with my hands, just—well, almost like the Spirit was moving me—that's how it felt because it happened without me even knowing it," he says. "And that's when I realize, when I—"

He takes a slow breath. My heart breaks for him. Once a powerful warrior, Earl came back from the war brittle and broken. Once happy-go-lucky, he returned sullen and disillusioned. Life could no longer be trusted. The illicit drugs had ravaged his once-fit body. Earl still held the push-up and sit-up record for his high school, but he had lost much of the vigor and muscle he had worked so hard to attain. I knew what was coming and did my best to make the confession easy on him. The mystery of the missing collection plate was about to be solved. I knew it would crush Virgil, but his grandson was doing the right thing now, and for that, he could be grateful. I soften my voice. "Sometimes good people slip up. It's why we need His grace and mercy, Earl, because we are human, because we do things we know we shouldn't. Even the apostle Paul struggled with this."

Earl's dusty brown eyes lift and meet mine. "That true?"

"Yes."

"And he was like the Richard Petty of Christianity, am I right?"

"A fair comparison."

"Not that I'm saying—well, NASCAR is a religion to some. It wasn't insulting, was it?"

"Not at all."

"The thing is, Pastor, I'm the reason those lady's teeth went missing back in '91."

"Excuse me, what?" I say, stunned by the comment.

"It started as a high school prank. I got double-dared, and you know how that goes." His eyes catch mine. "You ever been double-dared, Pastor?"

"Yes, many times."

"Took up on any you regret?"

"I think we all have."

"Not that I'm excusing myself, but a double dare in high school can be a powerful thing. I know where they're hidden. Virgil's gonna have a conniption, but I need to make this right. They're hidden under a floorboard in his barn. Thought I cleaned them at first, but I found out later I mixed up the Polident with the Alka-Seltzer, and well—I didn't want to risk pulling them out of the barn after yanking out that floorboard. My accomplices wanted me to ditch them at Wally's Salvage, but I thought we might get around to returning them if any of us had second thoughts, but that never happened. Then it became such a big thing in the town paper, we thought it best to let sleeping dogs lie, especially after the three ladies showed off how happy they were when they got their new ones."

"I understand," I say.

"Guess I should turn myself in."

"To who?"

"Poke. Virgil brought it up the other day. I guess Opal's been looking into it and thinks it's a conspiracy of sorts. Now Poke's opened up an investigation about it."

I sigh. "Listen, Earl, I wouldn't normally be in favor of sweeping something under the rug, but this qualifies for a quick broom. You were just a kid. This happened thirty years ago, and everyone's moved on. Let me get with Poke and Virgil. I think we can put this aside in short order."

"You think so?"

"But the deal is, you come back to church."

"That's exactly what I was going to do, anyway."

"Then what's done is done. See you next Sunday morning."

"Thanks, Pastor."

We shake hands, and after taking a few steps toward the door, Earl turns back to me. "I feel like I should ask for forgiveness from those three ladies."

"I'll leave that up to you."

After Earl leaves my office, I know I'll have to let Opal know the mystery of the missing dentures has been solved and the case is heretofore closed. Earl is well-loved by everyone in the church, which makes my job easier. I call Chief Poke and give him the lowdown. He decides it's best to keep the town folklore about the missing teeth a mystery.

"It's got a Big-Foot-Loch-Ness-Monster feel to it," Poke says. "Sort of diminishes the lore to find out it was just a kid's prank. I say we leave it as is and move on."

"Fine with me. Earl might tell Virgil and apologize to the ladies, but I don't think anyone will make a fuss about it."

"Let's hope not, Pastor. I like it as it stands. When people hear the biggest mystery a town has is missing dentures, it gives them a warm and fuzzy feeling that's good for all of us. But while we're discussing whodunits, you got any new information about your stolen collection plate?"

"No, and I'd still like to believe it's just missing."

"I appreciate that, but I don't share your optimism. I've talked to all potential suspects to said crime, and I've hit a dead end."

"Good. Case closed then. Maybe in thirty years, we'll get another impromptu confession, but until then, I'm in favor of dropping it. I'll let Opal know you've talked to everyone on her list, and now it's time to move on."

"Good luck with that, Pastor. Once Opal's set her teeth into something—well, you know how that goes."

"I do. God gave her the gift of tenacity. That I grant you. This will give her an opportunity to exercise her discernment, which will be its own blessing."

"Yeah. If you say so. Have a good rest of your day, Pastor," Poke disconnects the call.

I find Opal in the church, looking up at Jesus on the cross, signing to him in gentle movements akin to the ancient practice of Tai Chi. It may seem strange to some that the hearing-impaired might sign to God, but I have never seen a more reverent and beautiful way of prayer. Opal doesn't view her impairment as a disability. "You hear noise," she signed to me one day. "I hear God. I feel sorry for hearing people. The devil pounding pots and pans. All that distraction."

I step back into the vestibule to give her privacy. A few moments later, I peek out. Her gaze meets mine. It's awkward, but catching me gives her the upper hand. She smiles. "Peeping?" she signs. "That's disturbing."

"Hardly. I didn't know you two were talking, so I stepped out and waited. I didn't want to be rude. But I need to speak with you. It's about the missing dentures."

Her fingers move to her lips. Opal says more in a single expression than most can convey in a hundred words. If she were a speaking person or had lived in the age of silent movies, she could be a star. "You solved it?" she signs.

"It was a high school prank. Poke has agreed to let sleeping dogs lie, so"—I display open palms—"case closed."

Her eyes narrow. "Earl?"

"It's not important. It's best for all concerned that we drop the issue and move on. We have bigger fish to fry."

"What about the collection plate, did he—"

"No, nothing more on that, but Poke's interviewed all the suspects, and he's still at square one. I told him not to worry about it. We've filed our claim, and that will be that."

Opal's expression tells me that will *not* be that. As Poke reminded me earlier, once Opal gets her teeth into something, she doesn't let go.

I spend the week planning for my Fall sermon series. My thoughts lean toward forgiveness. I have seen a shift in society of late. It seems we have more judges who hold more grudges. When I see the hate and intolerance, my heart bleeds. I think of Christ, the one who had every reason in the world to hate, yet in the face of being beaten and spit on, even as they divided up his clothes by casting lots as he hung on the cross, His heart was on forgiveness. It is incomprehensible to me.

I wake up this morning to pouring rain. Matty was a fan of rain and rainbows. She had a tin roof put on the cottage so she could hear the rain on the roof. I have grown to love the pattering as much as she did. When she was with me, we would sit on the porch, sip tea, and watch the birds navigate flight in showers and downpours. As much as I loved sharing this with her, I was most happy when the rain stopped and the sun peeked through the clouds. I take a shower, dress, and walk to church with Moses in tow.

"Morning, Pastor!" Virgil says as he sweeps the steps leading into the chapel. "Got to keep Jacob's Ladder safe and dry."

"Much appreciated, Virgil," I say.

A rainbow arcs over the church, its colors as vibrant as I have ever seen. I take my phone from my pocket and take a picture. This one will be suitable for framing.

It takes extra time to start the service this morning. The rainbow has captivated us all, a reminder from God of the covenant between Him and His people. When everyone has settled in the chapel, Moses and I begin.

Chapter 27

Sunday, August 2, 2020
Summer Sermon Series: Week Nine
1963

Billy and I watched Pepsin step out of his car and scan his surroundings. He extended his neck and, like a periscope hovering just above the water, shifted his gaze left, and then right. He removed the bottle of nose spray from his shirt pocket, tilted his head back, and administered a squirt in each nostril. He put the bottle back in his pocket, paused, and found the intruder. A satisfied smile wormed itself onto his face. He walked to the middle of his lawn, bent down, and gripped the interloper in his fist before violently ripping it from the soil. Then he held up the weed like a decapitated head and admired his handiwork. His eyes shifted to us. His smile faded. He pointed at the weed and said, "A trespasser," before walking over to his garbage and tossing the weed inside.

"Man, that guy sure hates weeds," I whispered.

I imagined Pepsin's cold bony fingers coiling around my neck.

"Wait till he gets a load of the wreck out back," Billy said. "He's gonna have a coronary."

It was time for lunch. I made myself a fluffernutter while my mother advised Izzy on the fine art of hanging laundry.

"Hang the colored clothes inside out so they don't fade in the sun. Give the towels a sharp snap before hanging them and then drape the short end two inches over the line and secure each end with a clothespin. Hang slacks and underwear from the waistband and socks from the toes, or they won't dry properly."

"So precise, Kay. Good thing you weren't quality control at the gallows. The condemned would still be standing there."

"Says the girl who got a D in Home Ec."

"And it doesn't stand for domesticated. Unlike the sheep in saddle shoes at school, I refuse to button my lip or tow the clothesline. If I get married, it will be to a man who can darn his own socks and hang his own laundry. I don't mind cooking an occasional vegetable, but I'm not taking one on as a life partner." Izzy picked up the clothes basket and headed out the door.

"God help the man who marries that one," my mother muttered. "You doing okay, Nix? I know how unsettling this has been."

"Yeah, I'm good."

"Oh, I have the flyer for the talent show. It's in three weeks, so I hope you're practicing. Your father's counting on you." She grabbed her pocketbook and pulled out the flyer. "The winner gets a fifty-dollar savings bond."

Savings bonds were big back then. Grandparents were always giving their grandkids savings bonds and life insurance. Billy said it made perfect sense because, this way, if you died before your savings bonds matured, you'd still get something.

The truth was I had hardly practiced my ventriloquism, and the realization the talent show was only three weeks away terrified me. I finished my sandwich and went to my room. I grabbed Mr. Mercury and thought about what I might say. Then I realized something else. I didn't have a routine. Outside, Ellen was jabbering. I looked outside and saw her on her street skates pushing Harpey toward the cul-de-sac. She was pitched forward, putting everything she had into the effort. She wore a yellow terrycloth shorts set and her Yankees baseball cap. The metal wheels of her Roller Derby skates rattled on the pavement as she did her best to build up speed.

"Not too fast!" Harpey yelled, but Ellen had momentum and wasn't slowing down. The expression on Harpey's face was one of pure terror. I don't think he'd ever gone that fast in his wheelchair. Fortunately for Harpey, Ellen got tired, and they both rolled to a stop right in front of my house. She lifted her left skate and scowled as two of the wheels were coated in black tar. Her face pinched. "Darn you, Billy Finley!" she screamed, blaming the notorious tar bubble popper for her predicament.

"What's wrong?" Harpey asked.

Ellen, sitting on the curb, lifted her skate into the air. "Look at my wheels! Tar! I'm gonna push Billy Finley's nose in it when I see him!"

I smiled. Ellen was cute when hopping on her hopscotch board, but when she was hopping mad, she was adorable. Harpey had never seen this side of Ellen, and for the moment, he kept his distance. I put Mr. Mercury down and ran outside.

"What happened," I asked and plopped myself down beside Ellen.

"Billy Finley, that's what happened. Look!" She handed me the skate with the tar caked on two of the wheels and pouted. "Ruined!"

"It's not ruined," I said. "I'll get it off for you."

"How?"

"I'll ask my dad. He's an expert on adhesives."

"How is he?" Harpey asked.

"He's getting better. Baby steps, that's what my mother says."

"Are you still doing the talent show?" Ellen asked.

"Yeah. It's important to my dad, so I'm going to do it."

"What's your talent?" Harpey asked.

"It's not important."

"He can make his dolls talk without moving their lips. Like Chatty Cathy without the string," Ellen said.

Harpey's brows lifted.

"I don't have dolls," I said.

"Sure you do. I gave you my Barbie, didn't I?"

Harpey's gigantic eyes swerved toward me.

"Yeah, when you were a tomboy. Maybe I should give her back to you now that you've decided to be a girl." I regretted the words the moment they came out of my mouth.

Ellen's lips trembled. I thought she would cry.

"Some girls only look nice in dresses, but you look nice no matter what you're wearing," Harpey said.

Ellen softened at Harpey's words, and the hint of her smile appeared. "Thanks, you're a mensch, Harpey Mendelson." She turned to me with disappointment in her eyes. I wanted to say something, but the words stuck in my throat. My lips moved, but unlike Chatty Cathy, no sound came out. Ellen turned her attention back to Harpey. "I'm going to a birthday party at the roller rink tomorrow."

"That sounds like fun."

"You can come if you want. I get to bring a guest."

Harpey's brows lifted. "Really?"

"Sure. Everybody's on wheels there. You'd fit right in." Ellen took off her other skate and set it on the grass. "I can show you how I skate backwards and stuff."

My heart sank. Ellen Yancey had asked Harpey Mendelson out on a date. As an afterthought, she turned to me and said, "You can come too. You just can't come as my guest or have any cake."

I shrugged. "Maybe."

"I have to ask my parents," Harpey said.

"Why don't you ask now? I could go with you."

"Okay!"

Ellen peeled off her pink socks and stuffed them in her skate. "The pavement's hot. I need to get my shoes."

"Wear mine," Harpey said, "I'm not using them."

Ellen looked at the tiny black shoes on Harpey's feet, both tied in perfect bows, shoes so glossy they looked brand new. "I don't know if they'll fit." Ellen positioned herself on the grass in front of Harpey and lifted a bare foot. "Put your foot against mine."

"I can't," Harpey said.

Ellen focused on me.

"I'll do it." I lifted Harpey's leg. It felt like a chicken bone. Ellen placed her bare foot against Harpey's shoe. Their feet were the same size.

"Perfect!" She untied Harpey's shoes, removed them, and put them on her feet.

When Ellen stood up in those shiny black shoes, with her blue eyes beaming and the freckles across her nose dark from the summer sun, she looked like a doll.

"Snappy," Harpey said.

Ellen lifted the heel on one shoe, turning her knee inward as if modeling the footwear for a fashion magazine. "They fit okay. I'll lift my legs like a majorette, so they won't get grass stains." Ellen got behind Harpey's wheelchair and pushed him toward his house, high-stepping on the way.

Billy came out and met me on the cul-de-sac. We were discussing our secret mission when a police car rolled up the street and pulled into Pepsin's driveway. The color drained from Billy's face. "Holy crap." Billy cracked his knuckles. My mother told him it would give him arthritis, but Billy dealt with his nerves by popping tar bubbles and cracking various body parts. "You think he called the police about his greenhouse?"

"Maybe he's just making a report?" I said. "Or they're asking Pepsin if he saw anyone spray-painting the Mendelson's car."

Billy cracked another knuckle. A uniformed police officer and a man in a suit stepped out of the car and walked to Pepsin's front door.

"That's a detective," Billy said. He took his head in both hands and cracked his neck.

The uniformed officer knocked, and a moment later, Pepsin appeared at the door. They spoke for a few minutes and then the policeman and the detective turned, walked back to their car, and drove away.

"That was weird," I said.

"Yeah, they didn't even write anything down."

"What do you make of it?"

"I think you were right. They asked him about the Mendelson's car, but he was away on vacation."

Ellen walked up the street without Harpey. When she saw Billy, she made a beeline in our direction. "Better look out," I said, "she's mad at you for popping tar bubbles. It got on her wheels."

The last thing Billy needed was another violent encounter with Ellen. Billy pleaded his case. "They'd be even wetter if I didn't pop them, so it's not my fault."

He had a point. Freshly popped tar bubbles were worse than old ones, and if Ellen ran over the fresh ones with her wheels, they would've popped anyway.

"Maybe, but it's easier to see them if they're not popped." Ellen looked over at me. "Harpey can go."

"Go where?" Billy asked.

"To the Starlight."

Billy's brows crossed. "Harpey can't skate. He's a cripple."

"Don't call him that," Ellen said.

"He's in a wheelchair, isn't he? That makes him a cripple. And why does he have to go everywhere we go?"

"Don't be an anti-smite, Billy Finley. Because if you are, you're not my friend!"

"Have it your way. See if I care."

We sat there for a few minutes not saying anything. The only sounds were Ellen snapping bubblegum between her teeth and Billy's cracking knuckles. Our mood changed the moment Solly's van pulled onto the street.

"Shekels," Ellen said, and the three of us made a mad dash for Solly's van.

Chapter 28

Solly parked his van, leaped out, and danced around the lawn to the music blaring from the van's radio. When he saw us running toward him, he squatted like a sumo wrestler, pounded his thighs with his hands, and waved us toward him. His joy was infectious. Even Billy couldn't resist befriending him. Ellen jumped up, and Solly caught her mid-air and spun her around. Harpey came outside with his mother. Mrs. Mendelson went to the van and lowered the volume. Solly stopped dancing, cupped one hand to his ear, and crept toward the van as if he were about to listen in to a private conversation. He motioned for the rest of us to join him, and we shuffled across the lawn toward the van in a pantomime of clandestine eavesdroppers.

Harpey's laughter was high-pitched and sporadic. The muscles that controlled his breathing had been damaged. For Harpey, laughter wasn't the best medicine. Too much of it could be dangerous. Harpey was used to Solly's antics and rarely overreacted, but the sight of his new friends having fun with his uncle had caused a prolonged fit of laughter.

"Please, Solly," Mrs. Mendelson said, "you'll give Harpey an attack."

Solly stopped and turned to Harpey. "Don't laugh too much. You make nervous Nina nervous."

Harpey cupped his hand over his mouth and snickered.

"Much better," Solly said.

Solly opened the back of his van and put on his tool belt. We spent the rest of the afternoon adding a window, a wall, and a front door to the playhouse. Solly peppered Harpey with questions about Jewish life as we measured, cut, and hammered, never pausing for more than a minute for Solly to wipe the sweat from his brow. "Rabbi Mendelson, why does the woman dab her eyes with leftover wine during the Sabbath?"

"It shows how mitzvot are so precious to us. King David wrote that the Lord commanded the enlightening of the eyes."

Solly fitted a window into its opening. "Yes. And for our goyim friends, what is a mitzvot?"

"Commandments. There are six-hundred and thirteen, but six are constant in our lives."

"And these are?"

"To know God created all things. Not to have any gods besides God. To know God's Oneness. To fear God. To love God and not to pursue the passions of your heart and stray after your eyes."

After reciting the one about straying after your eyes and pursuing your passions, Harpey met my gaze. Nothing needed to be said. Izzy was Harpey's Bathsheba. He was having trouble following mitzvot number 6.

After we finished the playhouse, we got into Solly's van and drove to Dairy Queen. Billy got permission from his mom to go but was nervous the entire ride. His father had left earlier in the day to work a side job with a friend. His mother didn't expect him back until dinner. Still, Billy spent most of the time cracking his knuckles and looking around as if he expected his dad to show up any minute. We devoured our banana splits and arrived home just before Billy's dad's muscle car turned up the street.

"Gotta go!" Billy said. He took the long way behind the berm and cut through my yard so his dad wouldn't know he had been at the Mendelson's.

We put finishing touches on the playhouse. Solly completed the project by nailing the mezuzah low on the doorframe so Harpey could reach it, with the top end tilted slightly toward the playhouse.

"It's crooked," Ellen said.

Solly turned to Ellen and tilted his head to match hers. He stood back and looked at the mezuzah with her, extending his thumb to sight the mezuzah's placement. "Yes, it is perfectly crooked! Rabbi Mendelson, please explain."

"It's a compromise. Rabbi Shlomo Yitzhaki, known as Rashi, said the mezuzah should be hung vertically like the Torah is placed in the holy ark in the synagogue. But his grandson said it should be affixed horizontally, because the Ten Commandments and the Torah scrolls were kept horizontally in the ark in the temple. By setting it inward, we satisfy both grandfather and grandson by splitting the difference."

Solly slapped his palm to his forehead and held it there as he spoke. "Can you believe this boy? One day, he will be a great rabbi, mark my words."

"Hold on a minute," Ellen said and ran toward the Mendelson's front yard. A moment later, she returned. "Why didn't they argue about your doorbell?"

Solly's eyes lit up, and his bulbous face reddened with laughter. "Yes, this is a wonderful question! Don't tell your parents," he said to Harpey, "but when they're not looking, I will make their doorbell crooked to match your mezuzah!"

Harpey laughed hard again.

Mrs. Mendelson, ever vigilant about Harpey's condition, came out of the house. "Solly, please."

Solly held up his hands in surrender. "Yes, yes, for my nephew I will"—he took a deep breath—"whew, yes, we will contain ourselves."

Mrs. Mendelson went back inside. He looked at Harpey. "I love your mother with all my heart, but sometimes she is a pain in my *tuches*. But don't tell her." Solly put his fingers to the mezuzah, bowed his head, and said a blessing. "Baruch atah Adonai, Eloheinu, Melech ha-olam. Amen."

I loved the sound and rhythm of his words. His voice was musical, and much like my interest in the Rev's speech patterns, I was drawn to the cadence of Solly's prayer.

Solly rolled Harpey up the wheelchair ramp. Harpey kissed his fingers, touched the mezuzah, and rolled into the playhouse.

"Should we do it?" I asked.

"The mezuzah reminds us to live with God in mind. Do you believe in God?"

I shrugged. "As much as the next guy."

Solly laughed. "Well then, Nixon, sir, my prayer for you is that the next guy believes with all his heart."

"We go to Sunday school," Ellen said, as if this was the ticket that allowed her to take part in the tradition.

"It is a reminder," Solly said. "It's like putting a note on your door you touch each day to remind you to think of God and say your prayers and be good neighbors."

"I'm doing it." Ellen put two fingers to her lips, kissed them, and touched her fingertips to the mezuzah. "There," she said and walked into the playhouse.

I did the same and joined Harpey and Ellen in the playhouse. Solly popped his head through the side window. "We should pray that God will bless this playhouse."

"I say my prayers at night," Ellen said.

"Me too," I added, "right before bed."

"That's when he's listening," Ellen added. "And on Sundays."

Solly's laughter echoed off the walls of the playhouse. "Right before bed and on Sundays! Yes, this is so true. We should pray at night and pray in our place of worship, but God is always listening for our prayers." Solly squeezed his arms through the window opening. "I need to diet. My fat is taking over my thin. We will add this to our prayer, yes? That Solly will stop noshing between meals."

Harpey bowed his head. Ellen shrugged and closed her eyes. I closed mine, and we joined hands.

Solly prayed, "May God bless this playhouse with joy and laughter, a place where friendships will grow like flowers in the best of gardens, and...what am I forgetting? Yes, that Solly will stop noshing between meals. Amen."

"Amen," we all said.

Solly pretended to be stuck in the window opening. "Like a cork in the havdalah wine, this is your uncle," he said, before finally extricating himself from the window.

We spent the afternoon enjoying the playhouse, stopping only when we were all called home for dinner.

After dinner, I waited for Billy to come outside, but he never did. Something was wrong. Billy never missed a mission.

Chapter 29

———— ❦ ————

The next morning when I woke up, Billy sat on the curb waiting for me. He had a stick in his hand, and I could tell from the circular motion of his arm he was stirring the goop in a tar bubble. With his shoulders hunched forward, he looked like a warlock stirring a cauldron. *Toil and trouble*, I thought.

I got dressed, went outside, and sat next to him. He poked at the wet tar with his stick. The black-and-blue mark on his arm had not been there yesterday. Billy was clumsy, but I feared something more ominous had happened.

"You okay?"

He shook his head, swallowed, and focused on stirring the wet tar with his stick. "It got him. We're too late."

"Too late for what?"

Billy tossed the stick away. "It hurt my mom last night. Damn alien invaders." His chin quivered. "My mom wants a divorce. That's what she told him this morning. With ice cubes in a washrag pressed to her black eye, she marched right up to him and said it. Brave, huh?"

"Yeah."

"This is worse than any *Creature Features*, even *The Tingler*. My mom kicked him out, and he can't come back unless he promises to stop drinking and stay in the garage."

I put my arm around his shoulder. "We'll find the pods and destroy them, and your dad will go back to normal. Promise."

He looked up at me with resignation in his eyes. "It's already got him. My mom told him he isn't the man she married. She thinks it's because of his drinking, but he always drank, and nothing like this ever happened."

"I'm going to visit my dad today, and I'll see what I can find out. After that, we'll go to the Starlight to skate, and tonight, we can try to get Harpey to let us inside his garage."

His nod was tentative. "Better than nothing, I guess. Maybe there's a queen bee or something, and if we find it and destroy it…" His thought trailed off.

"Your arm, did he do that?"

Billy glared at me, his eyes suddenly feral. "Not he! It! Are you listening to me?"

"Yeah. You're right. It."

He hung his head again. "This is so messed up." He picked up a stone and threw it at the fire hydrant across the street. It pinged off the hydrant and landed in Addy's yard. "I tried to help my mom. It was beating on her, and it grabbed me and…" He paused for a moment then turned and looked at me. "If you would've seen its eyes. They were red, like a monster's eyes. Did your dad's eyes have that look?"

"Sort of. Sometimes it looked like my dad, but then it winked, and my dad never winked in his life."

Billy pulled his shirt out from the waistband of his pants and wiped his face with it. "Just talk like it's your dad. You can't let it know you're onto it."

On the ride to the hospital, my mother gave us an update. "If he keeps improving, they'll transfer him to the rehabilitation center in Franklin Park. Nix, make sure you tell him how much you've been practicing. That's sure to cheer him up."

"Okay." Of course, I had hardly practiced at all.

"Will he be able to walk and talk like normal again?" Izzy asked.

"There's a good chance. It will take work, but your dad's a fighter, so I'm optimistic. But it's in God's hands now."

Izzy looked at me and rolled her eyes.

"I saw that, Izzy," my mother said. "Do you have a problem with God now?"

"Color me stupid, Kay, but it was in His hands in the first place and look how that worked out."

My mother yanked the steering wheel to the right and skidded to a stop on the shoulder of the highway. Dust flew up around us. She shifted the car into park and pointed her finger at Izzy. "You're fifteen, Izzy. You know nothing! Nothing! Is that clear?"

Izzy pulled back as if my mother were a cobra spitting venom. "Okay, Mom, just calm down."

"I will not calm down!" my mother screamed. She slapped the steering wheel with her hands as tears, blackened by her eyeliner, streamed down her face. "You know nothing," she whispered and laid her head down on the steering wheel.

Izzy reached out to touch her but decided against it and pulled her hand back. "I'm sorry, Mom. I mean it."

"Such a mess," my mother said.

I leaned forward from the back seat and rubbed her back. "Like you said, Mom, he'll get better, and everything will be okay."

My mother reached back and patted my arm. "He's a proud man. I hate what this has done to him."

My mother waved Izzy toward her. Izzy slid over and nuzzled against my mother's shoulder.

"Goodness, mercy, I look like a raccoon," my mother said after checking herself in the mirror.

We laughed. It was a welcome relief. When we got to the hospital, my mother gave us further instructions. "I gave your father a pencil and a notepad. Sometimes he'd prefer writing to talking, so be respectful of that, okay?"

As the three of us walked toward my father's room, I picked up my feet so my sneakers wouldn't squeak against the tile. I had a wheel from Ellen's roller skate in my pocket. Asking my dad about how to get the tar off would help me discover if he was in control of his mind. Announcements blared over the intercom, and the odor of disinfectant hung in the air. When we were two doors away from my father's room, Izzy elbowed me. "Go right to the chair. I don't want to have to catch you again if you pass out."

"Funny."

As fate would have it, this time Izzy was the one who got light-headed. When we walked into my dad's room, a young doctor with an uncanny resemblance to Dr. Kildare was talking to my dad as he reviewed a chart. When he looked up and smiled, Izzy's mouth fell open.

"Hi there. I'm Dr. Morgan. I'm doing rounds for Dr. Fritz. He's under the weather today."

Even my mother was mesmerized.

"Oh, well, that's good then, that you're doing that for him," my mother said.

The doctor smiled at Izzy, who still hadn't closed her mouth. I'd seen Izzy go gaga over boys before, but this was ridiculous.

"Your dad's making progress," the doctor said.

Izzy stood there as if hypnotized.

"Izzy?" my mother said. "The doctor's speaking to you."

"It's nice of you," Izzy stammered, "with Dr. Fritz being on the fritz and all, covering for him, that's... I mean, we appreciate it."

If my dad expected to be the center of attention, it wasn't going to happen as long as Morgan was covering for Fritz.

"Well, I'm done here." He looked back to my mom. "We'll be releasing him tomorrow and transfer him to the rehab center in Franklin Park, which is near your house, from what I understand." He held up a note. "Less than a quarter of a mile is what it says here."

I glanced at my dad and he (or it) gave me a thumbs up. My stomach wrenched. First a wink, now a thumbs up. *Fine, let the battle begin.*

Izzy watched as her dreamboat sailed by and out of the room. My mother kissed my dad on the forehead and smiled down at him. "Progress, that's wonderful news."

My dad shrugged his shoulders. "Butter n' noth...in, I 'ess."

"Butter in nothing indeed." She adjusted the pillow behind his head. "Kids, doesn't your dad look better?"

"Much," Izzy said, still off balance from her encounter with Dr. Morgan.

We sat around my dad and didn't ask too many questions. My mother left the room to get information about my father's discharge in the morning, and Izzy said she was going to the cafeteria to get something to drink.

"Right," I said. "Bet you wish you had Harpey's Instamatic so you could take a picture of you-know-who to show Margaret Ann."

To her credit, Izzy ignored me. "You want anything, Dad?"

My father shook his head.

"See you in a few," Izzy said and hurried into the hall.

When I pulled the rag containing Ellen's skate wheel out of my pants pocket, the tar stuck to the fabric and ripped a hole in it. He lifted his chin toward the rag. "Wuzzit?"

I tore the rag off the wheel and lifted it up so he could see it. "Ellen got tar on her wheels. I told her you could tell me how to get it off."

He narrowed his eyes and examined the wheel. "Ale polish a-mover. If at dot work, W… D…four oh."

"Cool. I'll do it when I get home."

My stomach relaxed. Despite the wink and the thumbs up, my dad was still in there. I pulled a piece of paper out of my other pants pocket. Billy wrote questions down he wanted me to ask. "So I bet you can't wait to feel like yourself again, right?"

My dad's eyes watered, and he tried to speak but choked up. So he nodded instead. I looked at the paper again.

"Did you feel like yourself before you had the 'stoke?'"

My father's brows tugged together. Without thinking, I said, "I think he means 'stroke.'" Billy's lousy spelling got me again.

He stared at me, and the corner of his mouth lifted. It was an eerie, knowing smile that said, "I know what you're up to." Fortunately, my mother walked into the room, and its eyes let go of mine.

"Tomorrow it is," my mother said. "Nix, did you tell your father you've been practicing?"

"Not yet." I turned. "But I have been. I'm even working on a skit."

"Isn't that nice, Walter? He's working on a skit."

Izzy returned with drink in hand.

"What took you so long?" I asked.

She glared at me. "There was a line, okay?"

My mother kissed my dad, and we were walking out when my father called to me. "Ix?"

I turned, and he waved me back over to him. He hoisted one side of his mouth, attempting a smile. His eyes teared up. "I fight-in' as 'ard as I can."

A lump formed in my throat. "I know, Dad. See you tomorrow, okay?"

He nodded, and I left.

Chapter 30

––––––––––– ❧ –––––––––––

The church is quiet, and I let the silence do its work. Opal's revelation about the world of the deaf reminded me of how uncomfortable we have become when our days aren't filled with the clamor of everyday life. Psalm 46:10 says, "Be still and know that I am God," a reminder that the world is a distraction. Noise has always been an impediment to one's spiritual life. I look out over the congregation. They wait for me to speak. When Moses can stand it no longer, he tells the audience, "Well, you can't dance at two weddings with one backside."

Laughter wells up in the chapel.

"What does that have to do with anything?" I ask.

"I'm not sure. Sometimes I wander."

"Yes. Once for forty years."

I swivel his head toward me. "Hey, smart guy, we didn't have GPS back then."

"Point taken."

"That reminds me."

"What does?"

"I'm not sure."

"You're not—"

"Oh, right, the mezuzah. I'd like one on my trunk."

"We can arrange that."

I look over the congregation and remind them of the tile Matty painted and affixed to the wall outside our front door. It acts as our version of the mezuzah.

Our newest parishioner, Nicole, shoots up her hand and waves it.

"Nicole, you have a question?"

"Yes. I just love that idea, Pastor, but I was wondering—crooked or straight?"

I smile. "Ah, good question. Since we are not bound by the Talmud, your preference. Mine is straight. Matty was meticulous about things being just so."

Otis places his shaking hands on the rail of the choir box and pulls himself up. He's pencil thin with tired, bloodshot eyes. He sways, steadies himself, and points a twirling finger at Nicole. "And we could use you in the choir, young lady! We're running out of breath up here!"

Everyone laughs, including Nicole. We are relieved when Otis retakes his seat.

With the main service over, I wait by the lectern for the children to gather around Moses and me. Today, they heard the story of Moses parting the Red Sea, and I follow it up with a question-and-answer session with the man himself. When the children sit, a boy I had not seen before raises his hand.

"What's your name, young man?"

"Christopher."

"You have a question for Moses?"

"Yes." He points his finger at Moses and asks, "How old are you?"

Moses holds up five fingers. "One hundred and this many."

"Whoa, you're even older than my mom."

I widen Moses's eyes. The children and congregation laugh.

Gracie stands, presses down the pleats of her skirt, and asks, "Do you ever try to part the water in your bathtub?"

Again, laughter erupts in the chapel. Gracie turns to the congregation with her palms turned up as if to ask, "What's so funny?"

"No," Moses replies.

"What about in your swimming pool?"

I glance at Nicole. She smiles and shrugs her shoulders. Out of the mouths of babes.

I walk home with the Dern sisters. As much as the service lifted my spirits, the anniversary of Matty's passing weighs heavy on my heart. Pastors are masterful at masking their pain. As pillars of the faith, we feel obligated to show the love of God is always enough. If we falter, the guilt can overwhelm us. Sensing my mood, Winnie says, "There is something beautiful about sadness, don't you think? The Bible says there is a time for everything, and far too often, we try to move past what God has made a time for. Don't you agree, Pastor?"

Before I can answer, Francis says, "A time to weep, and a time to laugh; a time to mourn, and a time to dance."

I pull Moses's trunk behind me, and the clatter of the wheels on the sidewalk gives rhythm to my walk. We reach the Dern's home, and the scent of lilac fills the air.

"Now breathe in and smell those lilacs," Francis says. "Aren't they just lovely?"

Winnie pats my arm. "Remember, Pastor, His yoke is easy, and His burden is light."

The sisters shuffle to their door and go inside. I continue my walk home, stopping to count my blessings on the way. I'm lighter now, contented. I lug Moses up onto the porch. I kiss the tips of my fingers, touch our tile, and walk inside.

I eat my lunch and lose track of time. I need to get to the hospital, or I'll miss afternoon visiting hours. I place Moses in the passenger seat of the Chevy. I have a booster seat that positions my sidekick at the height of the window. I buckle him in to keep him steady. At times I travel with Moses in the car this way because it's easier than lugging him around in his trunk. I pass by Officer Becca's hiding spot, but she isn't there. Feeling bold, I speed and arrive at the hospital at my regular time. I pull into a parking space, grab Moses, and head through the front doors.

As I walk down the hall toward Benny's room, Brooklyn is seated in a wheelchair just outside his door and has reprised her role as a gargoyle. The mask covers her face, and her hands clutch the arms of the wheelchair like claws. Her knuckles are white, and the swollen blue/green vein receiving fluids from her IV runs like an anthill across the top of her wrist.

"Hey, Brooklyn," I say, "where's Benny?" She doesn't move. I peep into Benny's room. It's empty. The golem rests against his pillow. I turn my attention back to Brooklyn. Through the mask, her eyes shimmer with tears. I set Moses on the floor and kneel. I raise the mask. I remove a tissue from my pocket and wipe the tears from her cheeks.

"What happened?"

"His white blood count," she whispers.

"Where is he?"

A woman who has walked up beside me answers. "ICU." Her voice is soft and calm. I turn to look. The resemblance is unmistakable.

"I'm Victoria, Brooklyn's mother." She holds a tuna sandwich in a plastic container in one hand and a carton of chocolate milk in the other. "Benny's holding his own, but he's very weak."

"Pastor Bliss," I say, introducing myself.

"Yes, I know." She nods toward Moses. "I saw you last week." She looks down at Brooklyn. "I see you've gotten my gargoyle to respond. This is good, because she needs to eat and take her medication."

Fearing Brooklyn might retreat behind her mask, I say, "Gargoyles are disciplined creatures. She feels like the golem is safe, at least for the moment, so I suggest you make the most of the opportunity."

Victoria shifts her gaze to mine. "I see. Very well then." She opens the plastic container, takes out a half of the tuna sandwich, and offers it to Brooklyn. Brooklyn releases her claw-like grip from the arm of the wheelchair and takes it. Victoria smiles at me and mouths, "Thank you."

I want to check on Benny, so I give Victoria further instructions. "I will leave Moses here to stand guard while the gargoyle eats its lunch and takes its medication. If you commit to guarding the Old-New Synagogue, the gargoyle will do as you ask. But you must confirm your agreement with a verbal response. A nod will not suffice."

Victoria nods. "I agree."

"I won't be long," I say and head downstairs to the ICU.

I find a nurse seated at the nurse's station and ask her where I can find Benny Penzik. "I'm a pastor."

Her eyes narrow. She's a vigilant gatekeeper. "A pastor? I'm certain Benny's Jewish. I've met his rabbi." She lifts her brows and awaits my response.

"Yes, well, I am a pastor, but I am also a friend." I serve up my most disarming smile and wait.

"Near the end of the hall." She hands me a surgical mask. "You must remain behind the glass. Rules. Only two people at his bedside at a time."

"I promise." I don the mask and walk down the hall.

Benny lays in a hospital bed, hooked up to a superhighway of tubes, wires, and monitoring devices. These are the cold but necessary tentacles of modern medicine, machines that sustain a boy unable to support vital functions on his own. The circular bone of Benny's eye sockets pushes through skin so pale it's translucent. His sudden downturn stuns me. It's as if the disease is in overdrive. His mother sits at his bedside, her cheek resting on Benny's hand. No words can describe the pain reflected in her eyes. To hold your child's hand, helpless as he slips away from you, is the closest thing to hell I can imagine. An attractive woman who looks to be in her late twenties leans down and whispers to Mrs. Penzik. Benny's mother nods. The woman stands and walks into the hall.

"How is he?" I ask.

The woman has a timeless look. Her auburn hair flows to her shoulders, and her sea-green eyes, luminous and attentive, peer at me above her surgical mask.

"I'm Pastor Bliss," I say. "A friend."

"Oh, yes," she replies, her words muffled by the mask. "So nice to meet you. I'm getting a snack. Join me? I'll give you an update."

I follow the woman past the nurse's station and into the elevator. She presses the button for the third floor, removes her mask, and smiles. "I'm Rabbi Iris Zingel."

My jaw drops. If not for the surgical mask, it may have ended up on the floor.

The rabbi's eyes twinkle. "I know. No beard, no yarmulke. It's unfair."

The elevator door opens, and Rabbi Zingel says, "So a rabbi and preacher exit an elevator…"

I wait a moment. She smiles. "I have a sense of humor, though."

When we get to the cafeteria, she buys a salad, and we both get coffee. We find an empty table and sit. "Benny's condition has stabilized. His last blood count was up."

"That is so good to hear. He looks so pale."

"It's hard to see children this way, but there's a chance he may be back in his own room before morning."

"Such a sweet boy," I say.

We give thanks for our meal, and Rabbi Zingel picks through her salad, finds a radish, and stabs at it with her fork. "Indeed. And inquisitive. Benny knows as much about the Talmud as I do."

I sip my coffee.

"Benny told me you know all about the Golem of Prague," she says, "that, and resurrecting Moses, made quite an impression on him. Few pastors are well-versed on the Jewish mystics. My guess is that even fewer are ventriloquists."

"I had a friend when I was growing up who taught me about the golem. Benny reminds me of him, so much so that I find it uncanny." I sip my coffee and set the cup back down on the table. "Such an odd thing," I muse, recalling the moment I first met Benny. "My friend, Harpey Mendelson, he would hold court on the cul-de-sac of our street and tell us about the Bible and his faith."

"Us?"

"Billy, Ellen, and me. We were best friends back then. One day, Harpey told us that God loves to play hide-and-seek, and what fun would hide-and-seek be if the hider told all the seekers where He was?"

The rabbi smiles. "I love that."

"The day I met Benny, I told him I was sorry about his cancer and he said, 'Oh well, yeder mentsh hot zikh pekl.'"

"Everyone has his own burden."

"And the thing is, Rabbi, that's exactly what Harpey Mendelson said to me the day I met him."

"The Jewish mystics would have a field day with that one," she says. "I love the mysteries of life, things we can reach for but never quite grasp. And this Jewish boy, what was his name again?"

"Harpey, actually it was Isaac, Isaac Harpey Mendelson, but everyone called him Harpey because he couldn't fall asleep until his mother played harp music."

"The instrument of angels," she says.

"He made a point of letting me know he wasn't named after harpies, who he described as really ugly women."

The rabbi laughs. "He made quite an impression."

"I guess you could say Harpey was our rabbi. He taught us more about God than we ever learned in Sunday school."

Her smile turns mischievous. "Yet here you are on the other team."

"Yes, but I doubt I would've become a pastor if it weren't for his friendship."

"God puts a Jewish boy in the neighborhood and, voilà, a pastor!" she says, waving her arm like a magician over a top hat.

"Something like that."

"I have heard it said that God works in mysterious ways." The rabbi pats the sides of her mouth with a napkin and sets it on the table. "I'm going back up to be with Mrs. Penzik. Will you join me?"

"No. I promised Brooklyn's mother I'd be back to the room after checking on Benny. I left her to guard the Old-New Synagogue with Moses while the gargoyle ate and took her medicine."

"I'd be happy to keep you updated on Benny's condition if you'd like."

"That would be wonderful." I retrieve a card from my wallet and hand it to her.

"Thank you for being there for Benny. Shalom."

"Shalom," I say and head back upstairs.

I spend the afternoon helping Brooklyn guard the Old-New Synagogue. By late afternoon, we hear the good news that Benny's blood counts have normalized, and just before dinner, Brooklyn stands by the elevator, awaiting Benny's arrival. She clings to her IV pole, and I can feel her almost willing the elevator doors to open.

When the doors part, I'm reminded of Moses and the Red Sea. Benny's recovery is a much smaller miracle, but many times in life, the minor miracles sustain us. As an orderly wheels Benny's bed toward his room, Brooklyn walks beside him, the wheels of her IV pole rattling like a broken shopping cart.

Benny says, "I thought they were going to fix your wheel."

"Duh," Brooklyn replies. "I was too busy guarding the Old-New Synagogue and worrying about you to worry about a stupid wheel." She places her hand on his. I get Moses and, with a sense of peace I hadn't felt in weeks, drive home.

Chapter 31

———— ⟡ ————

I arrive at the church just as the Dern sisters hang the final letters of this week's message on the outdoor announcement board. It reads *Acting Perfect in Church is Like Dressing Up for an X-ray.*

"Oh, that's deep," I say.

"It beats what the Catholics put up this week. My Lord," Francis says, "I just about spit out my teeth. Maybe I'm old-fashioned, but putting *Lent Is Coming, so Get Your Ashe in Church* on your announcement board is just plain over the top."

"She's had her girdle in a twist all morning over it," Winnie says. "Said if it wasn't such a big jackpot this week, she'd stay home from bingo in protest."

"And don't you think I wouldn't!" Francis says. "I've protested a lot of things in my day. Reasonable things like cruelty to animals and bringing our boys home from Vietnam."

"She drew the line when her best friend, Betty Marie Oppenheimer, suggested they both burn their bras," Winnie says.

Francis slaps her hands on her hips. "I refused. I said, 'Betty, if we can't support both woman's rights and our boobs, we don't deserve either.'"

"She didn't have much up there anyway," Francis adds. "Be like a bald man burning his comb."

"Well then," I say, "It seems the good Lord saw fit to give you a righteous dose of discernment."

Winnie hands Francis the window cleaner. They are meticulous about the look of the announcement board.

I roll Moses into the chapel where I find Virgil wiping down the pews, Gladys cleaning Buster's rearview mirrors, and Opal walking toward the vestibule with a handful of flyers for today's service. There is a sense of divine purpose as they prepare God's house for worship. I spent the previous evening in my recliner reading my Bible, so the spring is back in my step. I never understood that phrase from a practical standpoint, but on my walk to church this morning, I have a bounce in my gait and feel more like myself, the man Matty respected and loved. Church attendance has improved and, with that, tithes and offerings. Even the building fund has seen a boost, so we might have enough to fix Beelzebub for winter. God is at work. Prayers are being answered. Benny's recovery is icing on the cake.

As I do every Sunday before my sermon, I pray God will give me the words and that my sermon will bring more of the flock into the fold. I think of my friend, Harpey Mendelson, and realize as I do every summer when I tell this story, what a profound influence he has had on my life. "Shalom, my friend," I say and roll Moses out into the chapel. I'm ready to deliver my sermon.

Chapter 32

Sunday, August 9, 2020
Summer Sermon Series: Week Ten

I rode my bike to the rink and locked it in the bike rack. I got there ten minutes late because the chain on my bike jumped off and I had to put it back on. I liked to roller skate but spent a lot of time in the penalty box for going too fast. Chester, the floor guard, was always trying to catch me so he could blow his whistle and kick me off the floor for ten minutes. Chester took his job seriously. His red floor guard's uniform was neatly pressed, and the boots of his skates had a high-gloss, military shine. Even the ball bearings in his red, Roller Derby wheels glistened. Chester lived by one rule: "If you're passing more people than are passing you, you're going too fast!"

I spotted Harpey in his wheelchair as soon as I got inside. He wore black pants, a white shirt, and a plaid bowtie. Harpey took to the rink like a fish to water. It never occurred to me that he had spent his life on wheels, so seeing other people rolling around made him feel more like one of the crowd.

The Starlight had a mirror ball, colored lights, pinball machines, and a snack bar. Ellen sat on a bench next to Harpey. Billy would be in the game room playing pinball. He didn't like to skate much, but he could play pinball all afternoon on one quarter. He put skates on because it gave him a better view of the pinball game. Before I could get to Ellen and Harpey, Pez, the beatnik organist at the Starlight, turned on the colored lights and mirror ball and announced in his low gravelly voice, "Couples, couples only, please. Couples."

Pez chained smoked Lucky Strikes, drove an old hearse, and played the organ as if pressing the keys caused surges of electricity to run through his body. When he made announcements, he did so reluctantly, like a political prisoner being forced to read propaganda. Despite this, Pez was a rocking organist who drew the teen crowd with his ability to play rock-and-roll. Ellen, dressed in baby-blue pedal pushers and a pink shirt with embroidered flowers on the sleeves, looked cute. Skates in hand, I walked over to the two of them. As if we were on a seesaw, Ellen stood up as I sat down. I had her street skates at home, wheels cleaned and good as new, but no one wore street skates in the rink. The metal wheels were made for asphalt not wood.

"Hey, Nix," she said then positioned herself behind Harpey's wheelchair and grabbed the handles. "You heard the man. It's couples only." She pushed Harpey onto the floor. I thought Chester would swallow his whistle. He skated toward them when Mr. Eddington, the rink's owner, waved him off. Chester deflated like a punctured balloon. Nothing excited Chester more than blowing his whistle and catching someone breaking the rules. I wished Ellen had never invited Harpey to the rink. He was hogging her attention. I was so mad about it, I asked a girl I didn't even know if she wanted to skate. She had jet-black hair that fell over her shoulders, dark eyes, and tanned skin. She was older than I was—maybe fourteen—and I regretted asking her the moment I did it.

"Do I look that desperate?" she asked.

"Well, no… I was just—"

"How old are you?"

"Twelve."

"You haven't had a pimple yet. Okay, what the (bad word, bad word)" she said. She grabbed my hand and yanked me out onto the floor.

Etta, my new skating partner, had a gutter mouth. She looked at me like she made an impulse buy at the store and wanted to bring me back. "What the (bad word, worse word) was I thinking? I robbed the cradle, and the only thing in it was a dirty diaper."

Despite Etta's garbage mouth, she was an older girl, and when Ellen saw me skating with her, I could tell it annoyed her. Pez played "Roses are Red" by Bobby Vinton, and Etta sang the lyrics, inserting her own salty vocabulary wherever she could.

"I shouldn't be (dirty word) out here with you," Etta said. "I have a boyfriend. He's seventeen."

"A boyfriend?"

"Don't worry, baby face. He's not here. He's in juvie for stealing cars."

My hand sweated in hers. I was skating with the girlfriend of a future inmate of America. I was relieved when Pez turned on the lights and announced, "All skate, skate slowly, please."

"Thanks," I said.

Then she lost her balance and fell. Pez was between songs, so when Etta let out a blistering barrage of foul language, Ellen and Harpey were close enough to hear it. Etta unlaced her skates in the middle of the rink, stood up, and marched off the floor with skates in hand.

Ellen rolled Harpey over beside me as Etta left the floor. "There's not enough Mr. Bubble in the world to clean out that mouth. Why would you skate with a potty mouth?"

Harpey was working so hard to avoid a smile it looked like he was in a wrestling match with his own face. Ellen noticed and chastised him.

"It's not funny, Harpey Mendelson. Boys," she muttered and pushed Harpey off the floor.

Right then, my life flashed before my eyes. My nemesis, Rory Pitts, was in the rink. I had never seen Rory at the rink in an afternoon session. Most teenagers went on Friday nights where they smoked in the bathroom and drank Boone's Farm Apple wine in back of the rink before they came in to skate. But here he was, in the flesh, with two of his friends. Rory didn't see me right away, but he saw Harpey, and he skated right to him.

"What's with the beanie?" Rory asked, tapping Harpey's head as though he was pounding piano keys.

It annoyed me that Harpey wore his yarmulke everywhere he went. It was like cutting yourself in shark-infested waters.

"You should know a person before you touch them," Harpey said.

"You telling me what to do, squirt?"

"Leave him alone, Rory," Ellen said.

Rory's eyebrows raised. "Mind your business, little girl."

Harpey continued, lifting a finger into the air to emphasize his point. "They might have a disease you could catch. An infectious brain tumor or muscle disease, for instance, that could leap from one person to another, God forbid."

Rory yanked his hand away as if he had touched a hot stove.

"Not to mention the fact that it's rude, obnoxious, and childish," Harpey added.

I skated up behind the group. I didn't want to, but it felt like someone was pushing me forward.

"Picking on a kid in a wheelchair, Rory? That's fresh," I said. I wanted to be a hero in front of Ellen but panicked when the words came out of my mouth.

Rory spun around. "Well, looky here…do my eyes deceive me?"

"Nope. It's your brain," Harpey said.

Rory spun back around and confronted Harpey. "What did you say, crip?"

"It's getting its information from your tuches."

"What?" Rory asked, confused by the Yiddish word.

"Your buttocks," Harpey said pointing at his behind, "tuches."

Unsure of how to respond to a boy in a wheelchair, Rory spun back toward me and got right in my face. His rank breath assaulted my nostrils. "Payback time," he said and shoved me to the ground.

Billy saw the entire thing and skated at us. Billy was great at pinball, but his balance wasn't the best, and once he got going, he couldn't stop. He ran smack into Rory, and both of them toppled to the ground. Rory was on his feet, ready to punch Billy in the face, when Harpey pointed a finger at Rory and yelled, "I CURSE YOU!"

Rory turned back to Harpey. "What did you say, crip?"

"Leave my friend alone! I have curses from the old country. Gypsies and Jews—we share things. Back away from my friend, or I'll say the words!"

"You're full of it," Rory said, "full of it up to your little Jew eyeballs."

Rory didn't sound convinced. You could tell he didn't know if Harpey was full of it or not. Rory knew how to give you a black eye, twist your arm, and shove your face in the dirt—typical bully tactics. What he didn't know was how to defend himself against a tiny Jewish boy in a wheelchair saddling him with a curse.

Harpey delivered the curse. "*Lign in drerd un bakn beygl!*"

Rory panicked. "Stop it!"

Chester blew his whistle and darted toward us. That got Mr. Eddington's attention. A moment later, both Chester and Mr. Eddington intervened.

"What's going on here?" Chester asked.

Rory pointed at Harpey. "The little Jew put a curse on me!"

"He started it," Ellen said. "He came over and started tapping Harpey's yarmulke for no reason."

"Did not!" Rory yelled.

Ellen slapped her hands on her hips. "Liar, liar, pants on fire!"

"Ask him about the curse! I want to know what he said in English!" Rory said.

Rory had two things going against him: his reputation as a bully and Harpey's ability to be instantly endearing to adults.

"Take your skates off and leave," Mr. Eddington said to Rory. "You're barred for a month."

"You think I care?" Rory sneered.

"Fine. Barred for life. Chester, get him out of the building and off the property."

"I'm not leaving until he tells me what he said!"

Chester grabbed Rory's ear and led him away.

"What a *schmuck*," Harpey said.

Mr. Eddington smiled at Harpey. "What's your name, son?"

"Harpey. Harpey Mendelson."

"Your yarmulke's crooked," Ellen said and adjusted it. "There you go."

"Just curious," Mr. Eddington said, "about the curse."

"Yeah, what was that?" Ellen asked.

"Lign in drerd un bakn beygl," Harpey repeated. "It means you should burn in hell for eternity and bake bagels that you may never eat."

Mr. Eddington laughed. "That's a good one."

Billy got up, brushed himself off, and extended his hand to Harpey. "Thanks. You saved me a black eye for sure."

Harpey shook Billy's hand. "You're welcome."

Whatever Billy thought of Harpey before that moment, Harpey had saved him from a beating. Standing up to Rory Pitts was the neighborhood test for putting your life on the line for a friend.

"Come on, let's skate," Ellen said.

We enjoyed the rest of the afternoon, but I knew my trouble with Rory Pitts wouldn't end. Bullies don't know when to quit.

When the session was over, Billy and I went to the bike rack. Our back tires were flat.

"Rory," we both said at the same time.

A horn beeped. We turned as Solly's van pulled up. Harpey was propped up in the front seat with his elbow resting on the open passenger side window. His eyes widened when he saw our bike tires. "Uh-oh."

Solly parked the van, got out, and hoisted our bikes into the back of his van. We explained to him what happened in the rink and how Rory had taken his rage out on our tires.

"What a *schmendrik*," Harpey said.

Billy stuffed his hands deep in his pockets. I knew what he was thinking. If his father was home, a flat bike tire would mean nothing compared to riding home in Solly's van. "Maybe I'll just walk it home."

Solly had a different idea. "No. We will go to the five-and-dime and buy tubes. I can have them repaired in twenty minutes."

"Thanks," Billy said, "but I don't have any money."

"Me either," I added.

"Don't worry. I set some of Solly's shekels aside for a rainy day."

Solly bought two tire tubes and had our flats fixed in no time. "There you go, boys. No need to *schlep* them home."

"Thanks," I said.

Billy admired his repaired tire. "Yeah, you sure saved my bacon."

"And you can have your bacon," Solly said. "We don't eat it."

"Wow, that's too bad," Billy said, stepping his leg over the bar of his bike. "Bacon's like my favorite food."

"Be careful on the ride home." Solly got in his van and drove away.

Billy and I biked home as fast as our bikes would take us. We didn't say it, but in the back of our minds, we both wondered if Rory might hide somewhere along the way. When we crossed the wooden bridge over the Park Stream, my heartbeat quickened. It wouldn't take much for Rory to morph into a troll, and as our bike tires bounced over the bridge's wooden slats, I imagined Rory's gnarled fingers reaching up to snatch my ankle. I never peddled faster in my life.

When we got to our street, we rode by Addy Wolf who sat on her porch next to a naked man. It stunned Billy so much he veered off the road and crashed into the Yancey's garbage cans. The metal lids flew into the air and landed like clapping cymbals when they hit the street. Billy hustled to his feet and set the cans back in place.

"It's a mannequin," I said, as Billy grabbed the garbage can lids and placed them back on the cans.

We watched as Addy carried on a conversation that included nods and laughter between Addy and the mannequin.

"Seems like Addy's back to her old nutty self," I said.

Billy's eyes widened. "Holy smokes, Nix, that's it! We're stupid, total ignoramuses. It was right there in front of us the whole time!"

"What was?"

"The mannequins. That's where they're growing. It makes perfect sense. They get to practice being in a fake body before invading a real one! It's not the Mendelsons or Pepsin—the aliens are right there!" He pointed at Addy's house as if identifying a suspect in a line-up.

Tiny hairs lifted on the back of my neck. It made sense, especially when you're two, twelve-year-old boys with minds obsessed with monsters and superheroes.

"We need to get in there," Billy said.

"When? She's always home."

Billy thought for a moment. "Except Mondays. That's when she takes the bus to the store."

I liked that idea. If we snuck in on Monday, it would be in daylight. That made confronting the aliens less scary.

After dinner, I watched from my bedroom window as Ellen danced around her lawn. She waved sparklers she had in each hand, making arm circles. Sparks flew as her parents cheered her on. Her laughter was beautiful, and I listened to it the way Izzy listened to her music, enjoying every note. When the sparklers fizzled out, Ellen and her parents went inside.

I used the binoculars Billy left on my windowsill to look toward Addy's house. I lifted the lenses, and looked straight into the eyes of Addy Wolf, who was peering right back at me! She sat next to a male mannequin propped up against a milk can on her porch. It wore a fedora hat tipped back on its head, a plaid suit jacket, and mismatched socks, one pulled up to the ankle and the other hiked up to the knee. But the eeriest thing was its face. Addy had drawn a lopsided smile with a smear of bright red lipstick across its lips. Its eyes were blackened, leaving thin red dots that peered back at you like tiny lasers. It was macabre. It sat in moonlit incandescence, smirking at me as if to say, "I know what you're up to, little boy." I snapped my curtains shut.

I woke up the next morning exhausted. I tossed and turned all night, thinking about the mannequin with the twisted smile and laser eyeballs. I imagined it creeping toward my bedroom window where it would tap on the glass and politely ask if it could come in. Dracula could be very polite before he sank his fangs into your neck and turned you into a human bag of plasma. When I looked across to Addy's porch, the mannequin was gone. I got up, ate a bowl of Trix, and got ready for church.

Sunday school went okay. Mr. Waycrest started off by saying the longest prayer ever and ended it by mentioning my dad. "In closing, Lord, we ask that you bring healing to our brother in Christ, Walter Bliss. Amen."

Billy whispered, "I hope God has a tape recorder, or He'll never remember all that."

Rory wasn't there. Another prayer answered. Mr. Waycrest discussed the Holy Spirit. When you invited it in, it helped guide you in the ways of the Lord. "It's like having a friend inside, a person who helps you make good decisions."

Olive Boyle shot her hand up and talked before he called on her. "Question. What's the difference between the Holy Ghost and the Holy Spirit?"

"Olive, and please wait until I call on—"

"Because ghosts haunt people. And I wouldn't want to be haunted."

"Spirits haunt people too," Billy said.

Mr. Waycrest put his thumb under his front teeth and pressed before speaking again. "This isn't about haunting anybody."

Billy turned to Olive. "It sounds like haunting to me."

Olive stuck up her hand again. "Can it leave you in the middle of the night and haunt other people?"

The vein that stuck out from Mr. Waycrest's toupee was pulsing again. "The Holy Spirit does *not* haunt anyone. Goodness, mercy, Olive, where do you get these notions?"

Lucky for Mr. Waycrest, the service let out. Once Olive started asking questions, there was no end to it.

On the ride home I thought about the Holy Spirit, how it was God, and since God was all powerful, maybe an alien invader wouldn't have a chance against it. When the Rev talked about the battle between good and evil, did it extend to alien invaders too?

When we got home, I got ready to ride my bike to the rehabilitation center. My mom thought it best if we visited my dad at different times during the day. "We'll spread the love," she said. I got the morning shift because Izzy rarely woke before ten, and my mother needed time to put her face on before she went out. Izzy told my mother if it ever took her that long to put her makeup on, she could expect Izzy to come out of her room with makeup, a clown suit, and floppy red shoes.

I had used the WD-40 on Ellen's skate, which worked like my dad said it would. I grabbed the skate and ran it over to Ellen, who was doing cartwheels on her front lawn while Harpey counted.

"Hey, Ellen. I have your skate. Good as new."

"Thanks."

She continued doing cartwheels as Harpey counted.

"Okay, well, see you later then. I'm riding my bike to see my dad. Then I have to get practicing on my act."

"Twenty-seven!" Harpey said. Then he asked, "What act?"

"For the talent show. Mr. Mercury's mouth doesn't move, so I don't know what I'm using for my dummy."

Ellen picked up her skate and examined the wheels. "You can use Chatty Cathy if you want."

Ellen said this with such sincerity that I had to control myself before answering. Chatty Cathy already caused me to say one stupid thing that made Ellen cry, but the idea I could get up in front of an audience with Chatty Cathy on my lap and not be teased for life was crazy.

"No, she's too small, but thanks for the idea."

"How about Harpey? He looks like Jerry."

"Who's Jerry?" Harpey asked.

"He's a ventrickulist dummy. When you first moved in, Nix thought you were him, right, Nix?"

Harpey asked, "Do you have a picture?"

"He has lots of them," Ellen said before I answered. She performed two more cartwheels, counting as she completed each one. Ellen was always in motion. If she wasn't hopping across her hopscotch board, she was jumping rope, skipping, skating, tumbling, or running. Even when playing the outfield in baseball, she would pound her fist in her glove or spit or adjust her ball cap. "Thirty-two," she said. "Nix can throw his voice and make you think someone else is talking. Show him, Nix."

"I don't have Mr. Mercury."

Ellen shrugged. "That's okay. I'll be the doll, and I'll move my lips."

Ellen went to the lawn chairs her parents used when they came out after dinner. "You sit here, and I'll sit in this one," patting the chair of each seat as she spoke. "Just whisper in my ear what you will say, and I'll move my lips." She sat in her chair and waved me to her.

I didn't want to disappoint her. "Okay." I sat next to her and whispered, "Two Dead Boys" in her ear. Ellen smiled. Billy, Ellen, and I knew the "Two Dead Boys" poem by heart. We recited it whenever we were sitting on the cul-de-sac with nothing else to do.

Billy came out of his house with a can of soda in one hand and a Moon Pie in the other. He walked over and joined us.

"What are you doing?"

"We're showing Harpey how Nix can be a ventrickulist," Ellen said.

"You mean, ventriloquist," Billy said.

Ellen rolled her eyes. "To-may-to, to-mah-to. If you want to be a part of the audience, you need to sit and behave."

"Fine. Whatever." Billy sat on the grass.

Ellen looked at me and smiled. "Ready. On three. One…two… three."

It didn't work. It played like a dubbed Kung-Fu movie, but both Billy and Harpey laughed and clapped as Ellen struggled to move her lips in cadence with my words. I halted after saying, "If you don't believe this story is true…"

"Then ask the blind man, he saw it too!" Billy said. "That was hilarious, Nix. You should do that at the talent show!"

Ellen's hands swept onto her hips, and she gave me her I-told-you-so look.

"With Harpey!" Billy added. "He looks just like that dummy."

Harpey shrugged. "It's a good shtick. I'll do it."

"I don't know," I said. "I think my dad expects me to do it for real."

"That's the beauty," Billy said. "After you and Harpey get the audiences in stitches, you do the real thing with a real dummy."

It was genius. Now I didn't have to go on stage alone and make it all up by myself. For the first time, I was excited at the prospect of performing.

"When is it?" Harpey asked.

"In two weeks," I said.

"Oy vey, we need to get to it. How about we meet in the clubhouse later to practice?" Harpey said.

"How about in your room?" Billy said. "It'll be too hot in the clubhouse."

Harpey shrugged. "Sure."

Billy didn't care about the heat. He just wanted another crack at Harpey's pinball machine.

"I have to get over to the rehab center to see my dad," I said. I hopped on my bike and headed out.

Chapter 33

I liked the rehab center better than the hospital. The lobby was carpeted and set up like somebody's living room. It even had an RCA TV. The lady behind the front desk looked like Della Street, Perry Mason's secretary on TV. She smiled when she saw me, twirled the pencil in her hand until the eraser side was pointing down, and tapped at a pad on the desk. The nametag she wore identified her as Rose.

"Good morning, young man. Are you here to visit a resident?" She wore glossy pink lipstick, and her thin, manicured eyebrows were as groomed as Pepsin's lawn.

I nodded. "Name?" Rose asked.

"Nixon."

She looked at the clipboard on her desk. "I'm not seeing a Nixon?"

"Oh, I thought you meant me. My dad's name is Walter Bliss."

She checked again. "There you are," she said. "Room 12. Down the hall on your right."

"Thanks."

I found my dad's room. When I walked in, he was busy rolling a tiny ball around in his weak hand. I stopped with a jolt. A mannequin's leg rested at the end of the second bed in the room. A man sitting there pointed a hooked finger at me. It had a yellowed nail that looked like it might slide off any minute. His skin was the color of Listerine and littered with those blotches old people get when their blood is too thin. "Who are you?"

"Nixon. He's my dad," I said and pointed at my father in the other bed.

"Well, that's good then," the man said. "My name's Larry, Larry Lamb, and that makes that—" he said, pointing at the artificial limb.

He waited for me to answer. I shrugged. He repeated himself. "And that makes that—"

I shrugged. "Your leg?"

"Leg of Lamb, son! Leg. Of. Lamb! Just got it yesterday. Ain't she a beauty?"

I looked at the leg. "Yeah."

"Oh, I get it. A man of few words like your dad. Fine enough for me. Don't need a chatterbox for a roommate."

A nurse's aide came in with a wheelchair and carted Larry off to a doctor's appointment. He left his leg by the bed.

I turned my attention to my dad. He looked different. He displayed a misshapen smile. My pulse roared. There it was, the alien. I expected it to speak, to look at me and say, "You're next, boy." But the smile melted into the confused expression of a man dropped on a distant planet with no notion of how to get home. It was like looking at a hologram. His expression kept shifting. Was the alien battling to take over my dad? I wasn't sure what to do, so I used Ellen's skate to start a conversation.

"Thanks for the advice about cleaning Ellen's wheel. It worked great."

"Or el-come," he said.

It pained him to speak because it embarrassed him.

"I've got a great idea for the talent show."

His eyes brightened. He took his pad, wrote something on it, and handed it to me. It said, "That's good!"

It was awkward at first, with my dad struggling to speak and writing things down, but as one hour turned into two, we got more comfortable with one another. At one point, he wrote, "frustrated" on his paper.

"I bet," I said. "I got like that when I decided I wanted to be a ventriloquist. You need to talk without moving your lips. It took me months to figure it out, and I'm still not that good at it."

He wrote on his pad. "How do you do it?"

"You substitute some letters for others and learn how to keep your lips from moving."

"Sha-owe me."

Had I heard right? Did my dad just ask me to show him how I throw my voice? "You want me to show you how I do it?"

He nodded.

"Okay. But I need a dummy."

A mischievous smile crept onto his face. He worked to lift his arm and pointed at Lenny's leg.

"That?" I asked.

He challenged me with an expression I had never seen.

He nodded.

The leg was made of wood and leather and had a PF Flyer on the foot. It gave me the creeps. I didn't want to touch it. Besides, it would be awkward if someone walked in the room to find me holding Lenny's leg. My dad sensed my reluctance and let me off the hook. He pointed to a closet where I spotted a spare pillow and blanket. I grabbed the pillow and sat in the chair by my dad's bed. "Okay, but we're missing an important part of the ventriloquist's trick. People use their eyes to find where sounds are coming from. So when the dummy's lips are moving and the ventriloquists aren't, the audience thinks the dummy is talking."

My explanation riveted my dad. He leaned in so he wouldn't miss a word.

"There's more to it than anybody thinks. Like the trick letters. There's seven of them: B, F, M, P, V, W, and Y. Those letters make you move your lips, so you have to use substitutes. Like, as an example, B equals D. So instead of saying, 'The bad boys buy a basket,' a ventriloquist says, 'The dad doys duy a dasket.'"

My dad watched and listened as I told him everything I knew about being a ventriloquist. He laughed, and I was so happy I forgot about the possibility that an alien invader might be tricking me. It was so unlike my dad, but it felt so right and real. He tried the practice sentence, working hard to replace the B with a D. He didn't get close, but he tried really hard. For him, the D came out as an R, so he said, "Rad roys ruy a rasket."

"That's so good, Dad," I said.

Time flew. For two hours, my dad and I practiced the tricky letters. Finally, he grew tired and needed to rest.

"See you tomorrow, okay?" I said, and he gave me a thumbs up. By the time I put the pillow back in the closet and set a fresh glass of water on the table by his bed, he was asleep. I shut the blinds to darken the room and left for home.

My ride home was exhilarating, one of those rides where the wind is at your back and you stand high on your pedals and glide as if the world is a hill and you are on the downside picking up speed. I was flying high! For the first time I could remember, my father and I had shared something meaningful just between us. I was on cloud nine.

Chapter 34

— ✐ —

2020

I wake to a summer rain and enjoy my morning coffee. A cool breeze wafts through the kitchen window. The soft glow of the sunrise illuminates the oak tree in my yard, its rays peering through droplets resting on the large oak's leaves. I am a morning person, my internal clock metered to the rise and fall of the sun. There is a stillness at sunrise that invites me to ease into my day. Light and its connection to the Sabbath fascinated Harpey. "And God said, 'Let there be light!'" he'd proclaim, while giving us his dramatized version of God's creation of the world. Harpey could watch the flicker of a candle for hours, and while kids like Billy, Ellen, and I asked for toys for our birthdays, Harpey asked for a dimmer switch for his bedroom. Billy was beside himself.

"You asked for a dimmer switch? Holy smokes, Mendelson, that's the dumbest present ever!"

"Don't be mean, Billy Finley!" Ellen said, always coming to Harpey's defense.

Harpey was unfazed. The ability to control light, even though it was just in his bedroom, felt magical to him. Harpey lived in a state of wonder, and if you didn't capture his enthusiasm, you felt you were missing something. It was as if there were a gigantic UFO in the sky and if you'd sign on to his view of it, you'd see it too.

A northern cardinal hovers at the window and then touches down on the sill. It flapped one wing, and then the other, shaking off the rain. The brilliant redbird with its thick bill and prominent crest lifts its feet and turns in a circle like a figurine in a music box. Then, as if on cue, it sings.

"That you, Matty?" I ask. The bird circles left and then right, as if to ask, 'Does this look all right?'"

Now that the year is up since Matty left this world for a better one, my prayers are for divine guidance and direction. I turn seventy this year, and although I am in good health, I wonder if it's time to consider retirement. Prior to Matty's illness, it was a fleeting thought. I have kidded about my eventual retirement in the past, and as much as I dread leaving the pulpit, I had to be realistic. At a church meeting, the elders were shocked when I brought it up.

"You're not serious?" Gladys said.

"Didn't think you had a thought like that on your mind, Pastor," Virgil said.

"Well, I turn seventy in November, so—"

"I was sixty-nine a year and a half ago, and I don't feel a day over sixty. You got plenty of tread left on those tires," Stanley added.

Having finally gotten her bearings, Opal signed, "Seventy is the new sixty!"

"Moses didn't lead his people out of bondage until he was eighty," Gladys said in the staunch tone of a schoolteacher delivering a reprimand.

The meeting ended with Opal signing, "We won't hear of it," followed by a terse "humph" to emphasize the point.

The notion of not having church business to fill my days unsettles me. I am a creature of habit, and the rhythm of my life, its recurring beats and tempo, synchronizes my days. To find joy in simplicity is a gift. Matty and I never needed more than God, each other, and the church. As we grow older, we learn to reap more from our moments and to take second helpings of the food that fills the soul. I smile, remembering the moment Brooklyn saw Benny Penzik, and their words resonate in my mind. I hear Benny say, "I thought they were going to fix your wheel."

"Duh. I was too busy worrying about you to worry about a stupid wheel."

It was a beautiful moment. The love of one friend for another is one of life's greatest treasures.

When I arrive at my office on Thursday, the check from the insurance company sits on my desk. I open it. They made it out for $5,475.14. The letter enclosed explained that it covered the original value plus appreciation. Appreciation indeed! I'm pleased at the sudden windfall, but the finality of receiving the check confirms the plate is gone, and just as quickly, I'm crestfallen. It was a moment akin to buyer's remorse. The plate had been in the church for over a hundred years and was lost under my stewardship. It had not only been passed through generations but from one hand to another as parishioners with generous hearts gave back to their church and their God. How could I have been so callous? As I stare at the check, I feel a profound sense of loss and, disproportional to the moment, think of Judas and his thirty pieces of silver. A wellspring of emotion that catches me off guard builds. My Lord, am I going to weep again? Opal taps out her Morse code on my door. I take a deep breath in and let it out. The door is already halfway open. Opal peeks in. When you work side by side with someone as astute and sensitive as Opal, any attempt to hide your feelings is futile.

"I'm still coping," I say.

Her eyes soften. She signs, "It's an emotional time."

"Yes, I suppose it is."

"Do you want me to give that to Gladys to deposit?"

I look down at the check then lift my eyes to meet Opal's. "Something doesn't feel right about it. Let's give it a few days, okay?"

"Maybe I'm the one who made too big a deal over it," she signs.

I shake my head. "It's an heirloom. We need to be sure we've done everything we can to recover it for the church. Sometimes I turn the other cheek to avoid uncomfortable situations."

"You had good intentions," she signs.

"Yes, and we know what road that paves."

Whenever I believe I'm at peace with Matty's passing, melancholy returns, taking up residence in a way I had not expected. Many pastors I know have suffered bouts of loneliness because they feel they should always be fine. God should be enough, and if He isn't, then what right do we have to preach He should be enough for others? I have had a few low points in my life, but Matty was always there to set me straight. "Such hubris," she would say. "I love you with all my heart, Nixon Bliss. But He is God, and you, my dear, are just a man."

It is a gentle but much-needed reminder.

Chapter 35

— ⟋⟍ —

On Friday morning, I drive to Mattresses Galore in Franklin Park. Opal is with me. As my resident personal health consultant, she insisted on coming along. Prior to our drive, she examined my current mattress and deemed it a health hazard.

"You might as well be sleeping on busted Slinkys," she signs. "A recipe for slipped discs and scoliosis."

Once in the store, I act as interpreter as Opal signs her demands. "High quality but not overpriced. I've been online, so don't price gauge me. If you do, we walk out. Understood?"

The salesman, Rusty, would not get one over on Opal. In less than an hour, I order a new firm mattress with shipping and an upgraded warranty included. I take Opal to lunch at Number 1 Chinese where she orders kung pao chicken and complained to the owner about the fortune cookie. It read, "Your kindness is a gift to others."

"That's not a fortune," Opal signs, and once again, I act as interpreter as Opal opens seven more fortune-cookies until she finds the following: "Your good deed will bring you an unexpected gift." The way the owner is sweating, you'd think she's the one eating the kung pao. Between the language barrier and the faulty fortune cookies, Opal has set the poor woman's nerves on edge.

"Bless you," I tell the owner, "lunch was delicious. Have a blessed day."

When I get home, I plop down on my busted Slinky mattress and take a nap.

On Sunday morning, I have my coffee and read from Proverbs. I remain in wonder of its collective wisdom. Harpey knew many of the proverbs verbatim and often referred to them when we were together. When Billy shared candy with us one afternoon and didn't count it out right, Harpey said, "The Lord detests dishonest weights, but a just weight is His delight."

"Yeah, whatever," Billy replied.

Oh, how I miss those days.

After a wonderful night's sleep on my new mattress, I walk to church, hitting each blessing step as I go. When I arrive at the church, I smile at the latest announcement on the board. *If Evolution Is True, Why Do Mothers only Have Two Hands?* I go inside and prepare to take the pulpit.

Sunday August 16, 2020
Summer Series Week Eleven

I remove Moses from his trunk just as Gladys presses the keys, and the first notes of "How Great Thou Art" touch my soul. As I make my way into the chapel, Nicole stands beside Otis, her powerful voice finding that sweet spot of harmony while maintaining its power and near perfect pitch. The hymn lifts people to their feet. Gladys leans into the keys, her shoulder blades moving like shark fins under the thin fabric of her dress, her knees lifting and falling as she presses and releases Buster's antique foot pedals. As voices soar, the chapel seems to break free of its moorings, to levitate above everything earthly, and for a moment, it exists in a different realm. As the last notes trumpet from Buster's pipes, voices swell, and when the song ends, the congregation pauses as if stunned by their accomplishment. Otis bares his teeth. Francis clasps her hands. Even Gladys, moved by the moment, swivels in her seat, closes her eyes and, as if the music has left a lingering fragrance, breathes it in.

"You may be seated," I say. "I feel the presence of the Lord."

Ms. Nellie stands. She has been a fixture in that pew, by herself or with her parents, since 1929. She takes a second to gaze around at the congregation before she speaks. "Well now, let me say that I hate old people who insist on telling you how old they are, so I won't. But we all know I only have so many breaths left in me, but that took my breath away, and I didn't mind it one bit. I almost peed my knickers, if you must know. I've never heard it sung so beautifully in all my years. Bless you all." Ms. Nellie sits, and a moment passes before I continue.

I open with a prayer and begin my sermon.

"I wanted to put words in my father's mouth, to hear him say he loved me. That is what motivated me to learn ventriloquism because then, I could give my father the words I wanted to hear, and all he had to do was move his lips. It seems so silly now, this musing of a boy who knew his father loved him, but even so, I felt a deep-seated need to hear the words. Just words, people often say, but words have power. With words, God spoke the world into existence. So imagine a little boy who has a fascination with words and ventriloquism when an odd Jewish boy tells him that God often speaks through others."

Chapter 36

1962

I met Billy later that afternoon to give him an update on my dad. He was just finishing up cutting his lawn when I got back home. Billy was the worst lawn-cutter ever. He couldn't mow in a straight line to save his life, so he always had to go back over the spots he missed. Billy's dad got mad at first, but when he saw how much it irritated Mr. Pepsin, he started congratulating Billy for a job well done. One time, he even stopped Billy from going over the spots he missed and left it that way for a week until Mrs. Finley made Billy fix it. Mr. Finley enjoyed irritating people, and nothing irritated Pepsin more than an unkempt lawn. When he got done with his lawn, you'd think Vidal Sassoon cut it.

When Billy saw me, he shut off the mower, and we sat on his stoop.

"Spill. He's different. Even more today than the last time."

I recalled that misshapen smile and his sudden interest in ventriloquism, and the elation I experienced on my way home faded. "It could just be the stroke."

"No way. We both know what's going on. My dad, Addy Wolf, and now your dad. It's them. You know it, and I know it."

My heart sank, knowing that the most fun I ever had with my dad might be because he wasn't my dad at all. "He kidded around. He even wanted me to use his roommate's artificial leg as a prop. And he practiced getting ready to throw his voice."

"Not *his* voice, Nix. *Its* voice."

213

I told Billy about the mannequin with the laser eyes and weird lipstick smeared across his mouth.

"It's practicing being human." Billy looked at Addy's house. "We know where they are. Now we have to do something about it. We can work out our plan after dinner."

We met at Harpey's a few hours later. Billy played pinball while Ellen showed Harpey how to administer an Indian burn. She placed both hands around his thin wrist and gently performed the wringing motion across Harpey's skin.

"That didn't burn," Harpey said.

"Because I didn't do it. If I did, you'd cry. Tell him, Nix."

"Like a baby. Ellen's Indian burns are legendary. One time, I ended up with a blister on my forearm, and my mother buttered it for a week."

"Play slapsies with him," Billy said, as he pounded at the flippers on the pinball machine.

"What's slapsies?" Harpey asked.

Ellen got that pursed-lipped, no-nonsense, you'd-better-watch-out expression on her face. She walked over to Billy and, while he was in the middle of playing pinball, gave him an Indian burn.

"Ow-uch!" Billy screamed, yanking his arm away from her. "What was that for?"

"You know good and plenty what it's for, Billy Finley! Playing with Harpey wouldn't be fair, and you know it!"

"What's the big deal? Give him a handicap."

Ellen's eyes flared.

"I mean, slap slower! You have to count to one, and he doesn't. Crap, look what you did. I lost a pinball."

"Harpey doesn't have time to play slapsies," I said. "I came over to work on the act."

Ellen's attention was diverted to the golem propped up on Harpey's pillow. She crawled on the bed and looked into its mouth. "What's in there? It looks like a fortune from a fortune cookie."

"It's a piece of parchment under his tongue." Harpey said. He rolled over to the bed. "The golem is brought to life by writing *Adonai Emet*, which means 'The Lord is truth,' on the tiny paper and slipping it under the golem's tongue. You deactivate it by writing the word *met*, which means 'dead,' and slipping it back where it was."

"That's neat," Ellen said.

Billy thought the golem was a lousy superhero. "I guess you forgot his best move is the socket touch. Now we find out he's brought to life by sticking a wad of paper in his mouth. Good luck with that."

"That's just the start," Harpey said defensively. "God shaped the very first golem! He kneaded the dirt and created Adam and gave him a soul!"

Billy slapped at a flipper, sending a pinball flying into the bumpers. Lights flashed, bells rang, and Billy earned a free pinball. "Adam? The guy who wore a fig leaf in the garden? Geez, Mendelson, a guy in a fig leaf against the Puppet Master and Mole Man? I don't think so."

"Your heroes are made up. The golem is real. Besides, there's more to it than just the parchment."

"Like what?" Billy asked.

"With two of his disciples, Rabbi Leow circled the golem fourteen times, seven clockwise and seven counterclockwise, reciting magical formulas the whole time!"

Ellen's eyes were a basin of wonder. "Whoa," she whispered.

"Totally stupid," Billy said. "By the time they got done circling the guy, Mole Man and Puppet Master would have destroyed the world."

"So?" Ellen said. "Clark Kent has to find a phone booth, take off his suit, and put on his elf tights before he can do anything. How long does that take?"

"They aren't elf tights, and he changes really fast."

"Who else wears red tights except Superman and Santa's elves?"

"Can we work on our act?" I asked. It irked me that Ellen sided with Harpey all the time.

"Sure," Harpey said. "I already worked something out." He rolled his wheelchair over to me and handed me a piece of paper.

"I read it, and it's really funny," Ellen said.

The sketch was a series of questions and answers. As much as I wanted to hate it, it was good. Harpey had a copy of it, so we did a run through for Ellen. Billy was too busy playing another game of pinball to watch. Harpey already had it memorized. I had to read it.

"So Harpey, what are you most afraid of?" I asked.

"Termites," he said.

Ellen's laughter was quick and genuine.

"Makes sense," I said. "And what do you most look forward to?"

"A good shellacking."

"I see."

"Hey, your lips are moving," Harpey said.

"That's because I'm talking."

"I thought your lips weren't supposed to move?"

"That's when I'm talking for you."

"Why don't you be the dummy, and I'll be the ventriloquist?"

"Because then it would only be me talking."

"Either way, I can't seem to get a word in edgewise."

"That is so funny!" Ellen said. "It's a good shtick, Harpey. You guys are gonna win, for sure."

Harpey swiveled his head back to me. "Do you like it?"

"It's okay," I said begrudgingly.

"At the show, maybe I should be on your lap?"

"No way."

Ellen shook her head. "That's not a good idea."

"Okay, side by side then," Harpey said.

By the end of the afternoon, I felt confident about our routine. Having Harpey on stage with me before I switched to the real dummy would give me time to settle my nerves before the main act. All I had to do now was memorize the lines and find a real dummy to use for the second part of my act. I went home and ate dinner, and then Billy came over to my house to discuss the plan. Addy's house was directly across the street from mine. Billy brought his dad's regulation field binoculars over, and we watched Addy's house as we talked.

"She always keeps her drapes closed so no one can see us when we're inside," he said. "We go in Monday afternoon when she leaves for the store. That gives us at least an hour to check out the house and the garage. We can get Ellen to be lookout. I'll give her one of my walkie-talkies, and she can let us know when Addy gets on the bus."

"How are we going to get in?"

"We'll go around the back. I'll bring one of my dad's screwdrivers. I can jimmy the lock on the laundry room door. I've done it at my house plenty of times. After we get inside, we grab the mannequin and sneak it into my garage. My mom never goes in there and my dad's gone, so we can examine it, sort of like an autopsy."

"Autopsy?"

"Like in *The Brain Eaters*. Remember how they found that parasite attached to the mayor's neck? Tomorrow, we do it." Billy set the field glasses on the windowsill and left for home.

I crept into my closet and listened in on Izzy and Margaret Ann.

"You should have seen him, Margaret Ann. A dreamboat on dry land. I'm going to take the bus to Princeton tomorrow to see if I can accidently run into him again."

"Wow, Iz, you're over the moon."

"I'll tell him how grateful I am that he saved my dad's life and kiss him on the cheek. Then I'll pass out and hope for mouth-to-mouth resuscitation. I'm bringing three packs of Certs just in case."

"You always have such good plans."

"You wanna come with me?"

"I would, but Harry had his wisdom teeth pulled, and I promised to spend the day with him."

"Didn't he just have his tonsils taken out?"

"That was two months ago. After this, he may have to have his adenoids removed."

"Teeth, tonsils, adenoids. If this keeps up, in a year, you'll be dating a guy missing half of his original parts."

I went back to my bed and peered out of my window to see if that mannequin was on Addy's porch. It wasn't. I grabbed Mr. Mercury and practiced throwing my voice.

"We're going in tomorrow. If we don't come out, alert the authorities."

It was hot in my room, so I got the oscillating fan from the hall closet, set it on the dresser next to my bed, and turned it on high. I liked the sound of the fan as it swept back and forth across my face. It sounded like a plane taxiing on a runway. I drifted off to sleep and didn't stir until morning.

Chapter 37

———— ⌘ ————

Billy and I met Ellen by Billy's house right after lunch. He handed her a walkie-talkie. She agreed to be our lookout, but only if we shared the name of the secret mission with her.

"Okay, but you can't tell anyone else. Operation A plus W Root Beer."

Ellen's head tilted to the side. "Root beer?"

"A. W. root beer," Billy repeated, now frustrated by Ellen's inability to get with the program.

"I don't get it."

"A for Addy. W for Wolf. Root beer."

"Oh. What's the 'root beer' stand for?"

"Geez, Louise, it's to scramble the code to make it harder to break if it gets in enemy hands."

"Who's Louise? Oh, wait. That's my spy name, right? What are your spy names?"

Billy ran both hands through his flattop.

"Frank and Joe," I blurted, doing my best to keep Billy from blowing a gasket.

"I don't like Louise. Can I be Annette?"

Billy pushed his words through clenched teeth. "Fine, Annette, whatever. Your job is to let us know when the target gets on the bus."

"Addy?"

Billy looked at me and threw up his hands.

"Yes," I said. "But this is a secret mission. We don't use actual names. You play hopscotch at the end of the street and then follow Addy and tell us when she gets on the bus. Then you wait there and warn us the moment she gets off."

Billy handed Ellen her walkie-talkie and showed her how to use it. "Keep it in the basket of your bike so the target won't see it."

"You mean, Addy?"

"Yes, Annette, AW, the target!"

Ellen's eyes narrowed. "If you keep being mean, you'll be looking for another lookout."

Billy glanced at his Dick Tracy decoder watch. "She leaves the house at thirteen-hundred hours. That gives us nine minutes. Everybody ready?"

Ellen put the walkie-talkie in her bike basket and hopped on her bike. "I need to go draw my hopscotch board." Ellen spotted Harpey coming out of his front door. "Can I tell Harpey?"

I thought Billy would have a bigger stroke than my dad. "No, Annette, you can't tell *anybody!*"

Ellen sighed. "Okay. Fine."

"And don't forget to radio me when you get in position. I put new batteries in the walkies, but we need to confirm communication."

As Ellen rode off, Addy stepped out of her front door. When she turned to lock it, Billy and I ran to his yard and hid behind his hedges. Harpey saw us and waved. "Hey, guys!"

Billy popped up like a clown from a jack-in-the-box and glared at Harpey. "Ix-nay, will ya!" He pointed toward Addy, put his finger to his lips, and ducked back down behind the hedge. Addy made her way down her driveway to the sidewalk. As she walked, her facial expressions changed from a smile, to a frown, to raised eyebrows, and back to a smile again. It was like she was trying on expressions to see which one fit best.

"What's she doing with her face?" I whispered.

"It's the alien. It's trying to figure out what it should look like around normal people," Billy whispered.

Then Billy's walkie-talkie went off. "Testing! Can you hear me, Billy?"

Billy scrambled to turn down the volume, but it was too late. Addy stopped in front of Harpey and turned back toward where we were hiding. Confused, she looked back at Harpey.

"Did you hear that?" she asked.

"No. And if I did, it was really low."

Addy pointed at the hedge. "It came from that bush. I heard words."

"So did Moses. But that bush was burning," Harpey said.

"You look like a puppet."

Harpey waved his arms. "Yeah, but look, no strings!"

"I need lettuce," Addy said and continued toward the bus stop.

Billy and I left our position behind the hedges and headed to the back of Billy's house to await Ellen's signal. Ten minutes later, Ellen was on the walkie-talkie.

"This is Annette. Addy just got on the bus. She needs a head of lettuce, and I need to use the bathroom."

"Ten-four. Make sure you get back out there to tell us when Addy gets off the bus."

Billy had his dad's screwdriver, and we both had flashlights. "We have an hour. Let's go."

Addy's backyard was hidden by trees, broken sections of fence, and a line of rose bushes that had thorns as sharp as barbed wire. We found an opening in a section of fence and squeezed through. We were about to cross a line neither of us had ever imagined crossing before. I thought I saw a shadowy figure move across the closed curtains of the kitchen window.

"Did you see that?" I asked.

"See what?"

"The shadow." My pulse quickened. "Maybe we shouldn't do it. We're breaking into her house. If they catch us, we could go to jail."

"Not jail, juvie, and that's if we get caught, but we're not. Besides, if the aliens take over, we won't even be us anymore."

An eerie stillness came over the yard, and I sensed it knew we were there. Not just the mannequin, but the house, like a spider had laid a silky web across its yard and felt the silent vibration of intruders.

"You coming or not?" Billy asked.

My mouth was dry. I nodded.

We stepped toward the house. I was sure the web was vibrating.

Billy tried the sliding glass door. "Locked."

We checked the windows with no luck. This wasn't a house anymore; it was a lair, a place where monsters hid. It felt alive to me, as if it sensed we were there, that we were touching it, trying to invade it.

Billy's face was awash in sweat. "We have to jimmy the laundry room door."

Billy pushed the screwdriver between the doorjamb and the latch, probing the lock. I expected to hear a groan, as if the tip were sliding between the ribs of a helpless old man. Billy rattled the door as he worked the tip of the screwdriver until it released the latch. The door squealed open.

Billy turned to me. "Ready?"

I nodded. We stepped over the threshold and closed the door behind us. Cloaked in sudden darkness, we paused and listened. The stillness remained. Billy slid the button forward on his flashlight. Nothing. He shook the flashlight. Batteries rattled, and a weak beam flashed on and off before going out.

"Dang," he whispered. "Use yours."

I turned on my flashlight and swept the beam around the room, heart pounding, expecting to see a mutant spider's red eyes radiating from the corner of its web. The beam moved over the washer and dryer and several baskets of dirty clothes. A heavy mildew odor pervaded the space. The stillness created an uneasiness, as if something inside the house were coiled and ready to strike. We stepped toward the yellow curtain that separated the laundry room from the kitchen. We paused. Listened. *Tick, tick, tick.* The kitchen clock? Or a countdown to an alien encounter?

"You lead," Billy whispered. "You have the flashlight."

My hand shook.

We kept our voices low, exchanging the hard whispers of soldiers in a foxhole. A curtain separated the laundry room from the kitchen. Billy eased it open.

"Wait," I said. "What happened to the ticking?"

"What ticking?"

"The clock? I heard a clock."

"I didn't hear anything. We're taking too long. Go." Billy pushed at my back.

"Cut it!" I said, swatting his hand.

I stepped into the kitchen, pointed the flashlight beam into the room, and came face to face with the mannequin's sickening smile. It sat at the kitchen table, poised with a fork halfway to its mouth, as if we had just interrupted a meal. I wanted to run, but my feet were stuck to Addy's yellow linoleum floor. Billy stood beside me, eyes bugged out, mouth open as if he expected the mannequin to spoon in a glob of ice cream. The motor to the refrigerator kicked on. The clock ticked. Did the mannequin control the appliances? It didn't move, and neither did we. Like gunslingers ready to draw down, we were frozen at the ready. Seconds passed. Then a minute.

"What do we do?" I whispered.

Billy flipped on the light switch illuminating the kitchen. A second female mannequin stood by the stove wearing a dress, a pearl necklace, and a blue-and-white gingham apron.

"Man, that's weird," Billy whispered. He glanced to his right and elbowed me in the ribs. "Look."

In the living room, two mannequins sat on the couch, one in a recliner, and one on a piano bench, its fingers resting on the keys of Addy's organ.

"If that thing plays—"

"We need to get out of here," I said.

"Not without one of them."

"No! We don't have time to take one out and get it back."

Billy looked at his decoder watch. "Darn. We've only got fifteen minutes."

"See? There's no way we can take one to your garage, autopsy it, and have it back here that fast."

"We'll take one and return it next week. Maybe she won't know it's gone."

"Are you kidding? They're her family. She might call the cops and report a kidnapping."

"No way. A missing person maybe, but where is she going with that? If she shows this to the cops, they'll put her on the looney bus and transport her straight to the nuthouse."

Billy's walkie screeched. "It's Annette. Target Addy is off the bus. I repeat, Target Addy is off the bus!"

"Crap," Billy said.

"Let's go."

Billy ran to the couch, wrestled one mannequin into a sleeper hold, and twisted its head off.

"What are you doing!" I yelled.

Billy examined the head and put it to his ear the way people do with seashells.

I parted the living room curtain and peaked out. Addy was at the foot of her driveway!

"She's here!" I said.

Billy panicked. He handled the mannequin head like a hot potato as he attempted to reattach it to the mannequin's body.

Addy fumbled with her house key just outside the front door. Billy tossed the head on the couch, and we ran, closing the laundry room door just as Addy entered her house.

No sooner had we met back up with Ellen when Addy let out a piercing scream.

"I bet she forgot her head of lettuce," Ellen said.

Billy and I knew it wasn't the head of lettuce that made her scream.

There was an unspoken truth between Billy and me after that day. We kept pretending, talked about aliens, and considered future missions to discover where they were, but beneath it all, a more frightening truth took hold—that Billy's dad had turned mean on his own. It meant my dad's stroke had caused changes in him that had nothing to do with aliens. Solly was right. For too many of us, a scapegoat is our favorite pet. It gives us someone to blame. It soothes us because we have named our enemy. Shades of gray crystalize to black and white. Battle lines are drawn. It becomes us against them, and hate becomes our weapon of choice. The Bible tells us to guard our hearts because everything we do flows through it. We would be wise to follow that advice.

"Amen to that, Pastor," Virgil says.

Gladys plays the first notes of "Blessed Assurance," and the congregation stands. I love this old hymn. Gladys stays with the classic rendition. The old hymns summon a magical nostalgia. The synthesis of "Blessed Assurance," written in 1820, and this building, constructed in 1861, gives life to ancient voices that echo in my soul. Buster is in his wheelhouse. His magnificent pipes—ranks of differing timbre, pitch, and volume—bellow with grandeur, lifting our voices, challenging us to sing in the province of angels. It's a transcendent moment, one only this old hymn in this old church can achieve. The last notes recede to a whisper, and for a moment, we pause in reverence as I lead our closing prayer.

Chapter 38

———— ✐ ————

After the service, Opal leads me through my yoga routine. My back pain seems to be improving.

"Let's keep stretching. I think it's helping," Opal signs in the middle of our tree pose. "How is your new mattress?"

"I've never slept better." I lose my balance. Regain my position.

Opal waves an extended pointer finger with the cadence of a metronome. Her expression softens. "I've stopped worrying about the collection plate. We talked," she signs, pointing to my portrait of Laughing Jesus. "He said, 'Opal, you are worried about many things, but only one thing is needed,'" she signs. Tears collect in her amber eyes. "Like Martha, I lost my way."

"You are a wonder, Opal. Truly. We are all so blessed to have you," I say.

She points to the check. "I should deposit it," she signs. "The building fund is in need."

"I think you're right," I say and hand her the check.

Still on a spiritual high from singing "Blessed Assurance," I stroll home. As I do, I remember Matty walking along beside me, measured steps that reflected a sense of peace with the world. Threads of memory become more prominent when someone leaves us. Details once hidden emerge. We build and deconstruct. Like a painter returning to a beloved work, we stand back and notice the character of each brushstroke. I cherish these as the most precious of mementos: the way Matty held her teacup in both hands, blowing delicately over its surface before bringing the cup to her lips; her habit of brushing her fingers over her ear when weighing the currency of conflicting thoughts; and how she patted the towel on her cheeks after washing her face, tapping delicately at the corner of each eye before applying her night cream. This is how I see her now. She blossoms in a menagerie of details that are the essence of both who she was and who she is now—a child of God living in one of many mansions and an adored wife in the memory of a loving husband.

After lunch, I take a brief nap before heading to the hospital. Stanley had his gallbladder removed on Friday, and although doing well post-surgery, the discovery of cysts in his stomach make additional tests necessary. My ride to the hospital is uneventful aside from a quick wave to Officer Becca, tucked into her usual hiding spot, hoping to catch a few Sunday speeders. I consider what the Dern sisters would categorize as "being naughty" by flashing my lights to warn oncoming cars of the speed trap but refrain. As Jesus said, "Give to Caesar the things that are Caesar's." I continue on my way.

I arrive at the hospital, and my spirits lift at the sight of Benny and Brooklyn. Benny sits in his wheelchair clutching the golem, and Brooklyn, for the first time untethered from her IV stand, hops on one foot, then two, and then one again, as Benny watches. I'm not surprised this time. I don't believe Benny has the soul of Harpey Mendelson or Brooklyn is Ellen reincarnate, but I do believe God has been playing hide-and-seek. I love Rabbi Zingel's view of life's mysteries, her ability not to wring her hands, knowing some answers lie not within us or before us, but in the mind of God.

When I get closer, I realize there is no hopscotch board on the tile floor. Brooklyn is hopscotching from memory and chanting. A doctor and two nurses stand alongside the imaginary board, singing out their lines as Brooklyn moves from one space to the next.

> Mother, mother, I am ill
> Call for the doctor over the hill
> In came the doctor
> In came the nurse
> In came the lady with the alligator purse
> "Measles!" said the doctor
> "Mumps," said the nurse

"Nothing," said the lady
With the alligator purse!

Laughter echoes through the hall, and Brooklyn's mother claps as Brooklyn collapses into a wheelchair next to Benny. Radiation and chemotherapy have taken their toll, but Brooklyn is still a beautiful girl, and Benny's eyes shine with adoration for his newfound friend. Theirs is a bond forged by the crucible of cancer, and I pray with all my heart they prevail and that their friendship will be for a lifetime. I join them in the hall, taking a seat with Moses on my lap, and for the next thirty minutes, my sidekick and I entertain the children. Kyle, the boy who said that terrible slur to Benny, is not one of them. Later, before I visit Stanley, I find Nurse Claire and ask her about the boy.

"Kyle's not doing well, I'm afraid. His cancer is very aggressive. He's been in and out of ICU."

"I see." I sigh.

"And I'm afraid he's run out of friends. This is a terrible place to be alone," she adds. "He has his parents, but it's not the same. I know how mean he can be. But when all is said and done, he's just a frightened little boy."

I stop by Kyle's room, but the door is closed. Brooklyn glances at me, her tired eyes fading as she fights against her body's need for sleep. She sits beside Benny, asleep in his wheelchair beside her. She waves me over.

"Kyle's white blood count is too high," she says.

I'm reminded of the world these children live in, one where they know the enemy within.

She adds, "He needs a stem cell transplant."

"Well, I will pray for him."

"Benny did. He said God cries when people say mean things to each other. Do you think that's true?"

I glance over at Benny. "I do. And I believe God brought you to Benny and Benny to you."

"Benny said hate is like cancer, except it attacks your soul."

"Benny is wise beyond his years, don't you think?"

"Sometimes it's annoying, how he knows practically everything. He's weird, but in a good way. He's sort of like an alien from another planet. I like him a lot, though. He's fun."

"I know he likes you too. Let's keep praying for Kyle. He needs friends now."

I enter Stanley's hospital room. Gladys sits at Stanley's bedside, working her knitting needles as Stanley busies himself reading an Elmore Leonard novel. The second bed is empty.

"Afternoon, folks," I say.

"Afternoon to you, Pastor," Stanley says and sets his book down. He shifts his position. Winces. "Still a tad sore from the excavation site."

"He's reverted to his construction lingo," Gladys says, working her needles at blinding speed. "Old dog, old tricks."

"One way to frame it," he says playfully.

"Might not be wise to needle me whilst I'm needling, dear," Gladys says.

"Fair warning," I say to Stanley. "How's it going?"

Stanley shifts again. "Doc says the gallbladder is an unnecessary organ."

"I can think of several more," Gladys says, poking fun at Stanley without missing a stitch.

Stanley and I both raise our eyebrows.

"She's in rare form today, Pastor. A regular Madame Defarge," Stanley says.

"Did women really knit while people were being executed by guillotine?" I ask.

Gladys is a former history teacher and still loves to ply her trade. "They were known as the *tricoteuses*. In English, 'the knitting women.'"

"Seems a bizarre task at an even more bizarre place," I say.

"It's a calming pursuit," Gladys says.

Stanley laughs. "Then they should have handed the needles and yarn to the condemned."

"We need to get you on *Jeopardy*," I say.

"Oh, she'd be a ringer for sure," Stanley says.

Gladys continues her history lesson. "The guillotine became a symbol of the Reign of Terror during the French Revolution," she says and then ceases to knit. "Think of the cross. An instrument of torture and death becomes a symbol of unimaginable love, hope, and eternal life. It's stunning when you think about it." She touches the silver cross that hangs around her neck. "Only Christ could turn a diabolical method of execution into the most revered icon in the history of mankind. We serve a miraculous God."

"Amen to that," I say. "About the cysts. Any update?"

"Doc isn't too concerned," Stanley says. "Should have test results late today or in the morning. Real sorry to have missed the sermon today. Gladys caught me up, said you were like a regular Hans Christian Andersen up there as usual. Like I said, lotsa tread left on those tires, Pastor."

"Retirement is out of the question," Gladys says. "The elders have discussed it, and we have decided it's time to hire a youth pastor for you to mentor. One day, he can take over."

"One day," Stanley emphasizes.

Gladys ceases to knit. "Leaving the pulpit wouldn't be good for you, God, or the church just a year after Matty's passing."

My thoughts are mixed. As much as I love the notion of a youth pastor, our funds were not at a level to afford to add a salary, but mentoring the next pastor was an appealing offer.

"I appreciate the plan," I say, "but I don't see how we can assure an ongoing salary for—"

Gladys held up what Stanley refers to as her stop sign. Head down. Right hand forward with palm up. "We are confident we can fund it."

A weight comes off me, one heavier than I was aware I was carrying. I didn't want to retire, at least not yet.

"Well," I say, "a year or possibly two sounds like a wonderful plan."

Gladys points a knitting needle at me. "Consider it done. The elders will begin the search. We'll be picky, and you'll have the final say on the candidate we hire."

I lead a prayer for positive test results for Stanley. I stay for a game of 500 Rummy with Stanley, leaving Gladys to return to her knitting, and then I head home. A sense of peace and contentment flows through me. I realize now how much having to decide to retire or remain pastor of the church has unsettled me. I haven't understood how much I depended on Matty to guide me when decisions needed to be made. Prayer is my first course of action, but the good Lord has sometimes left the decision in my hands.

After dinner, I decide it's time to take one giant step forward in accepting the reality of Matty's passing. I go to my study and replay the last words Matty spoke to me before going home to our Lord. "You can turn that blasted sound on now, my love." So I did.

The lights and sounds of the Thing remind me of carnivals and the roller rink. I shake it just enough to avoid tilt, slap at the flippers, gain points. By the time I finish, I have set a new record on the machine. As strange as this sounds, this winning game of pinball is a turning point. I sense Matty's presence and approval. I consider another game but choose to bask in my current victory for at least a day.

During the week, I tend to my domestic responsibilities. I rev up my Craftsman mower and cut the grass. I clean the windows inside and out; water the geraniums, hibiscus and rose bushes; and sweep off the back porch. Gladys calls to let me know they released Stanley from the hospital. His cysts were not cancerous and can be treated with medication and diet, praise God. The elders begin their search for a youth pastor, and I begin thinking about the year ahead. I spend time in the Word and in prayer.

On Sunday, I wheel Moses to the church with the realization that the summer series is winding down. As I watch the rise of hatred in our country, I feel history repeating itself and know that the story of Harpey Mendelson, now almost sixty years in the past, needs to be told. As I near the church, the Dern sisters are finishing up the new saying on the announcement board. Now it says *To Dyslexic Atheists: There is a Dog.*

Winnie covers her mouth and snickers.

"She's been in a mood all week," Francis says. "She's found herself an admirer at bingo. Comes right up to him and points at his nametag. Petey."

Winnie says, "But people call him Pete."

"Well, I would hope so," Francis says. "What grown man calls himself Petey?"

I widen my eyes in mock surprise.

"For short," Winnie says.

"For short," Francis scoffs. "One letter? And he's not seventy-five if he's a day."

"I'm a cougar," Winnie says playfully.

"Cougar, my behind," Francis says. "No fool like an old fool."

"She's just jealous," says Winnie.

Francis rolls her eyes. "Ridiculous. If I wanted a man—which I don't—I'll find one that knows how to trim nose hair and keep his eyebrows under control. And did I mention the earwax? Clean them or stick a wick in it, am I right, Pastor?"

"I think it best I not pass judgment," I say. "But it appears one of you has at least one new admirer at bingo every month or two."

The parishioners arrive, and another new family makes their way into the chapel. Virgil sizes up the children for the Christmas play as they pass by. He looks up, and our eyes meet. He tilts his head toward one of the boys and mouths the word "wise man." I nod my approval. Ten minutes later, Moses and I begin week twelve of the summer series.

Chapter 39

Sunday, August 23, 2020
Summer Sermon Series: Week Twelve

We heard nothing more from Addy Wolf about her decapitated mannequin. But it sat on her porch one evening, the headless fashion model beside her with its head duct-taped to its neck. We still wondered if Addy buried her husband on Crematory Hill after murdering him, but her interaction with her mannequins didn't scare us now. Billy came to believe that his father's behavior had nothing to do with aliens and Addy went back to being crazy, but Ellen put that in perspective.

"They're just big girl dolls," she said. "If she sat on her porch with a Barbie doll, that would be weird."

Billy's dad moved out of the house, and Billy became sullen and withdrawn. He'd half-heartedly play now and then, as if he were merely going through the motions. The police searched Billy's house, but they made no arrests concerning the words spray-painted on the Mendelson's car.

I visited my dad every day at the rehab center. The more time I spent with him, the less I believed an alien had invaded him. The speech therapist told us stroke patients take the path of least resistance when communicating. Gestures like winking and nodding were common. As he continued to improve, the odd looks diminished, and I became more accustomed to his mannerisms. We spent hours talking about and practicing ventriloquism. On my last visit before they released him to come home, he said, "List to dis." He took a moment to position his tongue, and said, "The dad doy duys a ras-das-dasket." His face lit up with pride.

"Holy moly, Dad! That's great!"

"I kna-know. Rega-lar Waller Wichell, huh?"

There are moments that change everything, and for my dad and me, that was it. My dad's ventriloquism practice had the added benefit of helping him gain control of his speech faster than expected. His speech therapist said his progress was remarkable and credited his trick letter practice for the improvement. He still had a long way to go before returning to work. I was fine with that. I worried his return to the tape factory would gum up his works and cause him to become less talkative.

With summer winding down and only two weeks left before the talent show, Harpey and I spent an hour each day practicing our act. Ellen critiqued our performances and continued to dote on Harpey. If his shoe came untied or his bowtie twisted, Ellen was right there to fix it. It annoyed me, but what could I do? Harpey Mendelson was an attraction all on his own. Once people met him, they were captivated.

Solly came into Harpey's room during one of our practice sessions and watched our act. I decided to use a stuffed dog as my dummy for my portion of the performance. It wasn't ideal, but by cutting a hole in the back of its head, I could stick my hand inside and manipulate the stuffed dog's mouth. It was one step above a sock puppet, but it worked better than Mr. Mercury. The movement of the dummy's mouth is a major part of the illusion. Without it, the act wouldn't work.

Solly's boisterous laughter echoed in the room. "Oh, my *kishka*!" he said, holding his prodigious belly. "I love this!"

"Nixon thought I was a dummy when we first moved in," Harpey said.

"You? The rabbi? A dummy?"

"Not that kind of dummy, Uncle. The ventriloquist dummy on TV. He showed me a picture, and it was like looking in the mirror."

Solly's eyes lit up. "Yes! Like Pinocchio. I have seen this."

"His name is Jerry Mahoney," Ellen said. "He's hilarious."

"This is good. This show, this ventriloquism. Very good," Solly said. "What soap is to the body, laughter is to the soul. But the furry dog won't do."

I shrugged my shoulders. "It's all I have."

Solly thought for a moment and said, "I can do this."

"Do what?" I asked.

"Build a dummy," Solly said.

"Sure, you could!" Harpey said. "You built the ark. You can build anything, Uncle!"

"I need pictures," Solly said. He turned to me. "Get me pictures, Nixon, sir, and I will get to work."

"You really think you can?" I asked.

Solly leaned toward me, his eyes ablaze. "There is an old Yiddish saying. *Az me muz, ken men.* If you have to, you can."

"I have a book with lots of pictures!" I said.

"Get it for me, Nixon, sir, and I will make this dummy."

Ellen said Solly acted like Santa Claus, and now he was about to give me a handmade gift that I would have easily traded my bike to have. I stood there, frozen. Solly extended his arms.

"Group hug and prayer," he said.

We gathered around Harpey's wheelchair, hugged, and prayed.

"Master of the World, who always ruled and always will, bless this endeavor, and may this presentation bring laughter and love to this tiny community. Amen."

My dad's speech continued to improve. My goal was to win the talent show and make him proud. The last few weeks of summer were a whirlwind. Harpey and I continued to practice our routine. Each day, I expected the arrival of Solly with the ventriloquist dummy he was working on in his shop. He gave us hints on how it was going.

"I have newfound respect for the woodcarver, Geppetto," Solly said.

"Do you need any help?" I asked.

"I did. I needed a helping hand, then guess what? I found it at the end of my arm. Don't worry, Nixon, sir, significant progress is being made."

Billy's mom agreed to go to marriage counseling with his dad, so she let Mr. Finley move back into the garage. Billy came over more and, like his old self, began popping tar bubbles and telling us what made perfect sense again. "My dad's in some program with twelve steps, and my mom says if he does all of them, he can come back in the house."

Izzy spent the last week of summer going gaga over Dr. Morgan. Harry gave Margaret Ann a promise ring, and she gave it back when Harry smiled at Karen Harvey who thought she was choice.

"Karen Harvey's too in love with herself to have room for anyone else," Izzy said.

Margaret Ann scoffed. "A lot of boys seem to like her."

"That's because low prices attract the most customers," Izzy said.

Harpey's battle to ignore his Bathsheba continued, and Izzy being Izzy, did all she could to energize Harpey's boyhood crush. She'd saunter over to him in her newest bikini, kiss him on the cheek and say, "Good to see you, darling," and Harpey would turn as red as a scarlet Crayola.

"Good to see you too!" he'd say, and then the tug of war with his eyes would begin.

Five days before the talent show, while Harpey and I were working on our routine in the playhouse, Solly came over with a crate and set it on the floor. "I have finished."

Harpey, Billy, Ellen, and I stared at the box as if it held a long-lost treasure. Solly waited and then cupped his ear and leaned toward the crate. "What's that you say? Oh, yes, I'll tell them."

Solly looked up at us. "He wants to know what you're waiting for. Nixon, sir, it's time to meet your new partner."

I knelt down, lifted the lid off the crate, and got my first look at the handmade dummy. I felt like I did the year I saw my Johnny Rebb Cannon under the Christmas tree.

"Whoa," Ellen said. "He looks a little like Harpey but without clothes on."

"Hey," Harpey said.

Solly laughed. "You are right, Ellen, sir—we need to dress him up before the show. Nina has been sewing clothes. But first, check out the mechanisms. You can move one arm and his mouth. I can add the other arm mechanism, but I thought you'd better start practicing."

This was the best present ever! I hugged Solly and took the dummy out of the crate.

"What's his name?" Harpey asked.

"I've been calling him Eugene, but you can name him what you wish," he said to me.

"Eugene's good," I said.

Harpey's mom brought his clothes out to the playhouse, and Ellen dressed Eugene in his suit, plaid clip-on tie, and kid's sneakers. When I brought Eugene home, my mom and dad were amazed. "My goodness, Nixon Bliss, that's quite something," my mother said. "You must take good care of it. I'll get you your own can of Pledge to protect the wood."

"It's varnished," I said, "it doesn't need Pledge."

My dad examined the glue points. "Ver good wis adheees-ive," he said. He winked at me and smiled. "Real deee-al."

"If that thing's staying in the house, I'm putting a lock on my door," Izzy said.

I was still nervous about getting up in front of an audience at the talent show, but having Harpey and Eugene there gave me confidence. I was excited. After all, what could go wrong?

If only I had known.

Chapter 40

———— ❦ ————

They held the contest at the Caribou Lodge. I kept looking at the door, waiting for Harpey. It irked me that he was being so secretive. He said he would hide in the car until the last minute so nobody saw him before the show.

"It's bad luck," he said. "Besides, who's gonna believe I'm the real dummy if I'm wheeling around all over the place?"

People pushed through the doors into the lodge. They rushed to get the best seats, snatching chairs and planting themselves as if the song just stopped during a game of musical chairs. Ellen came in with her parents, gave me a thumbs up, and grabbed a seat. I was feeling okay until Rory walked through the door.

The lodge was packed. My dad sat next to my mom down in front. It was a blessing he didn't have to get up in front of everyone and talk. He was getting better every day, but he still struggled with slurring his words.

"Look at all the people, Walter," my mother said as she craned her neck toward the back of the lodge. "They're packed in from Elwood to the official clock."

Elwood was the Caribou mounted on the back wall of the lodge, and they mounted the official clock on the front wall by the lodge entrance.

Rolly "Stretch" Monahan had volunteered to step in for my father as Master of Ceremonies. Stretch was six feet five inches tall with unkempt hair that sat on his head like a vacant bird's nest. He tapped the mic. "Testing" he said. "Am I on?"

The moment Stretch tapped that mic, I froze. Beads of sweat gathered on my forehead, and my heart slapped in my chest like a speed bag. I stepped outside as Harpey rolled up in his wheelchair with his parents and Uncle Solly behind him.

"You okay?" Harpey asked.

I wiped sweat from my brow with my fingers. "Yeah, just—there are a lot of people."

"Don't worry. We do our shtick, and we're home free."

We went inside, and I guided Harpey into the waiting area behind the makeshift stage. My stomach gurgled as my mind slipped into overdrive. What if I forgot my lines or barfed on stage in front of everyone? In front of Ellen! Stretch welcomed everyone to the event and then directed his attention to my dad. "A special round of applause is warranted for the person who made this successful event a reality, our Exalted Ruler, Walter Bliss!"

Thunderous applause rocked the lodge. I was proud of my dad, and his courage helped me muster mine.

Stretch introduced the judges. "We are grateful to the judges who volunteered their time. Joe Jenkins, Millie Katz, and Patti Price. So let's get on with it, shall we? First up is"—Stretch checked his clipboard—"Jennifer Alexander Klum! Come on out, darlin'!"

Jennifer Klum marched out onto the stage and bowed. She wore a red, white, and blue dress with a ribbon like Miss America contestants wear, but hers had God Bless America printed across it. "Ladies, gentleman, and distinguished judges," she said, "I will play that classic American favorite, 'Yankee Doodle Dandy,' on my kazoo while I perform a band-style march."

I thought it was an odd choice for a talent show since you didn't need a lick of talent to play a kazoo. Despite this, I admired the exuberance Jennifer displayed as she belted out "Yankee Doodle Dandy," high-stepping her way from one side of the stage to the other. When she finished and bowed, everyone clapped and cheered as if she had just played "Flight of the Bumble Bee" on a legitimate instrument.

Next up was Heidi Polaski, that kid at school who's so brilliant nobody can understand her when she talks. Heidi recited an original poem about Halley's Comet that didn't rhyme at all. Despite this, she got a long round of applause.

It was time for Harpey and I to take the stage. Our plan was for me to go out first, and then Harpey would roll out in his wheelchair. Stretch announced our performance.

"Next, we have Nixon Bliss and his sidekick, Harpey Mendelson, who will perform their"—Stretch squinted his eyes at his index card—"stick." Stretch turned to me and shrugged his shoulders. "Stick?"

"Shtick," I said.

"Right, that's what I said. Stick." He turned to the audience. "Let's welcome them, shall we?"

I walked to center stage and took a seat. A moment later, Mr. Mendelson appeared with Harpey cradled in his arms. He walked onto the stage, and set Harpey on my lap.

"For realism," Harpey whispered.

I couldn't speak. This was not the plan. I wasn't sure what to do with him. I was surprised at how light he was, a weightless boy who, if untethered, might float away like an astronaut in zero gravity. People laughed as soon as Mr. Mendelson walked on the stage, and the laughter grew as he struggled to steady Harpey who kept flopping side to side as if he had no ability to hold himself up. I grabbed the back of Harpey's shirt collar with my right hand and gripped his shoulder with my left. By this time, the audience was howling. After Harpey was balanced, Mr. Mendelson hurried off the stage. Harpey looked left, right, at the audience, and then back at me.

"Is it my turn yet?" he asked.

"Not yet. Do the routine."

"What?"

"The routine, do the routine!"

"Your lips are moving," he said, loud enough for the audience to hear.

"I didn't start yet."

"Well, hurry up, I gotta pee."

The audience erupted in laughter.

"Could you cross my legs for me?" he asked.

"What?"

"So I can hold it," he continued.

Now people were laughing so hard, they were buckling over in their seats.

"What are you doing?" I asked. I was rattled because he wasn't following the script.

The first spitball hit the left side of my face. It struck me like a miniature cannonball. I knew who did it—Rory Pitts. He was a spitball sniper, lightning fast and deadly accurate. He could hit you between the eyes from ten lockers away. He stored ammo between cheek and gum like a chipmunk holds nuts. People were laughing so hard they didn't notice. Harpey's shtick was giving Rory cover. A second hit me in my left eyebrow, clinging like a briar to a sock. The third round, though, caused the real damage, a one-in-a-million shot that entered Harpey's open mouth with pinpoint accuracy. The spitball reached the back of his throat, wedging itself in a spot that caused him to gag. Then Harpey stopped breathing. His eyes bulged, and like a fish out of water, he gasped for air. He clutched his throat and lunged forward. I had to wrap my arms around him to keep him from falling. It was as if he had swallowed a jawbreaker, and it had lodged itself in his airway. Harpey looked at me, his eyes pleading for help.

What I didn't know—what no one except Harpey's family knew—was that this tiny, saliva-laced projectile could be deadly to a boy with weakened chest muscles. Mr. Mendelson raced onto the stage.

"Call an ambulance!" he screamed.

Mr. Mendelson yanked a brown paper bag from his jacket pocket and put it over Harpey's mouth. "Breathe, son! Papa's here, just breathe!"

I spotted Rory heading for the door. "That kid!" I yelled. "He shot the spitballs!"

"Liar!" Rory screamed.

One of the men blocked the door and grabbed Rory by the collar. "Let me go!" Rory screamed. "I didn't shoot the Jew!"

With five words, Rory Pitts took the air out of the room. For several seconds, the sound of Harpey's chest wheezing was all you could hear.

"Please, son," Mr. Mendelson pleaded as Solly and Mrs. Mendelson ran toward the stage. It was a horrible sound, one I'll never forget.

Ellen was crying and called out, "Breathe, Harpey, please!"

And then, as if Ellen's voice had changed the dynamic, Harpey coughed, spit up the spit ball, and started to breathe.

Mr. Mendelson cried out, "Yes, yes, son, just like that!" Mr. Mendelson hugged Harpey to his chest and rocked him. People in the audience were wiping away tears. The ambulance arrived, and the paramedics checked Harpey out. They gave him oxygen, but he only allowed the mask to stay on his face for a minute before removing it. The paramedics determined Harpey was fine. Mr. Mendelson wanted to take Harpey home, but Harpey refused.

"Isaac, please—we should go," Mr. Mendelson said.

"Papa, I'm okay now," Harpey said.

I looked back toward the door where Rory was being held as Mr. Nagan, an off-duty police officer, now had him in tow and led him out of the lodge.

"Put me back on Nixon's lap, Papa," Harpey pleaded.

"You're sure?"

"The show must go on!" Harpey said.

Mr. Mendelson cradled Harpey in his arms, lifted him up, and set him back on my lap.

"I love you, Papa. You can go now," Harpey said.

Mr. Mendelson walked off the stage. A wide smile stretched across Harpey's face, and he swiveled his head from left to right, surveying the audience. Then he turned to me, hoisted his brows, and said, "Start moving your lips. I'm tired of being the dummy here. Go like this." Harpey moved his lips without making a sound.

People laughed. Harpey was a natural performer. His expressions, movements, and comic timing were so engaging that the audience couldn't take their eyes off him. Within minutes, Harpey Mendelson would be the lead character in both comedy and tragedy. I played along as best I could, moving my lips as I attempted to mimic what was coming out of Harpey's mouth. He looked out at the audience and introduced himself.

"My name is Isaac Harpey Mendelson, and I am a real boy. A Jew!" he said, "and we Jews love good jokes because God loves laughter." He swiveled his head to me. "Isn't that right, my friend?"

"Yes," I said.

Harpey turned back to the audience. "There was an unfortunate accident one day. A car hit a Jewish man. The paramedic put him in the ambulance and asked him, 'Are you comfortable?' And the man said, 'I make a good living.'"

The audience responded with a collective fit of laughter. Harpey told a few more jokes, and then I brought Eugene out of his crate, and with Harpey still on stage, I demonstrated my ability to throw my voice.

When I was done, Solly was the first one to stand. "What a show, eh?" pounding his hands together with the same vigor he used to pound nails. Soon the entire lodge was on their feet, applauding. I looked at the judges. Joe and Millie were all smiles, but Patti's expression was unreadable.

Solly bounded up onto the stage and scooped Harpey up in his arms. "You were good, Harpey, like Henny Youngman!"

The remaining contestants displayed their talents, and when it was over, Stretch stepped up to the microphone. "We'll have the results in a few minutes, folks!"

I looked at my dad. He lifted the left side of his mouth into a smile and gave me a thumbs up. Ellen pushed her way through three rows of chairs to get to us. "You should win, Harpey! You were great!" Mr. Mendelson retrieved Harpey's wheelchair and rolled it onto the stage. As soon as Solly lifted Harpey and placed him back in his wheelchair, Ellen hugged Harpey. "If you don't win, I will kick every judge in the shins, and you know what a great shin-kicker I am!"

I stood off to the side, feeling invisible. Once again, it was Harpey, not me, who had impressed Ellen. When Ellen looked over at me, she knew what I was feeling. It was as if she had a pair of those infamous X-ray specs they advertised in the back of comic books that promised you that when you looked at your friends, you would see the most (blushingly funny) amazing things! But what Ellen saw wasn't blushingly funny—it was my broken heart. She walked over to me and did her best to make me feel good.

"You were great too, Nix" she said.

Stretch got up on stage and positioned himself in front of the microphone. "Okay, if everyone can take a seat, I have the winner right here in this envelope. First off, I'd like to thank everyone for coming, and lodge members will be around the perimeter of the lodge, holding coffee cans for donations to the Disabled Children's Fund. If they entertained you today, we'd be appreciative if you could find it in your heart to contribute. Everybody settled?" Stretch looked around the room. "Here we go. The winner of the Savings bond is"—Stretch let a moment go by and then—"Harpey Mendelson and Nixon Bliss!"

The crowd cheered as Harpey and I collected the prize. I let Harpey take the envelope with the savings bond. When we got off-stage, everyone congratulated us because they thought we planned our routine. The only person irritated about the results was Jennifer Klum's mother. She was hopping mad. "The talent show's for disabled children, and a disabled kid wins. What a shock," she said, aiming her tirade at friends and family. "And dare I mention the other boy's father is Exalted Ruler? Talent? Both of their lips were moving the entire time!" No one agreed with her, not even Jennifer. It's tough for people to think your kid got ripped off in a talent contest when she played a kazoo.

I smiled. Granted, Harpey got Ellen's attention, but my dad was proud of me. It was one of the best moments of my life.

Chapter 41

M oses wipes fake tears from his eyes, first with one hand and then the other. He looks at me then shifts his gaze to the parishioners. "It's his breath. Onions."

"I have not had onions, and you shouldn't be ashamed to express your feelings," I say.

"In the old days they frowned on it, but I hear chicks dig it now."

"Chicks? That's the sixties."

"Right in my wheelhouse," Moses says. "Sixties to a hundred and twenty."

The congregation laughs. I look out over the congregation and smile. "To have someone express their pride in us for who or what we have done is one of the most uplifting feelings we will ever have. It was for me that day. Just a smile from my dad who worked hard to lift that weakened side of his face—I will never forget that moment. My heart was an idle bird whisked into flight."

"What happened next?" Moses asks.

After the talent show, we thought of how close Harpey came to dying. One minute he could be fine, and the next, because of his weakened muscles, he could struggle to breathe. Three months later, when Billy, Ellen, and I saw President Kennedy getting shot on TV, we thought of the incident at the talent show. Sickened by the death of a beloved president, it acted as a reminder for years to come of the terror caused by a spitball fired in the Caribu Lodge by another lone assassin. One event ended in tragedy, the other in victory. We clasped hands on Harpey's front lawn, and he led us in prayer for the president and his family. Looking back, I realize how unusual it was for us to be a part of something spiritual at that age. We were Christian kids with a rabbi, a teacher who made God real to us. Rory didn't get charged with anything, but the incident and his removal by the police from the talent show had a profound effect on him. He stopped bullying kids at school.

After the talent show, the Mendelsons insisted on a celebration. It became a block party. Music played, and we danced the hora on the Mendelson's front lawn. Solly taught the dance to my mother, Izzy, and Margaret Ann. My dad sat alongside Mr. Mendelson. Billy's mom came over to congratulate us, along with Ellen's mom and dad. It was a wonderful night. Little did we know our evening of fellowship would be followed by a night of blind hatred.

I awoke at midnight to the sound of sirens blaring. I bolted out of bed. Red and blue lights flashed through my window, careening off my face and bedroom walls. Izzy and my mother rushed from their rooms into the hall.

"Fire!" my mother yelled.

I saw the fire trucks before they did. They roared up the Mendelson's driveway. Firemen jumped out of their trucks, grabbing hoses and shouting to one another. Two firemen ran a hose to the hydrant by the curb.

"They're at the Mendelson's!" I yelled as I ran out of my bedroom smack into Izzy.

My father stumbled into the hall, using his cane to steady himself. "Wha-zit?"

"It's not us, Walter. It's the Mendelsons." My mother knotted the sash of her robe. "I'm going over!"

My mother ran out of the front door. Izzy and I followed.

The Mendelsons stood on their front lawn and watched the playhouse burn. A message spray-painted on the side of the house said MOVE OR THE HOUSE IS NEXT.

Police cars and an ambulance arrived. Soon, everyone was standing in the street watching as the fireman doused the flames on the playhouse. I turned as my father walked toward us, stabbing his cane at the ground. He stumbled and fell. I ran to him, followed by Solly, who helped my father to his feet. My father's eyes flared with indignation when he saw the words spray-painted on the side of the house. He looked at Solly. "Sic-in-ing," he said.

My mother and Izzy joined us beside my dad, who insisted on walking on his own to the Mendelson's yard. The Mendelsons joined hands to pray, and one by one, the neighbors who were outside joined that circle. Billy's dad stood across the yard. His eyes met Mrs. Mendelson's. Then he walked across the street and, in a moment I will never forget, joined the circle. Chills ran up and down my body.

People who lived on surrounding streets arrived. After the prayer, Billy's mother looked to the Mendelson family and announced, "This will not stand. We will not tolerate this." Ellen, Billy, and I stood beside Harpey as the fireman finished putting the fire out. The playhouse was destroyed. Tears ran down Ellen's face. Harpey took her hand in his.

"It's okay, Ellen," he said.

"No, it's not!" Ellen cried. "It's mean! Whoever did it should get a million years in jail and never get out for life!"

The police took photographs of the playhouse and the threat painted across the side of the Mendelson's home. For the next several nights, a police car kept watch on our street. Two days later, members of the Mendelson's synagogue and our church gathered to help rebuild the playhouse. Billy's dad never said much, but he was the one who painted over the words on the side of the Mendelson's house. Harpey had endeared himself to so many during the talent show, and many of those who attended showed up in the days that followed with food and well-wishes. Even Jennifer Klum and her mother came. Jennifer played "The Star-Spangled Banner" on her kazoo on the Mendelson's front lawn, and Mrs. Klum gave the Mendelsons a Bundt cake. She made a point of saying the recipe had won first place in the Betty Crocker cooking contest.

Ellen became even more protective of Harpey after the fire. We all did. Even Billy. He told Harpey he overheard his dad tell his mom when they found out who set the fire, he'd knock the guy's block off. Harpey wasn't a wallflower by any means, but he didn't hate. "God wants us to leave vengeance in His hands. We are called not to hate anyone—not even the schmucks." We all wondered who set the fire. That mystery would be solved one Saturday afternoon just before the end of summer, and it shocked all of us.

Chapter 42

As the parishioners leave, many tell me how much they have enjoyed the summer sermon and promise to return next week to hear how everything turns out. Most know already, but the story has a way of driving suspense, despite knowing the ending. The long-standing parishioners enjoy teasing the newbies.

"My Lord, don't miss next week," Ms. Nellie tells Nicole.

"Wild horses couldn't keep me away," Nicole says. "This has been such a wonderful experience. I can't wait to hear how it turns out."

I place Moses back in his trunk and wheel him back to my office. I take a seat behind my desk just as Wally Pritchett steps in the doorway. Wally rarely attends church, so I'm surprised to see him.

"Hey, Wally," I say.

He looks at his oil-stained work clothes. "Hope you don't mind me stopping in outside my Sunday best."

"Of course not. Come in."

Wally's hands are behind his back as if he's hiding something. "The thing is, Pastor, remember how I picked up your old fridge and dishwasher a few months back?"

"Sure. Out with the old and in with the new, as they say."

"Well, I was about to put the dishwasher in the crusher when I found this inside it." Wally moves his hands from behind his back and holds up the missing gold collection plate. "I thought everybody checked inside, but someone decided to wash this dish, and it got left. The oddest thing. A voice told me 'Wally, look inside,' so I did."

"Wally Pritchett, I could kiss you!" I say.

"Best if you didn't," he replies in his deadpan voice. "The way some people talk and others listen and all."

"I owe you lunch then."

"That I could do."

"Deal! This is an heirloom with a rich history, and I'm tickled to get it back."

"Well, that's good then," Wally says and hands me the plate. "You have a good day now, Pastor, and you bring that lunch by anytime you want. Make it Tuesday around noon. An Italian sub from Manny's would do."

"Consider it done," I say. "I'll see you then."

Moments later, Opal walks into my office and sees the gold collection plate. She stops and stares at it as if a UFO had landed on my desk.

"It was in the old dishwasher," I say. "Wally Pritchett heard a voice, checked inside, and voilà!"

"Wally heard a voice?" she signs.

"That's what he says. Can you inform the insurance company? We'll return the money, but I'm relieved to know no one stole it."

"Shame on me for believing it was," she signs. "But who in their right mind put a collection plate in the dishwasher?"

"One mystery solved is replaced by another," I say. "But it's wonderful to have it back in its rightful place."

I return to the hospital later that afternoon and find Brooklyn and Benny once again in their masks, posed still as statues, but this time, they stand guard in front of Kyle's room.

"What do we have here?" I ask but neither responds. I peer into the room where Benny's golem is propped up against a chair. Kyle's bed is empty, but his video games are on the nightstand.

Leah Penzik whispers, "They are guarding Kyle's room. He's been in ICU. They have prayed and asked God and the golem to intervene on the boy's behalf."

I look back at Benny and Brooklyn. Tears well in my eyes. This is what God wants of each of us. To love our enemies. To forgive. To show grace and mercy. I want to embrace Benny and Brooklyn, but you don't hug gargoyles. "I am in awe," I say and bow before these two amazing children of God.

I hold Moses up before them. "As do I," Moses says. "But I can't bow. My sciatic nerve, oy, if you only knew."

Brooklyn stifles a laugh.

I return home, my heart filled with warmth.

The elders accept applications for associate pastor throughout the week. The thought is to bring someone in who can lead our youth ministry and eventually take my place as lead pastor of our church. I'm excited about the prospect of a youth minister. The good Lord has seen fit to bless us with many young families this summer, so many that Virgil's casting has gone from famine to feast in twelve short weeks. I'm ready to take on a new year leading my little church. I am at peace.

The elders decide the last week of the summer series required something special, so they schedule an old-fashioned picnic to follow the service. When I arrive at church early the next Sunday, the church is bustling with activity inside and out. As Stanley and Virgil set up tables on the side lawn, Gladys follows, dressing each one in red-and-blue gingham tablecloths. Soon, there will be pies and sweet tea; lemonade; home-baked cookies and fudge; finger foods; and my favorite—the Dern sister's peach cobbler bars. It is a perfect day, partly sunny with a breeze.

As I watch parishioners arrive from my welcoming post at the chapel entrance, I'm reminded of an Amish barn-raising. People arrive from every direction. Twenty minutes later, Moses and I walk out to the lectern. The chapel is at capacity. Gladys plays her spiced up version of "Amazing Grace," and Buster has never sounded better.

"Let us pray," I say. "Dear Lord, thank you for this gorgeous day, for the people who have gathered here to worship you, and for the gift of story. You knew well the power of stories to touch the heart and move the soul. The Bible is a treasure filled with the greatest stories ever told. May my parishioners realize the power and beauty of the Good Book and realize what a privilege it is to hold a Bible in their hands. May they learn to love the Bible as much as my friend, Harpey Mendelson, who believed no greater book was ever written. Amen."

I look out at the congregation and smile before turning to Moses.

"Are you ready to bring this home?" I ask.

"Ready," he says.

I begin.

Chapter 43

Sunday, August 30, 2020
Summer Sermon Series: Week Thirteen

We believed in monsters back then—vampires and goblins, Frankenstein, the Fly, and the Creature from the Black Lagoon. And thanks to Harpey, the Golem of Prague. When you're a kid, you think evil has a face, that it announces itself with profound disfigurement, an odd walk, or a disembodied voice. Monsters were enormous like the Colossal Man, the Deadly Mantis or the Fifty-Foot Woman. They came from other planets, lived in caves, slept in coffins, or hid in murky water. They stood out. You noticed them. That's what we believed until the police cars pulled into Mr. Pepsin's driveway. We were on the front lawn playing baseball, and we stopped as four men in suits walked up to Mr. Pepsin who had just yanked a weed from his lawn. Harpey pulled off his umpire's mask and wheeled himself up beside Billy, Ellen, and me.

We watched as one of the men presented his badge. "Paul Roland Pepsin?" he asked.

"That's right," Pepsin answered.

"Agent Cosworth, FBI. You're under arrest for arson. Please turn around and place your hands behind your back."

Pepsin's eyes narrowed and became eerily translucent. He looked past the FBI agent to Harpey. A rictus of a smile crept onto his face.

"Now, sir," Agent Cosworth demanded.

Pepsin dropped the weed from his hand, arched his back, and whistled "God Bless America."

Agent Cosworth glared at Pepsin and forcibly turned him around to cuff him. Pepsin continued to whistle as they walked him to the car. The creepy sound of Pepsin's whistle haunts me to this day.

"I got goose lumps," Ellen said.

That was the day we learned evil could look normal. A year later, at his trial, Mr. Pepsin showed no remorse for his actions. He pled guilty, stood, and proudly proclaimed, "Jews are like weeds. They need to be pulled, poisoned, and destroyed, or they will take over every beautiful thing in humanity's garden." The paper reported that an audible gasp erupted in the courtroom. They sentenced Pepsin to twenty years in prison. It wasn't enough.

We gathered on the cul-de-sac on the last day of summer and did our best to make sense of what had happened, but we can never truly comprehend some things. That's probably for the best.

"The newspaper said Mr. Pepsin was a card-carrying member of a Nazi group," I said.

Harpey rolled his big eyes. "He carried a card around? What a schmuck."

"A super schmuck," Ellen added. She plucked a dandelion from the grass and blew on it, sending a wave of dandelion parachutes into the breeze. "If I were God, I'd never let anyone do bad things to anybody."

"But that would ruin everything," Harpey said.

"That's stupid," Billy said. "How could making people be nice to each other be bad?"

"Because we'd all be puppets," Harpey said. "God didn't want that. You can't make someone love you, because if you could, it wouldn't be love."

I looked at Ellen and understood what Harpey meant. I wanted Ellen to love me, but if I could secretly force her to, it wouldn't be the same. Izzy was always playing "Love Potion Number 9" on her record player, which made me think about getting my hands on the potion, mixing it in a glass of Tang, and getting Ellen to drink it. But it wouldn't be right. Love isn't love unless it's chosen. Our rabbi Harpey Mendelson taught us so much that summer, but nothing so important as that simple truth.

I smile at the congregation and turn to Moses.

"So how'd I do?" I ask.

"Not bad for a goy," Moses says.

I turn back to the congregation.

"We are all instruments of God set to play in a world in desperate need of His grace and love. He places people in our paths and sets His messengers before us, hoping we will hear their voices and not be distracted by the shiny objects of this world. He won't force us to see His way or walk His path because, as incomprehensible as it seems, the Creator of the universe, the one who spoke the world into existence, wants the one thing He cannot command—to be loved. This was God's kryptonite, and to have a relationship with us, He willingly sacrificed His supernatural power for a chance that we would love Him. How can we comprehend such a choice? When I think back on the superheroes we admired that summer—Batman, Spiderman, the Hulk, and the Golem of Prague—not one ever healed the sick, raised people from the dead, caused the lame to walk, or the blind to see. They had never refused to use their supernatural power in the face of humiliation as they suffered in agony on a cross to save all of humanity. It is the one time in history where the hero sacrificed himself for the villain."

I believe God placed Harpey Mendelson in my path, a Jew, who would lead me to become a man of the cloth. Harpey Mendelson believed his life, like every other, had purpose. Harpey was a boy with a destiny—to help others realize the gift of God's wisdom and love.

It's been fifty-seven years since the arrest of Mr. Pepsin, and the memory of "'God Bless America'" whistled through his hate-filled lips still haunts me. I remind myself we live in a fallen world, but it does little to calm the fear I have as, once again, I watch the rise of anti-Semitism around the world.

In 1972, the year before Harpey succumbed to his muscle disease, Billy, Ellen, and me, cried with him as eleven Israeli athletes were taken hostage and wantonly slaughtered by Arab terrorists at the Summer Olympics. We prayed together and begged God to keep them safe, but despite our prayers, they perished. Ellen wept until she couldn't breathe. Harpey beckoned her to his wheelchair so he could comfort her.

"Why, Harpey?" she whimpered, as he brushed the tears from her face that mingled with his own. "Why didn't God do something? I don't understand!"

"God doesn't want evil to happen," Harpey said.

"Then why does it?"

"Because people do. We need to pray for them now," he said, and we clasped hands and listened as Harpey prayed the mourner's *kaddish* prayer. "May God's great name be glorified and sanctified throughout the world which He has created. Amen."

It is the prayer I recite each year for my rabbi, Harpey Mendelson.

Also By Harold Schmidt
The Etching